THE
LAST
KINGS OF
SARK

THE LAST KINGS OF SARK

ROSA RANKIN-GEE

St. Martin's Press
New York

Lyrics appear from "You Never Give Me Your Money" and "For No One" by
The Beatles; "I'll Make a Man Out of You" from Mulan; "Let It Go,
Let It Flow Like a River" by Dave Mason; and "Closing Time" by Semisonic.

www.stmartins.com

Library of Congress Cataloging-in-Publication Data

Rankin-Gee, Rosa.
    The last kings of Sark : a novel / Rosa Rankin-Gee. — First U.S. edition
        p. cm.
    ISBN 978-1-250-04535-5 (hardcover)
    ISBN 978-1-4668-4400-1 (e-book)
    1. Tutors and tutoring—Fiction. 2. Sark (Guernsey)—Fiction. 3. Bildungsromans. I. Title.
    PR6118.A374L37 2014
    823'.92—dc23

                                                                    2014003161

St. Martin's Press books may be purchased for educational, business, or promotional use.
For information on bulk purchases, please contact Macmillan Corporate and Premium Sales
Department at 1-800-221-7945, extension 5442, or write specialmarkets@macmillan.com.

First published in Great Britain by Virago Press

First U.S. Edition: July 2014

10   9   8   7   6   5   4   3   2   1

1

The only real person in this book is DJ Silver Fox –
Roger – who was kind to us.

If this were a film, I would want it to start with leaves, and light coming through them. The sun would hit the camera straight on, and splinter out and catch dust. Light and leaves are how I'd want it to begin.

There would also be unmetalled roads and bright yellow butter on our table and the Coupée, thin as a spine. You'd see the sea, birds that flew faster, and women driving tractors, with potato cheeks, and legs cocked like cowboys. The Mermaid Tavern, with dogs in, and children. Roger with hips like a whisky flask, and fields through fences, school-jumper green. I'd put sun on all of this.

On our skin, too. Sun on our arms as we cycled along the Avenue, sun on Sofi, sun on Pip. I'd hold my hands up to the light and you'd see scars from sea anemones and other things.

The camera would pull out then, back past our skin, the stones, our bikes, the house and, eventually, you'd see that we were on an island. Then I'd go back to before I was on an island, and before I knew the island existed. I'd go back to the very beginning.

Thieves, bandits, pirates, robbers, ruffians and murderers, no worse than the very cannibal, they would certainly eat us alive.

Rabelais on the Sarkese, 1530

1

My name is Jude. And because of Law, Hey and the Obscure, they thought I was a boy.

Not even a boy. A young man, and someone who could teach their son. I was none of those things, apart from young. But a merchant banker called Edward Defoe flew me out to Sark on a private plane, together with frozen meat and three crates of Badoit, and that's how it started.

The plane was for the meat, not me. But he said there was no point in flying cattle class when I could fly with the food from Biggin Hill and escort the boxes through Guernsey. He'd send a cab, he'd book the ferry, he'd see me Friday. See you Friday exclamation mark. Just like that, sent from his BlackBerry. I remember thinking: he didn't even use all his fingers, how do you decide who tutors your son without using all your fingers?

Four days later, I turned up alone at Biggin Hill Airport. It was late morning on the second Friday of July, and I was wearing a suit jacket I'd borrowed from my mother. My shoes were wrong, and my stomach felt like a cold piece of paper, scrunched up. I didn't even have a ticket, all I had was his name.

A brunette with pink eyeshadow and a fluoro jacket came out and I said it: Edward Defoe? It was a question, and an answer and all I had. I thought she'd send me home – I think I hoped she would – but she smiled, teeth from temple to temple, and sent my bag off in a golf cart.

The departure lounge at Biggin Hill was a strange place, empty as an office in summer, with air-conditioning vents and London, Moscow and New York time on Rolex clocks on the wall. There was an unofficial-looking stall selling chocolate bars, and I wanted to stop for water, but I was taken straight through to the tarmac. The fluorescent lady introduced me to the pilot, Fred, who was eating a muffin and getting a stone out of his shoe.

He was younger than I wanted him to be. He had too much neck, in waves from his crown to his collar, velvety with stubble. It made me think of a sofa – over-upholstered somehow. And then I saw the plane, and that was when I thought: this has to stop. It was a joke plane, a child's plane. But I shook Fred's hand, and stood there, smiling until my gums were dry. Then, when he told me to, I climbed up the tiny steps. It was like a Smarties tube, just shorter and more metal. The fold-down seats in the back were stacked with the meat and Badoit, so Fred pointed to the co-pilot's chair, and said I was to sit there. It was mustard leather, with duct-tape kisses where the leather had cracked. I don't know why, but I got my book out, and put it on my lap, open, like an extra seatbelt.

Fred crushed in and gave me a cold, heavy headset to wear. He put one on too, and pushed the microphone nearly all the way into his mouth. 'Take off,' he said, flicking a switch, 'easiest bit, but most deadly.'

We didn't die. When we started accelerating along the runway, I didn't think we were going fast enough, but then we stepped up into the air, shaky, like it was just a jump, and gravity would remember us. But somehow the trees got further away, and two fields became four, five, fifteen, countryside.

I'd never been in a cockpit before. I didn't like the way the co-pilot's steering wheel shook, and the nose of the plane felt like my own – pale and too close to my face. I could even see it out of the bottom corner of my eye. I looked away, out onto England. It was gold because of rapeseed, and the clouds made islands of shadow. I looked at how big England was, and I kept on thinking about islands.

Fred pointed to places I'd never heard of, and then Portsmouth. Over the Isle of Wight, he showed me Shanklin; said he liked it. After that, it was just sea below and ahead, painted pebbledash, for miles.

Fred leaned out of his seat, looking all over the sky for light aircraft and birds.

'Radar's dodgy. And you can't trust the French – that's not racist. That's fact. What's the international language of air travel? English. What do they speak round here?' He summarized the air above the Channel and the vague direction of France with his finger. 'French. And what's that?'

'Easier?'

'Lethal. That's what it is.'

I asked him if he spoke French and he didn't reply. He showed me the cargo boats below, black little cuts in the sea, impossible to get in perspective. We also saw white ferries, but from 3000 feet up, on waves, they looked like foam.

After a while, we came to islands but I couldn't tell if they were big or small, or which one was Sark. I didn't know what to look for. When I asked, Fred said the one with a beach like a scar was Herm. And the other one, no, not very good at geography are you, that one's France.

Finally, there she was. That's how Fred said it: 'There she is.'

We saw Sark from the side. It rose out of the sea like a soufflé, with, all around the edge, these coloured-in cliffs, and on top a patchwork quilt of fields, stitched with hedges. I couldn't make out a single house. Because of where the sun was, the sea on one side shone, half-blue, half-pink, and on the other was almost black.

And then we flew past, on towards Guernsey. I didn't know we couldn't land directly on Sark because it's illegal, or that we couldn't even fly over it under 1000 feet, because we weren't royalty. Later, people in the Bel Air would tell us with dark eyes that even in a life-or-death emergency, air ambulances couldn't land, but I didn't know that then. In that plane, I was on my way to a word – Sark – an empty box, thin as paper, tinny.

Maybe I'd half heard of Farquart & Fathers, and that there were no cars – something about the war, Nazi occupation, feudalism. But I didn't know that even the doctor drove a tractor, or that we would steal internet and scallops. I didn't know anything.

2

I could tell straight away that Sofi didn't like me. I liked her as soon as I saw her. It's strange trying to remember when you didn't know someone, especially if they really didn't like you, and later they do. I want to shake myself and say, 'Be normal, why aren't you being normal?' I try to remember it for next time I meet someone new – 'Just be normal; go straight to normal,' but it's never like that.

Sofi didn't like me because I was wearing a suit jacket and using the voice I saved for my parents' friends. Also, she said, it was because I said no to a slice of her cake. She said she thought, *twat*, and plotted putting extra butter on my peas to make me fat. Still, I liked her right away.

But I hadn't got to Sofi and her kitchen yet, and I should say things in the order in which they happened.

Fred landed in slapping winds at Guernsey Aero Club. There was no passport control ('Customs only come if they don't like your surname,' Fred said as he yanked my bag out of the hold, then clarified: 'Arabs.'); just a taxi waiting, a people carrier – pearly purple – full of tree air fresheners and loud radio.

We drove out of the airport, so that first time I only saw Guernsey through glass. The roads were thinner than on the mainland, the pavements like pencils, but the buildings were proper ones, like you'd see in normal cities, and there were full-size offices, with proper signs, where real people must have worked. I don't know why I found this surprising, but I did. I just expected an island to be different. The driver played his radio, and hummed different tunes on top. He didn't try and talk to me and I was happy with that. A feeling kept on coming in waves; someone was running a rolling pin over the inside of me, making it so thin it almost went away. That was panic, I think.

I wanted the taxi to go slower. I prayed for red lights, and zebra crossings, and things that get in the way, but the singing driver drove me straight to St Peter's Port, and right up to the seawall. 'Defoe's lot,' he shouted out the window. 'Can I whack the boxes on?' Then he swung out of his car and hoisted my cargo onto the white and navy ferry for Sark.

It was called the *Sark Venture,* and it didn't leave for another thirty minutes. At first I was alone with the ticket man. I wondered if I could ask him questions. I wanted to know what Sark was like, and if he lived there. I wanted to know if he knew the Defoes. I wanted to know if it would all be OK. But I sat on a plastic seat below deck and wrote texts I never sent. I thought that if I tried to speak it would come out funny. I tasted my cheeks and even though I was still, I tasted iron, as if I'd been sprinting. Other people got on the boat, but nobody else was travelling alone.

It took all day to get there. By the time I set foot on Sark, it was evening and the air was heavy with fog. There's a lighthouse on the west side of the island, and its foghorn is thick and low. It only sounded twice that summer, but my first night was one of them. There was still brightness in the sky, but it couldn't light the sea any more, and I remember thinking that the water looked like tar. I pulled my suitcase up the harbour steps and I could have been anywhere. I'd had too much coffee and I hadn't had lunch. I could smell my mum on the lapel of the jacket, and I could smell the sea. I leant my bag against the cold harbour wall, and waited.

There was a blond boy sitting on the wall a few metres away, watching the people get off the boat. His jawbone ran like a metal bar under his cheeks, and he was shifting it from side to side. I watched it make shadows on his face, and then I looked away, and looked for a man. Defoe would be fiftyish. I hoped he'd be holding a sign.

But when everyone had got off the boat, it was only me, fishermen in overalls and this blond boy left. Finally, I wondered if this was the son, and said, 'Excuse me.' My voice sounded very high. He didn't look over. I said excuse me again, and then, when he turned around, I said, 'You're not Pip, are you?'

'Yes?'

'Jude.' I went to shake his hand. 'I'm Jude.'

'No you're not.'

'Yes . . . '

'Jude the tutor? No. Jude's a man.'

I thought maybe I'd slipped through a rip and walked into the wrong world.

'But I *am* Jude,' I said. 'And you're – you say you're Pip? Edward's son?'

'Eddy.'

'Still ...' I looked behind the blond boy for someone older. 'Is he here?'

'Yes, of course. He's waiting by the Toast Rack.' He said it like it was obvious.

All this time, he hadn't looked at me once. He focused on a point just left of my head, above my shoulder.

'This way,' he said. He led me through a tunnel. The Toast Rack turned out to be a passenger carriage strapped to a tractor, like a seafront train, but farmier. Edward – Eddy – had one foot on it, making sure it didn't leave. I think he said 'what the fuck' under his breath when he saw me, but when I got close, he said, 'Right. Well – hello,' and gave me a kiss on both cheeks. We sat on red seats under a corrugated iron roof and the Toast Rack took us up the hill. Slowly, so slowly, much more slowly than I'm going now, but I want to get to the kitchen, and back to Sofi.

When we arrived at the house, she was there. She turned her music down, but not off.

'If you're making a pot of coffee ...' Eddy tried, but she said, 'No,' blunt as a stone. 'Only instant.'

Then, when Pip walked in, she pulled him to her, said, '*Shirt*, schmuck,' and tucked it deep in with her hand. He blushed so hard you could see it underneath his eyebrows.

We were in the kitchen, and I was still holding the handle of my suitcase. It felt like if you struck a match, all the air would catch.

'I'm afraid Sofi's from *Poland*,' Eddy explained when we took our instant coffees through to the next room. She was also extremely pretty. Except pretty isn't the word – dirty blonde, dirty tan, denim-blue eyes. Her eyelashes were so long they touched her brows if she looked up, and her lips were so full that the only time I saw her in lipstick I thought she was joking. So, so, so, that was Sofi. Eddy, Pip and I sat in the sitting room, eating cake and not eating cake, and all of us could sense her next door.

Not feeling comfortable sometimes feels like being very cold. Individual parts of you can get warm but you're still cold, and your teeth feel hard and sharp as nails because all of you is clenched tight. I get cold a lot. But I did try; I smiled with my mouth and tried to make it reach my eyes.

Pip was silent, his Adam's apple poking out like a ring box. 'Just be normal,' I want to be able to say to myself again, 'it's *Pip*, you donkey.' But he wasn't Pip then. He was this strange creature, blond and bones, as tall as he was thin, who still wouldn't catch my eye. Eddy kept on trying to draw him into the conversation, saying his name with encouraging emphasis and punching his shoulder. But Pip just ate the icing off his cake and stared out the window. He looked like he'd cut his hair himself; it was long in different places.

My smiles worked better with Eddy. He was a man I'd already met in slices. Friends' dads, bosses, men in restaurants. He wore the uniform: navy polos meant for sailing, fat and buckled around their collar. His hair – straight and blond, the type of blond that rarely lasts into adulthood – was backing off his temples, but it was strong everywhere else, and so was he. He was so much sturdier than Pip. He had a slight belly, but expensive clothes and man's hands, signet ring squeezing his little finger. He settled into a bottle of Mâcon and talked to me about St Andrews. I'd just graduated. It was where his twin brother had gone; he didn't say how long ago.

'Used to visit Caleb. *Terrorized* that place. Spilt a glass of red over some girl's dress and still ended up bringing her back. Stellar university.'

I told him about charity rugby on the beach and stock-market drinking games. I praised his big house and he liked that.

After a while, Eddy brushed cake crumbs from the table onto his palm and said, 'Listen. Before dinner, I'd better have a word with my wife. She's not very . . . ' He finished his wine with his eyes on his son. 'Like I said, we were expecting a chap, you see.'

'Jude . . . ' He said it like he was chewing it. 'Never heard of a *girl* called Jude before.'

Just then, a woman appeared at the top of the stairs.

3

She was like a bird – dark, tiny, beautiful – straight away, beautiful – but she was wearing trousers which should have been tight, and her legs didn't fill them.

'Esmé,' Eddy said. He stood up so fast it was like falling over in reverse. 'This is my wife.'

She was staring at me. 'And this is Jude,' he said. He stopped, and started again, different intonation. 'Jude?'

Then Eddy said lots of things in one fast sentence: misunderstanding, didn't say on the CV, the agency's fault. Esmé was still at the top of the stairs and we were looking up at her like children. Pip was rubbing his hands over his face like smokers do when they can't have a cigarette. I wanted to say, please, I can just go home, let me slip out of the door, it's fine. In my head, I was begging.

'Pip, take Jude into the kitchen and have Sofi get her some olives,' Eddy said before turning to go upstairs.

I think I said, 'Olives sound nice'. When we got to the

kitchen, Sofi was already opening a huge glass jar with a knife. She plonked the jar down on the table undrained, and took a briny handful, dripping everywhere.

'Fuck, man,' she whispered to Pip, 'she is *not* happy.' He looked away.

There were two shut doors between us and the adults, but we heard their voices. It sounded like the type of shouting that makes faces change colour. Sofi ate olives, dripping, dropping. Pip chewed on a pit until it was dry, then eventually took it out and held it in his hand.

Then the shouting stopped. Eddy came downstairs. We heard him put his glass on the table. Pip looked as if he might get up, but none of us moved.

Eddy came into the kitchen to tell Sofi to set the table for three, and that's how we ate: Eddy distracted, flexing his fingers, Pip silent, me smiling. Sofi brought out plates, and Eddy touched the rim to see if they were hot enough. We had lamb chops. Sofi ate hers in the kitchen; Eddy, when he'd sucked the juice from the bone, took Pip's fat off his plate and ate that too.

After dinner, Sofi and I left the house together.

'I'm not being funny,' she said, 'but this is a joke.'

'I know. It's from Debenhams. It really isn't great on gravel.' Wheeling my suitcase was difficult in the dark and stones kept on getting stuck in it.

'Not the bag. The bag's a bag. It's this hotel thing. It's a joke.'

I jerked at the handle and tried to keep up.

'Share a room . . .' she went on, 'is he on crack? Don't *dare* tell me there are no free hotel rooms in all of Sark. I don't care if it's a bloody island. *Wanker.*'

Eddy had come back into the dining room as Sofi was serving us dessert. 'Just spoke to Bonita. No room at the inn, girls! But she says she gave you a twin, Sofi, so there's a spare bed in yours. You two will have to bunk together. Back to school, eh?' I smiled and said, 'Oh yes of course that's fine, *fun* even, I'm happy with anything.' Sofi slapped a sponge pudding down in front of me and said, 'Do you snore? Because it makes me psychotic.'

'"Back to school?"' she said now, writing speech marks with her fingers and a cigarette. 'I went to a comprehensive. The only thing we shared were these.' She ashed in the air. 'Bonita's lovely – Mexican or something – but her place stinks. Cold lamb. It smells like cold lamb in there. Mint sauce and flubby fat.' She took a deep drag. 'I hate cold lamb.'

I said mint sauce didn't sound very Mexican, and Sofi told me not to worry, there was a piñata in the hall, and dried chillis in the bathroom. She threw the stub of her cigarette into a bush. 'Listen, I'm sorry I'm being such a bitch. I'm not actually a bitch. It's just this hotel thing is a joke. Also, I'm on my period and it's like monsoon season down there.'

I tried to keep up with her but she walked so fast.

'Whereabouts in Poland are you from?' I asked.

'Ealing. *EA*-ling. I told him Ealing. I grew up in Ealing. I've only been to Poland once, and I was six.'

I said Oh. I had said Oh lots of times. Perhaps it sounded like I was disappointed, which I honestly wasn't. It was just that from the very beginning, something about Sofi, or simply Sofi herself, surprised me.

I was about to give up and start carrying my wheelie case like a baby when we finally arrived. I don't know why people had been calling it a hotel. It was a house, a small one, with bad plastering and four faded gnomes in the garden. There was a red sign saying 'La Casa Bonita', and one of the gnomes was wearing a sombrero.

The front door was frosted glass with metal rims. *Coronation Street* stuff. Sofi already had the key, and she led me upstairs to a door with a brass '3' on it.

'Bienvenida,' she said, 'it's the size of a fucking walnut.'

There were two single beds, a shared bedside table and little else – well, nothing else. 'Wait till you lie down,' Sofi said, flopping onto one of the beds, 'they designed the mattresses for anorexics.'

The curtains were like doilies. 'Dirty too,' Sofi said, putting her little finger through an old cigarette burn. She smacked a daddy-long-legs dead against the wall with her other hand, nail varnish all chipped, then scratched off a dark smear from someone who'd done the same before her.

She used words I hadn't heard in ages. Revolting. No one really says revolting, and not so affectionately, or about a coat hanger. 'But look, it's just *revolting*,' she said, pulling this puffy, pink thing out of the wardrobe to show me. 'I wouldn't even hang *myself* on that.'

She told me I could have the bed by the door because if a murderer broke in, it would be that bed they'd go for first. Then I unpacked, and she talked about Sark. She'd arrived five days before me. 'Four hundred people, that's sick. That's one single year at my old college.' She told me she was nineteen.

She whipped off her top mid-sentence and sat on the edge of her bed, legs open, in a black lace bra.

I turned my face away but you couldn't miss it. I folded my T-shirts in a pile without looking up. When it was time to change, I took my washbag to the bathroom and came back in pyjamas.

'I just sleep in pants,' Sofi said. 'But unless I get hot, I'll be under the sheet. So don't worry.'

We got into bed. Sofi was right, they were terrible mattresses, terrible – bony, and about the width of a bench.

We lay flat on our backs, counting the cracks in the ceiling. 'Sofi,' I said then – I've written it in with an 'f' but she was still 'ph' in my mind at that point, which makes a difference. 'Sofi,' I said, 'is Pip . . . all right?'

'What do you mean?'

'Is he . . . OK?'

'Dunno, man. Been here less than a week. He's sixteen, and he lives on an island. It's not normal.'

'But he's not – dangerous?'

She took in a long, slow breath that sounded like she was smoking again. I checked to see she wasn't. 'Lonely, more. He's just a kid. You'll be fine, you've done it before, right?'

That was the problem. It was so quiet that when I shifted, we could both hear the sound of the sheets.

Sofi turned off the light without asking, even though it was closer to me. And because we didn't know each other, that meant goodnight.

4

In the morning, Bonita gave us breakfast. Sofi had bacon, I had bran flakes. Bonita was how you'd expect her to be; round and smiley, with sausage fingers. The skin on her face had that pigment disorder where bits of it were darker than others, but her teeth were weirdly white for someone who was drinking cola first thing in the morning.

She came up behind Sofi and said, 'You sleep nice?' Then she kissed her on the crown. 'Beautiful girl, Miss Sofi!' she said to the room, though none of the other guests had come down yet. 'And you,' she turned to me with an open-faced smile, 'you must be the Jude! Mr Eddy call me, but what can I do? Full up to the eyeball.'

She said she was sorry that our room was so small, and that John would fix the light. At the word John, a silver sliver of a man with elbow skin under his eyes, coughed and raised his hand in hello. Her husband. '*Y chicas*, you're getting ... *oye* John, *como se dice*? You're getting kettle!' She pronounced it kett-lay.

I couldn't eat my bran flakes. Even though it was just us two, Bonita, and John with his crime book, it felt hectic in that breakfast room. I think it was the carpet. That kind of swirly pub carpet that makes your eyes go funny. The smell of fried bread swirled like the carpet and filled the room like the radio.

Sofi was quiet, even when Bonita brought her another bit of bacon on a fork, hand cupped underneath to catch the fat. 'Not a morning person,' Sofi said to me, spreading ketchup over bread with a finger. 'Oh God, and we walked here last night because of your bag, didn't we? Oh ... *pisser.*'

Every morning after that, we cycled to work from Bonita's. She let us borrow these two bikes: lilac-coloured, no suspension, dingy chains, and pedals your feet slipped off. But that first morning, we walked, and I saw Sark for the first time in daylight.

The sky was as white as this page, just so much brighter. You couldn't look directly at it. I found it hard to look at anything. Sofi was not a good tour guide. She pointed out that the post-box was blue when I was already staring at it. It was just like the old red Royal Mail ones – a chess castle, but blue. We passed a woman with a gargoyle face and a huge sunhat, and scaffolding erected by E&G Builders (on closer look, Ewan and Glenn). We saw red garden apples, shiny as yo-yos and about the same size, left out in cardboard boxes on front steps for anyone to take. I heard people saying hello, mostly men, and mostly to Sofi, who was wearing tiny denim shorts. But it wasn't like arriving on holiday, when you look at things so you can write them on a postcard, when you walk slowly. We were late and walking fast to somewhere I didn't want to go.

'You look a bit ill,' Sofi said, when we got to Eddy's gate. Her eyes floated over my face as if she were reading it. 'Pasty,' she said. 'Don't be scared.'

I told her I wasn't, I just got cold easily. I said I was fine, twice, in case she didn't believe me. I tried to smile and she opened the gate.

Pip – odd, eye-avoiding Pip – had done something to his hair. He'd slicked it back with water, I think. You could see the shallow dents of his temples.

'Sofi, I don't want eggs this morning,' he said as she pulled open the walk-in fridge. 'I had toast already.'

'What colour?' she asked.

'What colour what?'

'Toast. What colour toast did you have?'

'Brown.'

'With what on?'

He thought for a second.

'Nothing.'

'Not even butter?'

'No.'

'Gross. Doesn't it get stuck to your mouth? *What* have you done to your hair?' she said, combing back into place with her fingers. 'I'm making you eggs.' I watched her with him and she was just so easy. She put her hands where she wanted to. Pip still hadn't looked me in the eye once, but there she was, touching his head. We sat at the table and waited for his eggs. Sofi was singing. She didn't have a nice voice – pitch was a problem – but it kind of jangled like bangles on a wrist. What did she sing that first day? I don't remember any more. But she had a thing for Tina Turner, and also drum and bass. Pip's eggs came, scrambled to smithereens, and he ate them very slowly, clenching his eyes with every swallow as if each mouthful was a burr.

Sofi left the room and then there was silence. Fork on plate, sips of tea – louder than I wanted them to be – but silence, really. I was wearing shoes, but my toes bit the sole the way they do with loose flip-flops at the beginning of summer.

Finally, when Pip was done – apart from a curve of crust and a few pellets of egg – he took me through to the study.

'We have to do it in here,' he said. 'I'm not going to open the curtains, though, because the sun gets in my eyes.'

It was a dark room that smelt of books and unbeaten cushions. The ceilings seemed lower than anywhere else in the house. Pip pushed his hair back off his face again.

'You look smart today,' I told him. It tasted wrong as soon as I'd said it. Smart is such a dad's word.

He ruffled his hair out again, the way that Sofi had done. He shuffled in his chair, sat awkwardly, couldn't get comfortable. Still, his back was straight for a sixteen-year-old. He wasn't at all small. Even at the beginning of summer, his shoulders were wider than the chair's, it's just that he was sunken somehow. The mast and sails were there, but there was no wind.

I asked him to tell me exactly what he wanted to learn from me. I had a vague idea we'd write 'objectives' on a piece of paper. We could draw tick-boxes next to each one; the path through summer would be set.

'I don't know. This was Eddy's idea. I don't need a tutor.' He touched the top buttons of his shirt as if their being done-up was proof of this.

My face replied without me asking it to.

'I've never had teachers before,' he continued, 'and I've been fine.'

'"Teachers" doesn't just mean the teachers you get at school,' I said. I was speaking in sound bites and barely knew where they came from.

'I don't need anyone,' he said, but as soon as he said it, it seemed to both of us like such an impossible thing to feel that we moved on.

This time, he talked to my forehead. He told me he'd just done his GCSEs: four days a week at Sark School, but on computers mostly, in a room with no working windows. The majority of lessons were online for students over fifteen, on video feeds from schools in England and the States. He said they went too slowly and he hated American accents.

I later learned that when Pip chose to speak, he sometimes spoke very fast, like no one had ever let him speak before, so he was going to take his chance. This was one of those times. I asked him about his friends, if they were leaving Sark at the same time as him, if they were going to the same school. He said they had all left a long time ago.

'There are only three children my age at Sark School.' He was so tall, I found it strange when he said children. 'And the other two, they're not exactly ...' He touched his temple. 'They have special classes and stuff.' He looked at the heavy curtain, a square halo of sun pushing through at its edges.

Was he excited about leaving the island after the summer?

He picked at the arm of the sofa. Scratch, flick, scratch flick. Had he visited the new school he was going to be going to in England? He shook his head. The seconds stretched.

'What does Eddy *think* I have to learn?' he asked eventually.

Maths and science, I said, were the subjects his father had stressed. I'd bought books off Amazon and tried to read them. Long division, X and Y chromosomes; there was so much I'd forgotten.

'Look, I'm not trying to be rude,' he said. 'I just don't want to waste your time. Honestly. You have to believe me. There is no point in you doing this.'

'English?' I tried. It sounded like my last breath.

'You probably don't even like *books*...' he said, turning away to the heavy velvet curtain.

That was when I said, 'I do, I do, I do,' lots of times and very fast.

And that was when he looked up, and looked me in the eye. 'You do?'

I did like reading, it was true; I liked the idea of reading. 'I'm a great fan of Proust,' I said.

'You are?'

'Yes.'

'Me too. I read it a couple of summers ago.'

'The first one?' That's what I'd read. Most of it anyway, before I'd left it on a bus.

'No, the whole *Recherche*. It was Esmé's.'

I was nodding.

'I also like Borges,' he went on.

'Yes,' I said. The name was familiar. 'Excellent choice.'

'Only in translation, so far. I don't always like magic realism but I do like Borges. What do you think of *Ficciones*?'

'Hemingway?' I segued, 'I like Hemingway.' I had *A Moveable Feast* in my bag; I'd had it on my lap in the plane. It was a second-hand Penguin copy with an orange spine. I'd been carrying it around for a while, put it on the table when I sat in cafés.

Pip said he hadn't read Hemingway. I said he should, because he was really good. I think I even said he was one of my favourite writers. I got out the book and showed him the cover.

That was when Sofi burst in without knocking and called us into the kitchen for cake. I found myself wanting to say 'Pip and I both like reading,' so she knew we hadn't been sitting there silent, but I was perturbed by the size of the slice of cake she'd cut for me.

'I *know*,' she said, 'and it's not even nice. Fucking put *salt* instead of bicarb. And I was so lonely I also made quiche.' She said it 'quish' and put a tablespoon of cake in her mouth. Two chews in, she puffed out her cheeks and reached for the kitchen roll. 'Oh fuck, it's *rank*. No one eat it.'

I should say now that Sofi doesn't come across quite right on the page. Writing it down, it's not accurate. She did say 'fuck' a lot, but she said it lightly, like a laugh. It felt right when she said it. 'Do you know what it is?' she told me later, when we were standing close to each other over pink drinks at Dixcart Hotel's karaoke night. 'It's because I can't help looking at people's lips when they talk to me.' It was true, she'd look at your lips, even to see if you were listening. Anyway, right now she was rubbing at hers with kitchen roll and glugging my water.

'Ah, cake!' said Eddy, walking in, red polo shirt spotted with sweat rings. He had a bagged-up tennis racket in his hand and took a swing at an imaginary ball. 'Six–three. Too easy.' He clasped Pip's neck with his hand, which was supposed to be affectionate. 'Do you play?' he asked me, and then, before I could answer, 'Cake. Lovely. Lemon?'

'It needs icing,' Sofi said quickly, taking it away and putting it under a silver meat cover in the corner. 'And it's almost lunchtime. You can have a beer instead.'

There were days when Sofi's abruptness would make him bristle, but Eddy had just won his game, so he laughed, unbuckled his hand from Pip's neck and took his beer into the shower with him.

We ate lunch in the front garden, under a gazebo to the left of the croquet lawn. There was a slight slope, so Eddy looked a lot taller than Pip or me, who sat side-by-side opposite him, careful not to bump hands reaching for the salt. Sofi brought out a dish of hams; Eddy took most of it onto a plate with his spoon. I ate slowly. I composed small mouthfuls on my fork, held it up to my mouth then put it down again. I bade my time until the plates were cleared. I looked at other people's food, the quiche crumb on Eddy's lip, Pip's face when he swallowed, a wasp circling the salad bowl. The sun hit the table but the gazebo kept our heads in the shade.

Those first meals, I remember that the food tasted as if it had come straight from a fridge. The water made my glass mist, and the tomatoes were so cold they hurt my teeth. It's coldness I remember. Eddy asked me how the first lesson had gone, and we talked about Pip as if he wasn't there.

When Sofi brought coffee, I said thank you without looking at her.

We were always slightly better after eating, when the food had been cleared. Before it came, we didn't know what it would be; when it came, we might not like it. While we were eating, there were the noises, and the way that you can suddenly zoom out and find it strange to use metal things to bring food up to your mouth. Too intimate, embarrassing. We spilt things.

After lunch, another lesson in the study. Those I remember with my nose, the dust and the dark. Pip drew a diagram of a cell which was better than the textbook's, and I drank coffee till it coated my organs.

Occasionally Pip would ask me questions, but it was never about what he was supposed to be learning. How old are you? – Young for my year. But old enough. What is your surname? Have you been to Sark before? Do you have a brother? Husband?

I stalled, and then, soon, it would be supper, inside at the dinner table. Outside, inside, both were far too cold. 'Cold spell,' Eddy said, flicking his barometer with his finger as if he could change things. I counted beats with my teeth to try and make the meal pass. There were tall heavy cabinets, with feet which dug into the carpets. I imagined them falling over onto us. The air was heavy with the weight of having nothing to say. I don't know if I wanted Sofi there, or if I didn't. Would she have broken the ice or made it thicker? Either way, it was clear that she wasn't invited.

She made it easier for all of us by pretending it was her choice. 'Wouldn't want to sit with you anyway. Conversation round that table is dry as Ryvita. Dryvita. Not into it.' I know this wasn't true because later she told me she didn't like eating alone, that she found it harder to swallow. But she'd lay the table and bring us our food, and clear our plates, and prod Pip for leaving his carrots, and then eat in the kitchen, stool pulled up to the work surface, with her dirty white headphones in just one ear in case Eddy called out for anything.

'She's the help,' Eddy said, when Pip asked if we should invite her in for dessert.

'Isn't Jude helping us too?' Pip replied. I didn't like the way he said 'helping'.

'Yes, but that's different. Anyway, Sofi's ... Sofi's *Polish* ... She understands.'

Eddy turned to me, his hand with the signet ring held out for confirmation, and I smiled.

5

That second night, we came home to a kettle. 'Kett-lay!' Sofi sang as we walked into the walnut. 'Love a kett-lay.'

Bonita had left us two mugs and a Sandwich Spread jar, rinsed out and refilled with instant coffee. We'd been given caster sugar too, in an old curry pot with the label half scratched off, and there were teabags, loose, on the side. A handwritten note said 'tea and coffea', and Bonita had done some sort of origami with our towels. I think they were supposed to be swans, but Sofi lifted hers up by its long neck and said, 'She's done us *turkeys*! Such a gangster.'

Sofi sang songs I didn't know and dry-brushed her teeth for about fifteen minutes. I went to the bathroom on the corridor, and got changed in there too.

'They say you live for seven years longer if you floss, you know,' she said proudly. She wasn't flossing (she didn't even own any floss), but she was happy, so I didn't point it out.

'Night night, private dancer,' she said. And then, pants only, half-in and half-out of the duvet, she reached over towards me and turned off the light.

When I woke, it was my second morning on the island and I wanted to see it. I got out of bed quietly, careful not to wake Sofi, who'd cast off her covers overnight and was lying on her side with an arm taco-ed between her breasts. I put my trainers on and eased the bedroom door open slowly, because slowly means quietly. I made my way to the front door. The corridors already smelt of hash browns. Outside, the sky was soupy, but there was so much sun waiting behind it, I had to look down. Nearly every day started off like that – a bright white blanket. It took until eleven for the sun to burn off the clouds, or to catch their corners and turn them apricot.

Bonita's lawn was overgrown. The gnomes were waist-deep, and the dew got through to my socks. Once out the gate, I ran along a limestone road until I found a wooden signpost, shiny cream, place name and distance painted on in green. There were four arrows, and I chose the 'Window in the Rock' because it sounded like the name of a painting.

I say 'road', but that's not really right. Sark was scribbled with these long straight golden paths which ran thin between fields or along sparse rows of houses. Most were tree-lined, but the trees – they changed with the farmer – had grown up and bowed until they met at the top. Some of them reminded me of the driveway to Mandalay, but when I said this to Sofi, she said she didn't like Robbie Williams.

I ran past the school, and tried to imagine Pip there but couldn't. It looked like the kind of place you'd have a barn dance: big, wooden, mormon-y, but with rugby posts outside.

I ran past a restaurant called Hathaway's, where rain had poured smeary pinstripe onto a chalk sign saying 'Kidz eat 4 free'. I saw a woman on a tractor, and I wondered if my hair would go like hers when I got older; turn to wire, fall differently.

The Window in the Rock wasn't far, along a smaller path, through closer shrubbery, and then a clearing, a cliff edge, and a huge sign saying DANGER. Behind the sign there was a massive rock with a human-sized hole which looked like a giant bead, and opened out onto gunmetal sea and an archipelago of high rocks.

This was the Window and I walked into it, arms up in case I needed them, but not touching the sides in case they were dirty. I remember not being able to work out whether I felt very big, or very, very small. Scale is a strange thing on islands. I wanted to scream or make some sort of noise to fill the space and say I had been there, but no sound came.

Sofi was still in bed when I got back, sheets tangled around her ankles. She was lying in a cross like Jesus, breasts to the ceiling. I remember thinking that you shouldn't be scared of someone if you've seen them asleep, and that it wasn't true. I went to have a shower and used Sofi's shampoo (Palmer's, cocoa butter), then my own conditioner so she wouldn't know.

I remember that shower – that particular time I had a shower – because it was when I learnt to use the tap, to jam it with a hairbrush so it stayed on full, and I checked that the brown rings upriver from the plughole were rust and nothing worse. It really is just the first few days that I can still see this clearly, from start to finish, full-length and in order. After that, it became showers, lunches, everything plural. But I can give you those first days whole. They are self-contained and I can hold them, because everything was new and nothing had melted into shorthand. Beginnings are always slower.

6

It was at lunchtime of the second full day that Esmé re-emerged. Sofi had been taking Esmé's meals up to her room, Pip following behind with a bottle of Badoit he'd get from the drinks cabinet. They would swap places on the landing so that he was the one who knocked. Then, after we'd eaten downstairs with Eddy, Pip would go up to collect Esmé's tray. The plates always returned untouched, looking like glossy display meals at Japanese restaurants. The night before this one, I'd come out of the loo and seen Pip putting a chunk of Esmé's chicken in his mouth and hiding rice under a napkin before he took the tray down past Eddy. The only thing Esmé ever wanted was more water, and Pip would run back up, bottle of Badoit in hand.

That lunchtime I heard Pip talking to Sofi as she composed Esmé's tray.

'Just give her less,' he said. 'Smaller portions.'

'They *are* small. Look, I'm not going to cut a new potato in half.'

Pip was trying to get a look at the plate.

'I mean, is it me?' Sofi went on. 'My cooking? What does she normally eat?'

'I don't know. Things I make. Like *eggs* . . . or . . . other things I make. She's not always like this.' He pushed past Sofi and made for the potato. 'Just cut it in half.'

But this time when they went up with the tray, they came back with it too.

'She says she's coming down,' Sofi said, shrugging her lips. I stood up. Pip started cleaning the table with a cloth, putting down an extra knife and fork, and checking them for dust like a waiter on a trial shift.

Esmé was wearing black again, and her legs looked like pipe cleaners. That was what I saw at a glance, because I didn't know if I was actually allowed to look at her. I also didn't know where to put my hands. So I stood behind the chair I'd been sitting in and touched my napkin, stopped touching it, picked it up again, put it down. She walked to the table. Eddy was still in his office and Pip had gone to get her water. I looked at where he'd be through the walls, as if that might make him come back quicker.

We were alone. 'Hi,' I said, but really it could have been any one-syllable noise. She said 'Hallo' back (French accent, padded on the 'h') and then sat down. It didn't look like it was very easy for her to pull the chair out.

'Do you mind if I—?' I was starting to say when Pip came back in with a big glass of Badoit for her. I tried to catch his eye. 'Is it OK if I—?' He nodded yes, but he was looking around the room as if trying to check for anything Esmé wouldn't like. So I looked around too, except I didn't know what to look for.

It was incredibly awkward, as awkward as that word is spelled, two w's and a k, bramble round the tongue. It was the first time I felt relieved when Eddy joined us.

'Soup. Cracking. Chicken?' (It was cauliflower.) 'Never mind. Warm. Warming. Boy been good today, Jude? Got past two plus two?' He laughed, and got soup on his shirt. He only looked at Esmé when she wasn't looking at him, which is what I was like with everyone. Pip looked at his mother, though, watched her stir her soup. His back wasn't straight for once; he put his head down, so it was the same height as hers.

She was so thin – just bones pushing against skin – that I wondered if it hurt her to sit on a hard wooden seat. It's not that it stopped her from being beautiful, but her cheekbones were even more deeply carved than Pip's. A line drawing of a bird in flight.

Sofi brought out cold meats for the main course. Charcuterie, parma ham, fleshy piles of rillettes. It was all too pink, too close to animal. Eddy talked for us all, Eddy ate for us all. He spread butter on half gherkins; he asked for ice-cubes in his rosé.

Esmé spoke only once, to Pip. '*T'en veux plus?*' she asked him, while using her fork to safeguard the last bit of mortadella before Eddy reached for it. Pip said no, so she let Eddy take it. I could almost feel the workings of my watch, the seconds falling like the slowest drip.

After lunch, I asked Sofi to put the kett-lay on, so I could sit at the round table in the kitchen. Hers – and it did become hers: the knife marks she left from chopping without a board, the way she lay across it and power-napped after breakfast – was such a different table. I wanted to tuck myself under it like it was a bed, or place my head on it, like a pillow. She made me tea with too much sugar, but I was happy there with her.

'Batty, isn't it?' she said, blowing into her tea.

'Esmé?'

'Families in general. Batty, the lot.'

She put an ice-cube in my Earl Grey too ('to cool it down cos you don't have milk'), but after a few short sips, I had to go back to the study, and Pip.

Neither he nor I mentioned Esmé, but she might as well have been in the corner, soundlessly stirring her soup. It seemed impossible that before lunch Pip and I had laughed together (about the 'psss-*SHING*' noise Sofi made when she sneezed); impossible. I made him do a past paper – AS level Biology – and he did it in a quarter of the time, and got every answer right. 'Even more retarded than the GCSEs,' he said. After that, he sat doodling in his notebook. There was no sound apart from nib scratches. He used his fountain pen to colour in one of his fingernails. I pretended to read the back of a book in French and willed Sofi to sneeze again and bring us her light.

Halfway through the afternoon she did. She burst in, a short wooden spoon holding her hair in a bun, and said it was Friday, Eddy was on a clay shoot, and I was to come with her to the Avenue. I didn't even ask Pip, I just said yes, and she kissed me on the centre of my forehead and pulled me out of the house to the lilac bikes Bonita had lent us.

I can see her now, three metres ahead, her dress skirting in the wind, her wheels carving out a zigzag. She was very, very bad at cycling – that afternoon, she nearly crashed into a tractor with the number-plate ROSS 3 – but I can still see her, even now, cycling in front of me, cycling faster, looking back to check that I was still behind her.

The Avenue was Sark's high street. Except it wasn't a high street in any real sense, just a short string of shops and cafés, all low-rise and wooden, difficult to date or place. It made me think of Australia (I had gone there with my parents once, on what they called the 'last family holiday') although the voices here were French, Spanish, German, and ones from faraway Europe that I couldn't properly identify.

We wove through on the bikes. There was a NatWest, with purple hydrangeas in the front garden, and monkey-puzzle trees with fronds which u-bent like the necks of monsters. The souvenir shops spilt out onto the street, all selling the same hats – faded caps with 'Sark' sewed on, straw trilbies. Then beach-town necklaces and rusty racks of postcards that looked like they'd been dipped in tea. There was a new bakery being built out of wood, varnished like a Chelsea bun.

We cycled straight to the Island Stores, and leant our bikes on the dusty kerb opposite. The shop was rectangular, white, paint on roughcast. The window was a mosaic of flyers for open gardens, dog-walking, and the annual Service on the Sea. I stood outside for a second, but Sofi wafted me in with her shopping list.

The shop was subtitled 'supermarket', which was aspirational, as it was about the size of a classroom. There was a newspaper stand (all a day old – current affairs ferry-lag), sliced long-life bread, then chest freezers full of black forest gateaux and polythene packs of wontons. Sofi went straight to dairy and filled her trolley with eggs. 'Sark' was written in blue biro on the cartons, all capital letters apart from the r.

'I was here last week,' she said, leaning on the push bar of the trolley so her feet came off the ground. 'My first day. Everything's changed.' She pointed at the girl behind the till. 'She had *tips*, last week . . .'

'You have to tip in shops here?'

'No, you spacker. Purple. Purple tips. Like she'd dipped the ends of her hair in bog bleach.'

She went from that to hummus. 'Hummus?' She picked up a pot. 'Last week they didn't even have *onions*. Eastern bloc, man. Or whatever wartime. Rationing days. There was about one thing on each shelf . . .' She broke free from me and trolley-scooted up the aisle. 'Fuck *me*! Herbs!' She pierced a packet of fresh tarragon with her little fingernail and smelled it through the bag. 'It's for the tourists, isn't it? I love herbs.' She was talking very loudly, which could have been embarrassing, but when you're beautiful, and do what you do with the confidence of the sun, no one seems to mind.

Sofi was a hedonistic shopper. She didn't look at labels, she didn't deliberate, she just threw things into the trolley, denting tins, bruising apples. She ate grapes as she weighed her onions, and told me to get biscuits.

I walked round. I liked looking at the prices, because they were impossible to guess. Golden Syrup in that tricksy green-gold twenties tin, by Royal Appointment, for £1.37, and then right next door, glacé cherries in a thin plastic pot, £8.31 or something silly.

'If you're going to take a fortnight choosing, at least get two packs,' she said when I came back. 'Rich Tea? That's *bread*, not a biscuit. Rich Tea? Oh *pisser*.' And she sent me to get cleaning products instead.

Sofi had no sense that heavier things should go at the bottom of a trolley. She started the shop with eggs, and crowned the load with huge two-litre bottles of full-fat milk. When we got to the till, she paid in British fifties and Jersey pound notes, forest green and with the Queen looking younger. We cycled back to Eddy's with bags in our baskets and balanced on our handlebars, Sofi in front, faster, wobbly, and me in her slipstream. It would often be like this.

7

I can't tell you when 'we went' became 'we would go'. There isn't an exact number of days which pass before something becomes a routine; six, perhaps; maybe a week.

We would get up. Sofi would shower, and dart back to the tiny room naked, towel on her head, one arm half-holding her breasts ('as a sports bra, not a shield'). I'd go into the bathroom after her. The floor would be soaking and I'd have to stand on the loo seat to put my socks on. The mirror would still be steamy. Sometimes I wouldn't wipe it, because we didn't wear makeup in the day, and I thought it was better not to look.

Sofi would go ahead to the house to make breakfast and I'd say I'd eat at Bonita's, though I never did. It felt forced talking to Bonita without Sofi. She'd say something like 'Miss Sofi left early this morning,' and I'd say, 'Yes, she was wearing a really nice top,' and that would be it. So I'd skip breakfast and arrive in time for Pip's lesson. Sofi would bring us coffee in the study. Pip took it milky, and Sofi would 'cappuccino it' with Cadbury Highlights and a heart-shaped cookie cutter.

Pip frowned when he was working, and rubbed at his lips (they got dry because of this, and Sofi gave him her Vaseline, which she applied with her own finger). His foot metronomed the floor. I'd make him stop because the speed changed, so you could never relax into it.

More and more often we started to spend time with Sofi in the kitchen, We'd bring our work with us, past papers and lists of equations. Sofi's clattering and swearing and singing made just enough noise for us to concentrate. She called the kitchen her office. The cupboards were red, and she wiped the doors meticulously clean, even though inside there was soy sauce on the spines of spice racks and crumpled curls of garlic paper.

Mid-morning, the dishwasher from breakfast stopped. When Sofi opened it, steam would flood out that smelled like hot tomatoes and breathing. We'd watch her cook. Slapdash, like her shopping. Sometimes she'd make it into a perform-ance – she'd use the pot of paprika to knock cumin into the sauce and then vice versa; she'd chop fast and all the rounds of carrot would come out different sizes. She'd lick cake-mix off the spoon then put it back in the bowl. She grated her finger-nail into the dauphinoise once (that was an accident). And she used scissors a lot, for snipping broccoli, chopping through meat, cutting the hard, creamy fat off bacon. I didn't like that; there was something wrong about snipping flesh. It's the clip, and the way the scissors bounce back, and how they make you think of paper and garden hedges.

We always ate lunch with Eddy, but only very occasionally –

three times, perhaps? – with Esmé. They were different types of deeply unpleasant. Pip wasn't used to having his father there. When it wasn't summer, Eddy worked during the week – 'and weekends,' Pip said into his soup – in London. Eddy didn't know where everything went; he asked questions which gave it away. At least he made noise, but he'd go on and on about Pip's new school, talking about fagging through fat chunks of bread. I was hopeless, hopeless, ever-smiling. I'd be the first to see if Eddy wanted the salt passed. I'd ask if he wanted more potato salad – 'could I tempt you?' I'd say. I can hear myself saying it.

When Esmé was there, the only thing I remember her eating was radishes. That harsh crunch they make. If Eddy told Pip he wanted him to be in the first fifteen for rugby or something like that, Esmé would say, with her thick accent, *'Plizz.* Let the boy eat.' The few words she uttered would be in English if she spoke to Eddy, and French if she spoke to Pip (though he always responded in English). She never said anything to me or Sofi.

I don't like to think about those lunches. I suppose I blocked them out. That's the thing about summer, when you think back to it, the sunlight bleaches out the bad, and you don't remember it ever raining. Those first lunches though ... Salads, soups, cold meats; all of it bitter as rocket.

But afterwards, when Esmé had retreated to her room, when Eddy was away again, sailing or emailing, Sofi and I began to stay on at the table and talk. One day, Pip gave up waiting for me in the study, and came back to the kitchen.

'Are you having tea?' he asked.

Sofi pointed at our mugs.

'Can I have one?'

She changed the direction of her finger to point at the kettle.

Pip started to walk towards it but she sprang up, blocked him and pushed him onto her seat. 'Only joking. I'll do it, knobber.'

While the kettle boiled, she stood behind Pip's chair and absent-mindedly massaged his neck.

'How's it going then? Is he learning a lot?'

I felt a prickle on my cheeks. 'Tea's hot,' I said and blew into it.

Sofi knocked on Pip's hairline with bony knuckles. 'Oi, are you learning? I'm doing an investigation. Ofsted.' She went back to massaging. Sofi couldn't see it, but he was wincing with each squeeze.

'Ahh – Sofi – ahh, in a nice way . . . it really hurts.'

'Poof.'

He shrugged away from her. 'Not a poof. Your nails are long.'

She looked at them, couldn't really argue, and walked back to the kettle.

'I'm giving you the mug with the crack,' she said. And she blew into the bottom to get rid of the dust.

We all sat round the table, hands cupping, but not quite touching, our mugs, like you do round a campfire.

'So this is nice,' she said. We both looked at her. 'No, it is! Why does everybody always have to be sarcastic all the time? I *like* this . . . Let's have *biscuits*.' And she flared her eyes like she was suggesting something exotic.

'Whereabouts in Poland are you from?' Pip asked as she hoisted herself onto the work surface to get to the top shelf of the cupboards.

'Fuck's sake. Ealing. *Ea*-ling. Haven't you told him anything? It's just the z's and c's in my surname.'

'Oh. Right. That . . . how do you say it?'

She turned so she was facing us. 'Try.' She was standing in the sink now, Converse soles on enamel.

He shook his head.

'No, I'm serious, *try*, please.' She did praying hands. 'It's my favourite game.'

He thought for a second, then said something that sounded like 'leek soup'.

'No.' She started laughing. 'Try again.'

He refused and looked at me instead. 'What about you, Jude? Where are you from?'

'The country.'

'Where?'

'Just – the countryside in the country. But I went to uni in a city called St Andrews.'

'I thought it was just golf there,' Pip said. 'Golf and tea shops.'

How did he know about St Andrews? 'There is golf there. Some golf. But also a lot of nightclubs.'

He looked confused. 'And shopping,' I added. 'Shopping malls.'

'Biscuit?' Sofi said. 'Am I the only one eating? Don't you like jaffa?'

Pip said he wasn't hungry.

'You don't eat because you're *hungry*. We're not in Africa. Jaffa – *now*.'

Pip picked up the packet and said he'd never had one before.

'Tell me you're joking,' Sofi said, putting both palms flat on the table.

'No.'

'He doesn't joke,' I said.

'Infidel! Like this.' And she showed him how to chip off the chocolate, peel off the orangey bit and then suck the base till it stuck to the roof of your mouth and turned to paste.

'Do you like it?' she asked him, tongue battling against clags of cake.

'Not really.'

'Well, you're going to learn. You are going to learn a lot.' She scraped a finger round the back of her molar and looked contemplative for a second. 'Have you seen *Mulan*?'

'No.'

'*Jesus*. What's wrong with you? Watch *Mulan*.' She turned to me. '*You've* seen *Mulan*, haven't you?'

I said yes, but I hadn't. She started singing 'We'll ... [dramatic pause] make a man ... out of you.' She mimed a sword fight and tried to get me to join in. Obviously I didn't know the words, so just repeated 'out of you' slightly after she'd finished.

'They're OK actually,' Pip said. 'They grow on you. Do you want one?' and he scooted the packet across the table until it knocked into my teacup.

That became what we did after lunch. Jaffa Cakes and talking. We asked one another questions. What ifs, and would you rathers. What we were scared of, and where we wanted to be in ten years. Brothers and sisters (none, we were all only children), and how we felt about that.

There's a moment when you realize you're going to spend a lot of time with someone, that it's worthwhile to ask questions, and all right to answer. We asked the same questions more than once and the answers changed, because they do when you're young. We'd start with a story, then move forwards, backwards, sideways, between us. You'd get scraps of grandparents and never remember which side they were on.

I have no chronology for either of them. We dealt in moments. Mostly Sofi's: running away at Christmas and spending it at a McDonald's; a nipple-piercing which got infected. After her stories, ours seemed drawn in the dimmest pencil. Pip told us about breaking his leg harbour-jumping at low tide, I said I'd run a half marathon in Leicester. I just couldn't tell stories in the same way as Sofi. She told us about when she was eleven – puppy fat, pyramid hair and polio shoes – or about the time her period leaked during a presentation at college. I did say some things, but I couldn't use my hands like Sofi, or tell stories against myself the way she did.

The one advantage I had, was that I was older. The magic of being in the year above at school. They asked me different types of questions, and they asked me like I'd know the answers. Sofi: How much does a chicken cost? Like, a *raw* one (alive was what she meant). Pip: Did I think a great painting could go undiscovered, or did I think that after enough time, it would be found?

It's not a choice whether you bluff or not, it just happens. I said chickens were cheap and that art was arbitrary. Arbitrary and reductive, I used those words a lot. Sofi asked me how I knew this stuff, so I said you learned as life went on; you hit a certain age and then you just know.

When I talked, Pip listened intently. Maybe he'd already worked out that I didn't know much about maths or science – and that if he was going to learn anything from me, it would be about other things.

Most of the time, though, we listened to Sofi. She *adored* things or *hated* them (either one accompanied by a burst of her fingers). But there was more *adore*. Pip spoke too, sincerely, seriously; usually, I was quiet. But quiet was fine, because Sofi would be julienne-ing carrots, or giving us potatoes to peel, or she'd sing, and all these things would fill in the gaps. I wondered what my listening face was like. I thought about it, and tried different ones. I don't know if these faces worked, but *it* worked, it somehow worked, the three of us, tea after tea, tale after tale at the table.

8

On the eleventh day, everything changed. When we got to the house for breakfast, Eddy was already in the kitchen looking for a teabag. Sofi found one in a cake tin (she sniffed it, nostril touching, before putting it into a cup). When the kettle had boiled, Eddy announced he was off. Business trip, *had* to go, three weeks, Monaco and some other place.

Once again, it was difficult to know what to do with my face; did he want me to look sad that he was leaving, or sufficiently capable to be left in charge? *Was* I being left in charge? I didn't know. I did a bit of both: sad, capable.

Eddy was blowing into his tea to cool it, but took an over-ambitious glug and scalded his throat. He looked at his watch, face battling against the burn.

'Today?' I said.

'Yup. Ferry's in five. Suppose we better do *au revoir bisoux.*'

His French accent was like Pip's – unsinkable English in that way Churchill had.

He kissed our cheeks – Sofi on one side, me on both – and left on the first boat, before Pip had come down for breakfast.

'Must have a new intern,' Pip said over amber eggs – they'd all been double-yolked that day. 'A pretty one.' He put down his fork. 'Also explains why he put *this* under my door.' He pulled a scrap of magazine paper out of his pocket and laid it on the table. It was a timetable for the Rugby World Cup championships on the television. Eddy had written *IMPORTANT* in fountain pen on the shiny paper, and the ink still hadn't dried. Pip smudged it into a navy blue blur with his finger.

After his eggs, Pip announced that he wanted to spend the morning reading (I'd lent him the orange Hemingway; it was hard to get into so I said I'd finished it). I said that that was fine, because it meant I could spend the morning in the kitchen with Sofi. I sat with her while she had her 'ten-sies' – yesterday's cake flicked with milk and heated in the microwave. When she went to the shops, I opened cupboards and looked in them, because you're not supposed to do that in other people's houses. Eddy must have left on a Tuesday, because it was also the day Sofi met the Czech boys.

'They – were – *great*,' she said when she came back, fingers flaring out like fireworks. 'Three of them, builders or something, kind of grubby. *Friendly*. They said we have to come out with them.'

'Not "we",' I said. 'You. They haven't met me.'

'I told them about you. I said you were sweet. That's not the point. It's a free country.'

'It's an island,' I said. 'Come out where?'

'A place called the Mermaid. You've seen it . . . have you seen it? We've cycled past it, it looks hideous.' She said it like that was a good thing. 'We have to go. They were Czech, Jude. They had *dreadlocks.*'

The first night without Eddy, we stuck to the routine. Sofi had dinner on the table at seven. Esmé's miniature meal went up on a tray. I ate alone with Pip, and for some reason he lit a candle. Sofi sat in the kitchen, though she talked to us through the wall and put her iPod on speaker. 'What's Love Got to Do with It', and 'some heavy stuff from Bristol'. After the meal, I helped with the washing up. We'd had lamb, and when I tried to wash up the tray there was so much fat it splintered into glitter.

Sofi took out the Mâcon Eddy had opened the evening I arrived.

'It's nice, isn't it? It's a good one, isn't it? Eddy only drinks good ones.'

It was days old now, eleven days old, and tasted of olive rather than grape. But it was so cold it fogged up our glasses, and Sofi drew a heart on hers and we clinked. She said I had to look into her eyes: otherwise, it was seven years bad sex luck. Sofi slurped, I started slowly, but we both felt the way the first sip sears. That light, lifting prick in the chest: possibilities, maybe it's all possible.

We took our wine to the bathroom and started doing our makeup side by side in the small mirror. Our heads were touching and she said we looked like Siamese twins. 'Unidentical, obvy,' she added, taking a bit of my hair and holding it next to hers. Then she said my hair was the most beautiful she'd ever seen; that she wished her hair was the same colour, and that it made her think of guitars and pianos. The great irony of compliments: I felt so shy after that. I sat on the lip of the bath and let her do her makeup first. I didn't want her to see where I put my concealer, or if I held my face differently in the mirror.

When we came out, Pip was drinking milk from the bottle. He looked up, top lip tippexed, mouth slightly open. He asked us what we had all over our faces.

'Makeup,' Sofi said. 'It's supposed to be nice.'

I tried to look at my reflection in the window of the microwave. It might not have been a good idea to borrow Sofi's bronzer. Pip asked where we were going, and for a second I thought Sofi was going to invite him, so I said, 'We're late! See you tomorrow, Pip. Don't give up with the Hemingway, it's worth it,' and we left him alone with his milk at the table.

'It's much safer without a torch,' Sofi said to me by the lilac bikes, finishing the Mâcon from the bottle and frisbeeing it into a bush. 'For me, anyway. I just look up. In the air. I can tell where the path goes from seeing the sky along the line of the trees.' She gave me her headtorch, 'Take it, *take* it. Don't be gay,' and went first, zigzagging by the moon.

The paths seemed bumpier at night, but we were lucky because that afternoon it had rained, so the biggest potholes were filled with water and caught the light. I remember thinking they were like islands of water, and that on the path the world was in reverse: the sea was the land and the land was the sea. I had no idea where we were going, I simply followed the red bindi of Sofi's backlight, until she suddenly veered off into a brightly lit inlet, shouting, 'Right! Right! The one you WRITE with!'

She cycled straight and shamelessly into a large crowd of people. When I saw them all, I got off my bike and started wheeling it, but Sofi stood up high on her pedals and cycled on, saying 'beep beep', and then 'ding-ding-ding' (she had a bell, but always preferred her voice). A path cleared, I followed her. We leant our bikes against an old oak tree at the back. Only when we were walking away did we see a girl in a sequinned top, skirt up, squatting beside it.

'If she wees on mine, I *swear*...' Sofi said, looking back worriedly but not stopping. She took my hand and led the way to the door. It should have been £2 entry, but the man at the door – thinking about it, he might not have been a bouncer, he might have just been a man at the door – said we were pretty as princesses, and we went in for free.

I'd never been anywhere like the Mermaid. It was a tavern, but there were dogs in there, and children. It looked like a church hall, with pews round the edge, and plastic tables with metal tube legs, the ones you get in primary schools. There were women staring at empty pint glasses like crystal balls. There were age gaps, fringes, fat girls, shouting, lots of people kissing. Most of the couples looked wrong somehow, as if the whole club had been shaken up in a colander and only the oddest pairs had slipped through the holes together. Sofi bee-lined for the bar, parting the dance floor like Moses.

She asked for two double vodka and cokes, 'big mother ones'. The barman had shoulders like a carthorse, and stubble that was almost teal. He poured our drinks from an enormous bottle into small glasses without ice. Sofi took a sip from both glasses to see which was stronger, then chose that. The bar curved in a semi-circle, and halfway round there was a wooden wall with a small arch through to a sort-of VIP area. The VIPs looked like they'd been there a long time. Resident alcoholics, cigarette smoke as a hairspray, unwashed T-shirts, unwashed women.

Sofi downed her drink and was sucking on an ice-cube when she dropped my hand and long-jumped into a man's arms. He swung her round in a circle by her waist, Liesl, but golden-haired.

'Sofya!' he said. She took a big sip from his pint as two more men clambered to kiss her on the cheek.

I stood just behind her, holding my drink and her bag. Lemon. But then she turned back to me. 'Sorry, sorry. Boys, this is *Jude*.' I remember how she said my name, how she pushed it at them, as if I was famous and they should have heard of me.

'You are friend of Sofya?' asked the main one, the one with the dreadlocks.

'I work with her,' I said, because I didn't know what we were.

'You're cook like Sofya?'

'Oh no, no. No, I'm a tutor.'

'What is tutor?'

'She teaches,' Sofi said. 'She's very clever. Not like a cook.'

Which wasn't what I meant, but I couldn't explain because it was too loud and smoky. The song changed and a group of potato-faced ladies at the next-door table started singing along and bashing the beat with their fists on the table. They were sat under silver bunting which said 'Happy 30th!', but they looked much older than that.

We went outside and stood in the cool, the boys rolling thin cigarettes with rough fingers. I tried to tell Sofi that all I'd meant was that I couldn't cook.

'You're such a *spoon*. I don't care, dude. And it's true, you aren't a cook.' She kissed me on the cheek, 'And you are clever.'

She looked over at the boys, who were playing football with one of their shoes. 'Isn't Vaclav beautiful? Teeth are a bit funny, but his *eyes*. He must be a gypsy. I love that. What about Armin, for you ... do you like him?'

'The one who's headering the shoe? No.'

I said that he smelt, and she asked what I meant.

'What do I mean by "smells"? I mean: he smells.'

'Which one?'

'What?'

'Which smell has he got?'

'*All* of them, Sofi. All the smells. Breath, armpit ... *hair* ...'

She laughed at me and told me I was fussy.

'But it's not from exercising,' I tried. 'It's *dirt*.'

I went to the bar. Sofi stayed outside with dreadlocked Vaclav. When I came back with drinks she was telling him his eyes made her think of tequila and lime.

'You want to drinking my eyes?' he said. She had her hands on his forehead in order to inspect him. His eyebrows bushed out at the ends and fanned together at the nose and she patted them down with her fingers, then pushed him away.

'Then we will drink tequila, the drink tequila,' he said.

'Tonight is birthday of the DJ. Who is Silver Fox. Who is Roger. Who is seventy-three. Who is wonderful DJ.'

We finished smoking in the doorway (just for the breeze, the ban was flouted) then we moved inside. The others started dancing, except it was really just jumping and singing into each other's faces. I sat on a stool, and tried to look as if it was a choice. My drink was already finished so Armin bought me another. Roger, DJ Silver Fox, was in the corner, nestled in a booth next to overflowing coat hooks. He looked fittingly formal in stonewash jeans, but with his striped shirt tucked in, under a shiny leather belt. His hair was blow-dried back into a low-rise Elvis, and he had Pied Piper hands – he pointed, and eyes followed. There were gold rings on most of his fingers.

I was trying to edge away from a breathy conversation with Armin, when the music went dead and a woman started ringing a bronze bell by the bar. She was very short and kept shouting 'Oi'. She'd turned it into two syllables. Oy-yuh. After several of those, she said it was Roger's birthday. A group of boys 'a-wooga'-ed. The short lady pulled out a box of Ferrero Rocher and presented it to Roger, and we all sang Happy Birthday. Sofi went over to join the fat girls at the thirtieth who were doing harmonies.

After that, a chant started for another song. Vaclav and Armin shouted particularly hard, 'Vun moh! Vun moh!' Roger silenced the crowd with a ringed finger. A riff started up. I knew it from somewhere – grainy guitar, seesaw piano. Slow though, nostalgic in some way, but for something that hasn't happened yet. Sofi came over to see if I was OK, and then the chorus came in. It was Semisonic, 'Closing Time': 'I know who

I want to take me home'. I'm sure everyone knows it, but still, I wish I could write down how a song sounds. The chorus soars somehow, it really does, and yet it's still so sad. Sofi sat down next to me and laid her head on my shoulder. Boys in caps found girls to kiss, and a dog lapped up spilt beer. We stayed until the song was over.

Sofi sang the chorus on the cycle home, just that line, her zigzag following the beat. She shouted that when she was drunk she could completely see in the dark. Then she screamed as her front wheel dunked into a pothole. When we got to a stretch of downhill she took her feet off the pedals, her hands too at one point, so she could stretch her limbs out into a star.

You can't imagine how dark it was. Thick ink black. It wasn't like it is in cities, or anywhere in England. And there were the bumps and the hills and our borrowed bikes with shaky brakes. I'm not sure how we survived those bike rides home, when it was dark, and we were drunk. I think that maybe you come much closer to dying when you're young than when you're old. It's just that you sail home safe somehow. I cycled behind Sofi, trying to keep up, trying to keep my distance, and I remember thinking there were so many ways in which cycling was like flying.

When we got back to Bonita's, Sofi took a handful of peanuts from the big bag in the hall meant to refill the bird-feeder. She said she needed it more than the birds did, and sat on my bed in her bra, throwing each nut up and catching it (mostly not catching it) in her mouth.

'What about Vaclav?' I asked a couple of moments after lights-out. 'Why didn't you kiss him?'

'No, I did, but he had the most terrible erection. Too big. *Monstrous.*'

'Oh,' I said. I lay there silent, and I could hear my heartbeat in the pillow.

She must have had a few peanuts left, because she threw one at my head.

'Goodnight, Jude,' she said. 'Nice night, Jude.'

When I woke up, my bed was full of soft white peanuts, in halves now, with bits of their red papery sheaths flecked all over the sheets.

9

It wasn't a conscious decision that everything would change when Eddy went away. That first morning both of us blamed the night before.

I didn't wake up until Sofi shook her hair out post-shower and it felt like it was raining.

'Teefed your shower gel,' she said. 'Nice. *Minty.*' She smelled her arms, knelt down next to me, swept my hair off my face like a curtain and said good morning.

It was already midday. The sky was blue but there had been another storm in the night after we'd gone to bed and our bike seats were sopping. Sofi whipped out a tampon from her bag and used it to wipe hers down.

'Do you want yours done too? There's room in here,' she said, making the tampon swing like a pendulum, waterlogged only on one side.

The paths were sodden, but Sofi pedalled fast, mud flaring out in a flamboyant V-shape from her tyres.

When we got to Eddy's, I barely stayed in the study with Pip at all. We were supposed to be doing triangles – equilateral and isosceles and how the sides and angles related to each other. I was looking at the textbook, trying to read fast so I knew what I should be saying, but the paragraphs were just fuzzy blocks.

I was sure I looked hung-over. My face had that kind of gelatinous sheen, a bit like pregnant belly before an ultrasound. I must have looked odd somehow because Pip kept on looking at me.

'What?' I asked, finally.

The answer to that is normally 'Nothing', but Pip said, 'What?' back. And so I said it again, and for a moment, we just swapped 'Whats?'.

'Nothing,' he said, in the end. 'But it's hypote*nuse*. You keep on saying hypothesize. It's different.' He put his lid on his pen, then took it off again. 'Was it fun?' he asked. I shrugged.

At 1.15, I told him we were done. We went back to the kitchen, Sofi's kingdom.

We had lunch on the sofa, with the telly. Sofi had made Pip so much pasta she had to serve it in a salad bowl. She sat down in between us, with the remote.

'Sofi's choice,' Pip said. And then he leant over and prodded me, 'Sofi's choice ... like the book?'

I told him to start eating before it got cold. Sofi put on *Jeremy Kyle*, but, pointing up to Esmé, turned the volume right down. She moved off the sofa to watch it on her knees, right by the screen, leaving a dip in the seat between us from where she'd been sitting.

After all the pasta, Pip said he was tired. He was going to stay inside, but Sofi forced him out into the light for vitamin C.

'*E*,' I said. 'It's definitely E.' And she said 'B, E, C, A, Z' – the sun was good for it all.

We had all been in the house too long. In a way, it became its own island on an island. I looked out of the window at Pip asleep on the lawn now, post-prandial, his face still for once. His leather notebook was making a tent on his chest, rising slowly every time he breathed in.

The sun must have been almost exactly above the house, because it wasn't coming in through the windows. We needed to be outside too, so I told Sofi to be careful not to make too much noise, and we pushed our bikes over the grass past Pip and left.

We cycled by signs, but mostly by Sofi. She said that even after five days she could picture Sark from above, and that was as good as having a map. We stopped at the Island Stores and Sofi bought an avocado. She had it on a bench, biting off the top, peeling it like an orange and eating it like an apple.

'It's so funny how you watch me,' she said. 'Is it that you want some?'

'No,' I said quickly. 'No, not at all. It's just that you've got green all over you. How did you get it on your forehead?'

She lifted up her T-shirt high to wipe her whole face. 'Better?'

After that, we cycled to the Coupée. It's this teetering path between Big and Little Sark – ninety metres long, ninety metres high, three metres wide. You're not allowed to cycle over it so we walked our bikes. Right in the middle, Sofi asked me what held it up, and how it could be so thin, and so high, when the huge, heavy sea was clapping it from either side. I told her to stop taking her photo and walk quickly to firmer ground. Like planes staying in the air, it's best not to think about it mid-flight.

It was our first time on Little Sark. It was different, a bit like Scotland is to England, bleaker, with bracken, gorse and purple flowers. You had more the sense you were on an island – that king-of-the-castle thing – and that cliffs were near, wherever you were. The strangeness was more concentrated. We passed a boot-brown man sitting in his doorway, dipping carrots into a red pot of Saxa salt. And the people walking through fields together . . . you couldn't imagine how they'd ever met, even less become friends, lovers or whatever they were.

It was uphill for a while after the Coupée and we cycled slowly. Sofi used her left hand to push down her knees and make it easier. She changed colour even on that one bike ride. When we got off our bikes, she was golden. She held a croissant against her leg at breakfast the next day, and they were the same colour, they really were. But anyway, we walked to the furthest edge of Little Sark, arms paperchained. We kicked rocks and picked flowers, and we didn't say much. I worried that she'd notice, and think I had nothing to say. But then – on a bench, looking out onto Guernsey – she put her hand up to my chin and kissed me right on the jaw. She said that she was happy, so happy Eddy had gone, and that she loved the sea.

She told me she got these bursts of happiness, that some-times her whole soul – did she believe in souls? she wondered for a second – but yes, her whole soul felt like it was too big for her body and she had to touch someone.

She was covered in sun. It seemed to put a spotlight on her. And I wanted to stay sitting on that bench with her until the wood was cold. I looked at the sea, then Sofi again, and I didn't know what I could possibly say, so I said that we had better head back.

10

We got used to life without Eddy very quickly. The sky was bluer when we left Bonita's, first at ten, then soon ten-thirty. Sofi turned showering into an art form, the floor into a floodplain. We left with wet hair and it dried on the ride.

I dipped with Pip into the dark of the study, but we always came back out into the kitchen.

'Shall I do the lessons then?' Sofi asked. 'You want to learn how to cook?' She took one of Eddy's white shirts from the laundry and put it over her head like a ramshackle chef's hat. '*Fine*. If Esmé comes in, I'm teaching you how to be me.'

She told us how to use the weight of the eggs, rather than the number, to measure out the other ingredients for cakes. She said you could tell how cooked a piece of steak was by comparing its firmness to a place on your own hand. 'I never get that right though,' she said. Occasionally, she'd suddenly get irrationally protective: 'Not a chance! I can't give you freeloaders *all* my secrets.'

One day, halfway through a demonstration of how to make

breadcrumbs by bashing a bag of bread against the table leg, Sofi accused Pip of looking at her funny.

'He's looking at me funny. Why's he looking at me funny?'

Pip put his head straight. He'd been looking at her from an angle, more with his left eye than his right. He did the same to me sometimes when we were in the study.

He mumbled something.

'What do you mean "death"?' She almost shouted. 'Is he trying to curse me?'

'*Deaf,*' he clarified. 'Deaf in my left ear. Just a bit.'

After that we switched seats so that we were always on his hearing side.

We ate lunch lying on our fronts on the croquet lawn, or round the kitchen table on days when it was too hot. After lunch, Pip would get tired, which Sofi decided was because he was growing. As soon as he was asleep, I'd say there was no point in staying and we would escape and leave him. We went to the Venus Caves, and lay in uncut grass which stayed erect in the gap between us, like a little fence. We walked to a cliff edge over Derrible Bay – the sea ahead spread like a jewelled carpet – and sat in the wind, feet dangling.

'Next time,' Pip had asked me, 'could you take me? There are some places I'd like to show you. I could come.' But when he fell asleep after lunch, I didn't wake him.

The following day, however, he said the same thing in front of Sofi. He wanted to show us Little Sark. I said we'd already been a hundred times. His face fell, so Sofi said, 'We love it though, let's go again. Vaseline,' and she reached into her pocket and dabbed some on his lower lip.

Pip didn't have a bike, so he ran along behind ours. Because of the way his spider legs moved – knees to the sky – it looked like he was pedalling too.

The afternoons were different with Pip. He knew which one was Jersey and which was Guernsey. He told us that the Coupée was a wind trap, and that, during the most terrible storms, kids from Little Sark used to have to crawl across on their bellies to get to school. He answered Sofi's question about it staying up: it was 'an isthmus'. And the beach we'd looked at, the one that curved between the cliffs like the in-between-toes of a webbed foot, was called Grand Grève. We sat looking out at its white bay, and he told us other things: about the silver mines at Port Gorey; and that Sark was the last place in Europe to abolish feudalism. He paused.

'In 2008,' he finished.

Sofi said she'd guessed. She bit a fingernail. 'So who's the king?'

'No king,' Pip said. 'He's called a Seigneur,' and he told us how the Seigneur 'semi-rents' the island from the Queen for £1.79 a year.

'*Cheap*skate!' Sofi said. 'That's the price of a cup of tea in Costa. What jokers.'

She asked Pip if everybody knew everybody knew everybody knew everybody knew everybody. Pip said he didn't know, and then, 'mostly'.

'Like them, for example. Do you know them lot?' She pointed, using her elbow for subtlety, at a family having a picnic down below us on Grand Grève, a father and three sons. The youngest two – one olive-oil blond, the other rustier –

were filling their pockets with shells and having competitions to see how far they could throw rocks into the sea. The father and the oldest son had deckchairs, and looked like they were giving the stone-throwers marks for each shot. The wind was strong enough to make each stone fly in a bow-shape.

'Bend it like Beckham!' Sofi yelled then, subtlety forgotten.

'Them? The Millers? No,' Pip said. 'I think they're only here for the summer.' The dad had dark curls and he was laughing – his laugh big, coloured, kind – at something his son had said. Pip's head was tilted as he looked at them in his concentrated way. He looked slightly sad. 'They look nice though. That's the thing, most of the people young like me only come here for a few weeks.'

Pip took us further onto Little Sark, past a place called Cider Press Cottage. The sign was a shiny slice of trunk; the words carved using the sun and a magnifying glass. Sofi was worried Pip would burn, so she rubbed suncream into his neck. She played a three-note piano on his moles and then blew on his skin to dry it. He didn't even say thank you, he just bounded ahead, looking back to check we were following every few paces.

When it got too brambly, and too steep, we left the bikes and used our free hands to pick blackberries.

'You won't have them yet,' Pip said to me, 'in the country-side where you're from. They won't be ripe.'

'We get them from Sainsbury's.'

'Oh, right, well . . . we get them early. Microclimate.'

I used my thumb and forefinger like chopsticks, one berry at a time. Sofi plunged a hand in, and groped. She didn't get many and said it was because she was from the city. Pip told her to look behind us; there were always more blackberries if you looked back in the direction where no one walked. He said that every path was more walked-down in one particular direction, which confused him, because if you walked one way, wouldn't you have to come back?

Perhaps not. We had just reached a precipice; sixty feet high, a jagged drop.

There was a rope which ran from where we were all the way to the rocks at the bottom of the cliff, studded at various points on the way down, pinned under boulders or tied round rusty metal loops. The rope was waterlogged green from old rain. Sofi gave it a tug.

'Seems all right.'

I wish she'd given us more than 'all right', but she'd already taken off her flip-flops and tucked them between her teeth. Sofi went first, and Pip followed her down the rope, both of them doing this sort of poor man's abseiling.

'Don't put the string between your legs!' Sofi yelped. 'It's gnarling up all my ovaries.'

Why had I brought such a silly bag? Nothing in there was mine. It had Sofi's chocolate orange, Sofi's cigarettes, her suncream. I took hold of the soggy rope, taut from the hands of the other two, and headed over the edge.

By the time I got to the bottom – the insides of my fingers burning – Sofi was standing barefoot on a big, bald rock. She was balancing on one foot, squinting. 'If you stand right, and get your eyes right, you can see out to sea through that cave there, and this one here.' The two caves out to the sea were wide, but they curved, and so you could only see out through slits, and only exactly where she was standing. Pip had showed her.

'You have to *align*,' she said. 'There's something pagan about it. Something . . . Mayan, I don't know . . . One of those ancient things.'

She stretched out her arms, and shut her eyes, her own ritual. Pip was wiping mud off his feet on a low rock, slick with algae. I could tell he was glad to have shown Sofi something she liked. I poked Sofi in the thigh and pointed to a flat, pigeon-grey rock, where someone had written 'Spank me hard dady' in permanent marker.

'There's your ritual,' I said, and something about dyslexia.

Sofi laughed – except it wasn't quite a laugh – and then stepped down off her Mayan rock. We made our way through the slit on the right, and climbed up onto a rock platform right by the sea. It was flinty, and Pip said that when he was younger, Esmé used to bring him here.

'Serious?' Sofi said. 'She took that rope?'

'Yeah. We used to come and pretend this flint bit was a tile on a giant's roof. That we were on top of everything.'

We lay on our bellies, our tops pulled up so the bottoms of our backs were in the sun. Sofi got her chocolate orange out of my bag, battered now, and cracked it open on our rock. She ate it two pieces at a time, sucking first and then scraping the pieces back out of her mouth against her teeth. Her bottom lip was brown, and she coloured in the top, like lipstick, with a stubby segment of chocolate orange. Pip took his top off, shoulders pale and broad as a canvas, collarbone like an anchor.

He sat cross-legged. He'd taken his notebook out of his back pocket and was writing in it, pretending not to listen to our conversation.

'Would you rather your hand be stuck – for the rest of your life – in an unbreakable jam jar ...' (this was Sofi, every other word italicized) '... or that everything you ever eat again for the rest of your life taste of tuna?'

'Tuna,' I said.

'So quick to answer! It's not with mayonnaise, you know. It's plain, *tinned*, tuna.'

'Tuna.'

'It's in *brine*.'

'Not being jam-jar-hand. It would wither.'

'I know, but tuna ... *fuck*.' She looked out to sea, shaking her head.

Sofi took these questions so seriously. We'd wake up in the morning and the first thing she'd say to me was that she'd changed her mind. She'd decided it would be better if her dad walked in on her and her dog, rather than vice versa. I'd be half asleep, and it would take a while to work out what she was talking about.

'Fine,' she said now. 'The tuna. Fine. Maybe that's better. But, would you *rather* – sleep with *Armin* – or the Ross man who has all the tractors?'

'No more, Sofi, no more.' Though there were always more. I suppose they were ways of asking the questions you wanted the answers to. I asked her if she'd ever been in love, and she said no.

'I want to go to Paris,' she said then, as if it was the logical step in a conversation about love. 'Have you been? I so want to go.'

I'd been there on a school exchange. We'd partnered with a convent but one of the nuns died while we were there and we didn't get to go to Disneyland.

'It's OK,' I said. 'Bit overrated.'

'Not for me. I've seen films, it's perfect for me. *La Haine*. All of that.'

'Sofi,' Pip chimed in, looking up from his notebook, his shoulders red despite the suncream, '*La Haine* is about Algerian immigrants in tower blocks. We watched it for GCSE. It's about murder.'

'That's what I *mean*. I like it whatever. Whatever. Look.' She was holding a segment of chocolate orange between her fingers, using it firmly, like a teacher, as if it made her argument stronger. 'I am going to Paris and none of you bastards can stop me.'

'No one's trying to,' I said. 'You're having a fight with yourself. If you go, I'll come and meet you under the Eiffel Tower one day.'

'Really?' she said. She softened. She realized the piece of chocolate orange was softening too, and that it was the last one, and she offered it to me.

I shook my head about the chocolate. But about Paris: 'Really,' I said. She put the top of her forehead against my arm, and stroked me with it, like a cat, clumsily. Her head was so hot, you could almost feel the activity going on inside it. 'I'll be there, jam jar on hand, eating tuna, whatever.'

'I might be there too,' suddenly, from Pip. 'I've got family there. Mum's side.'

We had never heard him say the word mum before. It felt too easy a word for Esmé. He pressed his pen hard into his notebook.

He mentioned his grandfather, and said a name that neither of us recognized.

'Painter,' he said. 'Quite a famous one. But yeah, the whole lot go to the Sorbonne. Grandfather, great-grandfather. Uncles too.'

'Just the men, then,' I said.

'And her. She went.'

'Sorbonne sounds like sorbet,' Sofi said.

'Why do you need to go?' This was me, practically at the same time. 'Don't you already speak French?'

'Oui,' he said, 'but my accent's terrible.'

I nodded, though it didn't need confirmation.

'She says I get it from my dad.'

'Well,' Sofi looked back at him on his high rock. 'I think that would be great, Pip. More the merrier. Us three. Pa-ree.'

'It's not like I just suddenly thought of it,' he said to me. 'She grew up there, in the sixteenth. I've thought of it before.'

'Sixteenth what?' asked Sofi.

'Arrondissement,' I said. I knew that.

'I didn't think it was century. Arrrr-ond-eess-mont!' said Sofi, affecting Frenchness by stretching her top lip downwards. 'I love it. I can't wait to go. Baguettes, man. Reunion. Shitloads of wine.'

Sofi bared her chocolate-orange teeth. She'd shifted and was lying on her back now, T-shirt shuffled up to her bra. She scrunched a bit of the orange tinfoil into a ball and balanced it on her stomach. She was using her hips to try to roll it into her belly button, like one of those pinball toys you get in a Christmas cracker.

The little ball rolled in a wobbly path off her waist and she threw it into the sea. We both watched it go. There was more sea – golden-blue, but choppy, hard-looking – than when we first lay down. A lot more.

'Pip,' she said. His eyes were shut now, lashes flickering in the heat. 'Oi, white boy. How do we get back up that cliff?' She worry-burped, and blew it up towards the sky. He said we had to climb.

'Fuck that for a bag of chips,' she said. 'I'm flying.'

'No,' Pip replied, as if it had been a genuine suggestion. 'You can't. The only way's to climb. Or swim, maybe.'

Neither of us liked his answer so we decided not to hear. The sun was coming in thick beams in the breeze and I asked it to blow me to sleep. I'd got to that stirry half-awake, when Sofi called my name. She'd wiped the chocolate off her mouth with my bag and was using both arms to do enormous waves. It was like breast-stroke, but standing up, and she jumped up in the air every time she brought her arms down. 'It's *them*,' she kept on saying, '*them*'. It was the Czech boys: Vaclav and Armin, in a little red dinghy.

They shouted 'Sofya!', and then 'Judy!'. Pip started laughing when they said it a second time.

'Judy's – brilliant,' he said. 'Can I call you Judy from now on?'

I said, sure, fine, and that I'd call him Pippa. 'Your shoulders look like crayfish, by the way.'

When the Czech boys got close enough, Sofi stuck out her thumb like a hitchhiker, then stuck out her chocolate tongue. Vaclav jumped in the water to pull the boat close enough to us. He and Sofi kissed each other on the cheeks, three times, maybe even four. We got in, Pip last, carrying my bag and his leather notebook between his teeth.

The boat wasn't meant for five people. It sat low, very low in the water.

'Why do you have a boat?' Sofi asked, drawing finger tattoos on Vaclav's forearm. 'Are you pirates?'

It was when Vaclav said they worked for Farquart & Fathers that Sofi's hand dropped off his arm.

'But Sofya, it's not choice thing. It's job – money thing. What you can do?' He put his hands up in the air like he hadn't fouled in football. 'But I give you promise. Armin. Vaclav.' He pointed. 'Good men.'

All I knew about Farquart & Fathers was that they were rich. Pip clarified things later: absurdly rich. The family had just gone up from nineteenth-richest in the world to eighth. There'd been a boom in their pubs – the recession – and their funeral parlours had bought up Co-op.

Armin held the tiller, and Vaclav did the talking. He told us they were handymen. Cash-in-handymen, Armin interjected (high-five with Vaclav). They'd found their job online, on a summer work website. They mowed the Farquarts' lawns and sowed vegetables in their greenhouses. Then there were stranger things, like bringing back bundles of gorse to burn, and collecting sea glass from the beach to fill the driveway and make it shine.

'They want to feel like they walk on diamonds,' Vaclav said. Sofi's fingers back on his arm now. 'And this witch patch—'

'Perch,' Pip said, and explained that it was an old superstitious tradition, a stone plinth on Channel Island chimneys for witches to rest on mid-flight.

'This witch patch or perch or whatever thing. They are putting one. But every wind it falls off. Five times, we've stick the patch back on.' He slapped the back of his right palm against the palm of his left, the way Italians do. 'Ten times! I say to Armin, witches too fat. Only thin witches from now, please.' They high-fived again.

When we got to the shore, the boys – all three of them – pulled the dinghy up onto the sand with me and Sofi still in it. We climbed out, kissed Vaclav and Armin goodbye and left them sitting on the edge of their red beached whale, lighting a damp spliff Armin had kept tucked behind his ear.

As we walked, Pip told us the Farquarts were buying up half the island. He'd said he'd heard they were trying to import foreign cows and that there were rumours of an underground bunker. People on Guernsey were starting to call it Fark rather than Sark.

That's when I remembered the graffiti scratched into the toilet walls at the Mermaid: 'Fark off!' which I'd thought was just bad spelling. When we got to the Avenue, Pip told us to look. 'This side Sark,' and he pointed at the normal shops that we went to, 'and that side Fark': the Chelsea Bun bakery and restaurants with terraces, ye this, ye that, all new with old names.

It was late by then, home time, and we left Pip by the blue postbox.

'You're sunkissed,' Sofi said, and kissed him. 'And kissed. And you've grown! Fuck, Jude – kiss him. He's a giant. He's grown in a *day*.' Pip looked down and knocked the sand off his shoes against the bottom of the postbox.

As we walked home, Sofi asked if *I* had ever been in love. I was glad we were walking. 'Of course,' I said, then when she said, 'Really?' said I didn't know.

Back at Bonita's, our hostess was asleep, melting into the sofa in front of a Costa Rican telenovela. There were three empty cans of Coke next to her, one still dripping from the lip. She was snoring, making the most unimaginable noise. We'd heard it from the front porch and Sofi had gripped my wrist and dilated her eyes. When we got to our tiny room, we could still hear Bonita, in baggy chorus with husband John next door.

'Fuck,' Sofi said, head hammering against my arm. 'Oh fuck. It's like a fucking *farmyard*.'

I started to laugh.

'Oh but it just won't *do*!' She laughed too now, and when we laughed together, the light flickered. She kicked the wall with the side of her foot. 'I said, I *said*. Didn't I *say* it makes me psychotic?' She explained: it was because there was no fixed beat, so you couldn't set your heart to go in time to it. Like Pip's metronome foot, for me.

'My heart and my breathing. It fucks both of them up. Oh bugger *off*, Bonita,' Sofi said as snores poured in. She lay in bed for a few minutes, wrestling with her sheets, laughing, then not laughing, then really, really not laughing. She got up and said she was going to the garden. She said she'd sleep outside. She took the laptop and watched films I suppose, the stripy sunlounger dragged close enough to the fence to steal next-door's internet.

There were a few nights when she ended up doing this, and although I saw her go I never went with her. It was night-time and night-time had rules. Even if I was perfectly awake – feet hot, then cold, thinking about Sofi outside, nothing between her and the sky – even if I was perfectly, perfectly awake, I just obeyed it.

11

Thinking about it, that was the only summer since I'd got a computer in my room that I didn't check my emails.

The laptop was mine, but it was thicker than the Bible and took three minutes and strange sounds to turn on. Sofi used it more than I did. Outside, at night, and sometimes outside in the morning, before we left for the house.

Eventually, she found that the strongest signal could be reached from within the flowerbed, and so fashioned a chair from the toughest branches of a large lavender bush. She used to touch the screen – jab her finger at it and make dents – and she said it was because she was used to her parents' new television.

The way she typed made me laugh. From her purple throne, she balanced the laptop on her knees. Then she typed so fast and aggressively it looked as if she was galloping.

'But where are you trying to go, Sof?' I'd ask her.

Tappity, tappity, tap, tap. Elbows up as if to hold reins.

'To the end of the internet?'

She didn't reply.

I wondered who it was she wrote to and what she said about the island, if she ever even mentioned it, or me, at all.

That day, I told her to pass the laptop over. I was curve-backed on the sunlounger. It may have crossed my mind that she'd leave her inbox open and I'd be able, at least, to look across the subject lines.

'It suits you,' she told me when I had it in my hands. 'You look very modern.'

The screen was set to BBC News.

'It's the news you read?' I asked her.

'It's rude not to have it *open*,' she said. She was chewing something.

I scanned the page. It had been so long since I'd thought about the rest of the world that I was out of date with all the storylines. The proper nouns – politicians' names, ceasefires, celebrities – looked like a different language.

Most of my emails were from eBay and Amazon. Deals of the day, low insertion fees, lots of them. I looked down the bolded lists for names that meant more.

There was one from my father:

Is it going OK? Family's not the Farquarts, is it?
    Not much to report here. The council is still trying to close down the library.
    Love Dad

and a longer one – two actually – from my mum, signed from both of them. She was doing a lot of yoga and had an

American teacher who was apparently a guru. She said she'd photocopied my graduation certificate and sent it to all the aunts. She was the only person I knew who still used Xs with Os. I marked it as unread and imagined I'd reply later.

The last email I looked at was from a boy called Seb who'd been in my halls at university. He'd taken me to a Thai restaurant in our final year, and it turned out he was very reactive to spice. I'd told too many people about the way he'd poured the wine until it reached the rim of our glasses. It had been a bit awkward since then.

Hey.
I heard from Dan that you were spending the summer on Sark? I'm in Jersey, we're visiting my grandma. It's a bit dull if I'm honest. I'd kind of like a night out. I thought maybe I could come say hi? I looked at ferries.
　Hit me back,
　Sx

'Your face has gone funny,' Sofi said.
'No it hasn't.'
'Do you have a rash?'
'Just this boy I know wants to come to visit.'
'Here?'
'Yeah. For a night out,' I laughed.
'OK, but is he hot?'
'No. Absolutely not. He's ginger.' I looked down at what he'd written. 'He put "Hit me back".'
'He sounds nice. I like gingerbread.'

'You can't have it. He's not coming.'

'*Is* lavender edible, by the way? For eating?' It was already in her mouth.

I slammed the computer shut without replying to the email. I never did to anyone, and we left for the house, nearly three hours late, with small bunches of lavender tucked behind our ears.

12

So where was Esmé in all of this?

In a way, she was the rain that you forget. If Sofi asked about her, I told her not to; it was best to block the blackbird out.

Pip took up the tray and Badoit alone. 'It's just sometimes,' he'd say when he came down. But that summer it was nearly always. She stayed upstairs, alone, in the dark. Once, when Pip thought we were outside doing back crabs in the garden, we heard him come down with a bag of clanking bottles.

'There's something in the water,' Sofi said one evening when we were getting ready for the Mermaid, ear by ear in the bathroom.

'There's always something in the water on islands.'

'You know what I mean,' (index finger to the ceiling) '*Her* water.' She mimed drunkenness by crossing her eyes.

I finished my mascara and said that it was none of our business.

During the day, at our round table, when one of us talked too loudly (Sofi), the other two would point to the ceiling. Esmé's bedroom was directly above us, and a finger to the sky became shorthand. Esmé above was a strange crown, though not exactly a thorned one. She made us quieter, but she also made so many things funnier, the way it is in school assemblies, when you know you're not allowed to laugh. And we were not stupid. All of it – the morning rosé, the sunburn, our laziness – all of it felt safer with some sort of parent around.

On Sunday morning, every Sunday, she went for a long walk. She always left at eleven, and when we asked Pip why, he told us that it was her version of church.

'Where does she *go* though?'

'Just around.'

'Around where?'

'The island.'

And she did. She walked almost the full perimeter of the island. Sometimes if we went out on a Sunday, we'd see her in the distance – near the powder blue hydrangeas of La Sablonnerie, or on the slopes down to Bec du Nez – and change our path. Sofi asked if we shouldn't say hi, but Pip said it was best to leave her, that it was her way of thinking.

'It's weird though,' Sofi said to me, when we were alone. 'I always thought she was anachrophobic.'

'What's that?'

'Scared of the outdoors. *Space*.' When she said space, she made her eyes big too.

'*Ag*oraphobic.'

'Exactly.'

Even if we didn't see her, I thought about Esmé on her walks. I imagined her not taking paths, and how small she'd be against the open fields. In my head, it was always windy, and she walked with her arms around her waist and her head dipped. The wind was almost strong enough to blow her over. I always felt a strange relief when she came home. I think we all did.

She was important. Sofi didn't smoke inside, because Esmé would have smelt it. We slept at Bonita's and mostly observed mealtimes and washed up, because somewhere, there was Esmé. We used her when she was needed. It was Pip who mentioned *Lord of the Flies*.

13

By then, it was early August. My ticket home, three weeks to go, had been stuck to the fridge, but Pip had put it away in a drawer. Even with Esmé upstairs, the house felt open, ceilings higher, windows wider. And we were hardly ever there now. Esmé upstairs and home time in the drawer: we didn't want to see any of that. The world was blond, the wind was warm. These were the days that were golden.

Sofi made Pip do pull-ups on his old swing in the garden. Some days he didn't wear T-shirts, and we all stopped wearing shoes until it got dark. One day, Esmé saw Pip in this state of undress.

'What did she say?' Sofi asked him.

'She asked why I was naked.'

'And what did *you* say?'

'That I didn't know where my clothes were.'

'*Why?*'

'It just came out of my mouth.'

'And what did *she* say?'

'*Gamins*,' he said, flatly. 'Kids.'

In the evenings we sat round dusty cardboard boxes of Chardonnay at the Mermaid: three litres, £18; wine as warm as the dance floor. Vaclav squirted it out into cups for us, once, twice, then straight into Sofi's mouth, a slave holding grapes for an empress.

There was the time Sofi saved DJ Roger from a girl who'd accused him of stealing her diamanté denim jacket. Sofi had a word with the girl and she left very quickly. I asked what she'd said.

'I told you. I'm from *Ealing*. I'd take any of these island leprechauns.' (She said it leper-corns.)

Anyway, because she'd saved him, Roger invited us over to his house one afternoon. I told Pip to go and see if Esmé was OK, and Sofi and I, girls, went alone to Roger's house. It was painted red, and named after a song from a Disney film.

'See?' said Sofi, when we were hovering outside the front door. 'That's what I mean. He has *taste*.'

He had mounted plates of race horses and Malay sunsets, and a whole wall, skirting board to ceiling, of CDs.

He asked if we wanted coffee, ran a ringed finger over necks of whisky bottles, plumped for Bell's, and belly-flopped it out of the bottle instead of milk. He told us he used to run a nightclub in the cliffs called Bootsies, and he told us about the Sark Lark. 'Taxes and that. Nominees. Plaques. People made their money. Weren't nothing but for fun.' He told us about human table football – 'a little Sark tradition' – where players' arms were strapped to scaffolding poles. He spoke in exclamation marks and question marks, muffled by years of smoking Royals Red. When we left, he gave us cassette tapes, *Now 19* and *Now 21*, the ages we were that summer, to take away with us.

We were drunk by then, and went to the Island Stores for food to fight it.

'Do you think they'll know?' Sofi asked. 'Smell my breath.' She did three short breaths from the back of her throat right in my eyes. 'Can you smell I've been drinking?'

'No, I can smell prawn crackers. Sofi, you can't open them before you've paid.'

She said that shops brought out the worst in her. That it was 'all those aisles'. So we went and sat on the bench outside, the bench between two phone booths. We watched kids count coins in their palms, then buy sugar cigarettes. We sat in the kind of happy silence where you feel you're talking.

'An apple,' Sofi said, after a while, 'an apple of all things.'

'I like apples.'

'Is it even *nice* though?'

'Well . . . no, not this one.'

'I can see. It's *onion-y*.'

She tried to touch it.

'It's floury, isn't it?' She retched. 'Crapple!' she said, and stuck her tongue into her lassi to get the last drops out. 'Do you think I'll make it to Paris, Jude?' she asked, licking her top lip then looking straight at me.

I could tell she wasn't looking at the surface of my eyes, but somewhere deep behind them. She had this way of looking at you so intently that you had to look away. I did.

'And Pip. Pip said he might go for a whole year. That would be cool. Do you think that would be cool?'

The thought of Pip getting to be alone with her, far away, felt like heat. 'Yeah, maybe,' I said. My voice see-sawed, intentionally unsure.

'A year's a bit long,' she agreed.

'And you and him . . . *there*. It just might be a bit *weird*. It's fun here. But there, and afterwards, it would – it wouldn't be the same. It would be like some kind of photocopy.' I paused. 'Bad photocopy,' I added, to make sure.

She went to put her wrappers in the grey street bin a couple of metres away. When she came back, she seemed to be thinking about what I said. The tips of her eyes looked unhappy.

'Of course you'll get there,' I said. 'You'll get to Paris. And I'll come. Of course I will.'

We went to the post office and fiddled with the kitchenware they sold, one-person Le Creusets and skewers for corn-on-the-cob with patterned handles. We had to leave when they said Sofi was trying to shoplift a notebook (she said she was just putting it in her pocket 'to see if it fitted').

After that, we went to church. It appeared to be empty so Sofi put her arms in the air and walked up the aisle singing 'Calypso Carol'. That was when a woman popped up from behind the altar with a yellow duster in her hand. Sofi sat down very quickly in a pew and pretended to be praying.

'No worry,' said the woman from the altar. 'Nice to see young people. Day trip?'

'No,' Sofi said, letting her prayer hands fall. 'Here for the summer. Working for a family.' She said Eddy's surname.

The woman went back to dusting for a second. 'The mother – yes, the mother used to go to the other church, I think.' She said there were two churches, this was Anglican, but there was a Methodist one too.

'Do you lot fight?' Sofi asked.

The woman laughed. No. And actually, she said, the two churches came together at the end of every summer for a service on the sea. She told us this year's was soon, and we should come. We said we would, and Sofi apologized for walking in singing the Christmas song.

One time, back at the house, when the three of us were sitting in the garden, backs propped against Eddy's big shed, Pip asked what my dad did.

'Why her *dad*?' Sofi shouted. 'You're so medieval.'

'No I'm not. She just said that "all dads want a shed" so I was thinking about dads.'

'*Sex*-ist,' Sofi said anyway, and raised her hand as if she were going to hit him. He flinched away from her – a sprinter ducking to cross the finishing line, the stock image of fighting siblings.

'He's like your dad,' I cut in. 'In business.'

In business was true, but they were in very different tax brackets. My dad wore a suit. Eddy's collar was always undone. 'Neck's too fat,' my dad would say about men like Eddy.

'Insurance. That kind of thing,' I finished.

'And your mum?' Sofi said.

'She worked at the same company as him. That's how they met.'

'Nice,' Sofi said, chewing on a pen, though it wasn't that nice. '*My* parents met at language school. In Dover.'

She paused, but we could see from her face that she wanted to continue.

'He took her to France on the ferry. Calais. The bright lights. And that was it, he proposed right there.'

'Really?'

'Swear down. At an Italian restaurant, just like that. Wham bam, thank you man.' She dusted off her hands and smiled and her bottom lip got a tiny bit stuck on her teeth.

'That's sweet,' I said.

'Kind of like mine,' Pip said. Then, when we turned to him, 'Kind of.'

'They met in *Dover*?'

'No. No, but France . . . '

'Really?' Sofi said tentatively, catching my eye.

'What?' Pip said. 'It's a nice story, actually. Eddy tells it at dinner parties.'

'Fuck off, do you have dinner parties here?'

'Yes.'

'But with *other* people?'

'Yes. No. Well, we had a couple. I remember a couple when I was younger.'

'Anyway, go on—'

'They were children when they met.'

Sofi made a face.

Pip shut his eyes and swallowed, ignoring her. 'In the moun-tains behind Nice. Eddy's family had their holiday home next door to where Esmé grew up. They were neighbours. Every summer, they were neighbours. You know the big photo in the conservatory with two children picking olives?' We nodded. 'That's them.'

'They're tiny,' I said.

'Is Eddy the one without any teeth?'

'Yeah. No teeth. Anyway, Eddy's dad sold the house. The way Eddy tells it, he only found out when they spent the next summer in Greece. He says he tried to kill his father by dunking him in the pool.'

'Shit.'

'Not really. He was twelve.'

'But what happened to *Ez*?' Sofi demanded.

'He wrote her letters.'

'Bullshit.'

'No, really. For years. She wrote back. I've seen them, the letters. Hundreds, a whole box. What's strange is you can see how the handwriting turns grown up.'

We were still sitting down but Pip had stood up and he lightly kicked at Eddy's shed with his heel. 'They met again when – I think he was nineteen and she was seventeen? And well . . . voilà.' With his voilà – his English voilà — he raised his arms to gesture to the garden, the house, the marriage. His voice, which had been upbeat, anchored. 'I don't know if they knew each other at all, really. Not at all. I think she was still a kid.'

That night we rode out to the Czech boys' field. Pip ran beside the bikes, faster than before, using the backs of our seats to push us uphill whenever it got steep. The field was quite far from the thatched Farquart castle but there were still signs warning about guard dogs, in English, French and another language which looked textspeaky, with lots of apostrophes. 'Sercquiais,' Pip said. '*Wankers.*' (That word was a gift from Sofi.) 'No one local speaks it.'

The boys had made a shaky wooden table out of old oyster crates for their poker games. Sofi and I lay on the grass nearby with our shoes off. There wasn't a single cloud, and Sofi wasn't used to the stars.

'It's not like I'm a rabbit, stuck down some little hole. There *are* stars in Ealing. They just don't look like this.' It was so dark, but if you looked hard enough at any piece of black you could find a star. She tried to find the 'bit' of sky which was her favourite, but it kept changing. She pointed her way through the whole universe, and neither of us had seen stars like that.

What else happened? All the stories stack up on top of one another and the pile is so thick I can't see most of them. I climbed a tree for the first time in years. The three of us sat in its catapult and smoked rollies the thickness of a thumb. We cycled in the wind and it didn't matter what we said because the wind threw our words into the next-door fields. I remember the smell of shells; the sound of seagulls, tractors, horses. Pip took us to navy-black caves and showed us how to jump into where the water rushed. I went last, but I did go. I cut my hands on sea anemones, and I wanted the scars to stay, like rings.

Sofi kissed me on my cuts and told me to look at Pip. 'His neck. He's got a man's neck. Aren't we doing well?'

Sofi taught him how to sew and made him 'power bowls' of

bananas and nuts. He ate without wincing; his ankles were less thin. He had freckles now, messy stars on his cheekbones, dots on his lips. He gave Sofi piggybacks without blushing, and he could look at me straight. He pushed his hair out of his eyes, and got good at looking; good looking.

If it rained, sometimes we would go back to peristalsis, and osmosis, and all those 'ises' I was supposed to teach, but Pip knew it all already. And besides, it never rained.

The grass was warm enough to lie on in cotton and there was sugar in my coffee. We left Esmé her tray and Badoit, and took crisps and cans of sweetcorn for clifftop picnics. We drank Eddy's good wine from the bottle as the sun burnt into the sea. I don't know if the sun tricks you into feeling things, or if it makes you see things more clearly. But that's what I mean when I said it was golden. Our skin got darker and our hair got lighter, and summer passed like sand through our fingers.

14

Three Fridays after Eddy left, he texted the house phone to tell us he was coming back. Sofi put the answerphone on loudspeaker and a jerky automated voice read out the message:

'Home tomorrow. Bringing Caleb et al.'

'Such a creepy voice,' Sofi said. 'So *nasal*. And who's Al?'

Eddy had sent two messages, and at the end of the second the service de-abbreviated his LOL. 'P.S. Chateaubriand pls,' the computer voice said. 'Laughing Out Loud.'

'I think he meant the love one,' Pip said. 'Idiot.'

We had breakfast at lunchtime. Scrambled eggs Sofi-style, which were more of a condiment – half-egg, half-butter. I leaned back in my chair, stretched my arms out and took up space while there was still room.

Sofi's huge Nokia started vibrating on the table. It was Vaclav. She picked up and said, 'Yeah. OK. Yeah. *Jiggaman!*' looking at me with good-news eyes. She hung up and said the Czech boys were going scalloping and wanted us to man the boat while they were in the water. Wo-man the boat, she corrected herself.

'It's illegal,' Pip said. 'Can I come?' He looked at me. We hadn't been to the study for nearly a week, but I was still teacher. I looked at Sofi, because she made the decisions.

'You know what they say,' she said. 'When the cat's away, the cheese will play.'

Pip chopped the rest of his scrambled eggs into a noughts-and-crosses grid of pieces and ate them with his fork, determinedly, quickly, happily.

We threw our things into Pip's school rucksack, and met the boys down at Creux harbour. Armin was carrying tanks down to a tied-up speedboat. Vaclav was standing up at the bow, wobbling because he was waving, and so was the sea.

Girls kissed boys, and boys bashed shoulders. Pip pointed out where he'd harbour-jumped and mangled his leg, and on that note we went down the wet steps and clambered into the rocky boat, a manoeuvre impossible to perform with grace. Something humiliating about it, like changing your shoes on the side of a street.

Vaclav, tipping the boat like old-fashioned kitchen scales, held his iPhone up to the sun. 'Reception is crazy shit on island.' He'd googled 'how to drive boat', and was waiting for an instruction video to load on ehow.com.

'Dory boat, not dinghy boat. Is different.'

Vaclav asked if anyone had a pen and Pip got out his notebook. I went to take it, so I could be scribe, but he pulled it away and said it was private; he'd write. We all stared at the little iPhone screen.

The video was presented by an American man in wrap-around sunglasses. You can see it if you go on the website. We couldn't, however, because of the glare of the sun. So Vaclav held the phone to his ear instead, screwing up one eye to show he was listening.

'Turn on bilge blower, write! Write! Turn on bilge blower.' That was the only instruction he gave from the video. And when it was over he said, 'What is bilge blower?'

'And what is dead man's switch?' Armin cut in. 'You find out dead man's switch?'

Vaclav looked at his phone, shrugged, and pushed off from the harbour wall. He said we'd manage, it couldn't be that hard, and we ad-libbed into the ocean, chipping past parked boats. Vaclav pointed to nowhere and said that was where we were going.

Sofi was chirpy and ran a finger through the sea, so it looked like we had a mini jet-skier beside the boat. Pip looked ahead with the same face he had when he was reading: concentrating, happy, lips which might be about to whistle. And Vaclav and Armin argued as they always did – unless that's just how Czech sounds.

When Pip corrected Sofi's pronunciation of scallops, she asked if she could see his hand, then bit it.

'Why are we doing this, again?' she asked Vaclav.

'Moonlight job,' he said. 'Tourists. They love it. Love this fish.' We stopped at some sea he was happy with. He shook talc into his crotch and started yanking his wetsuit up in fistfuls. He handed me a radio in a waterproof sheath and said that the emergency channel was twenty. Teacher again; I held it tight.

They'd dropped a light-looking anchor, which led up to a bright orange buoy. It was tiny. 'Young buoy,' said Sofi, then dunked it.

Vaclav took the red springy emergency break cord off his thigh and attached it to Sofi's, taking longer than seemed necessary. They put on masks and tanks with hisses of air and clanks of metal. I didn't want to think about whether they'd done it before, but Sofi asked. Vaclav said he had, when he was younger, in his uncle's swimming pool, and Armin had practised with the kit in their field.

'I thought this PADIs was Irish thing, not Professional Association Diving or whatever,' Vaclav said, perched on the edge of the dory. 'But I think this: you can try thing, and hope. And normally is working.' He touched Sofi for luck and threw himself, massive red scallop bag clipped to his waist, into the flat blue sea behind him. Armin kissed the back of his own hand, and followed his friend into the water.

Our job was just to stay near, to watch out for the coastguard if nothing went wrong, and to call for them if it did. Pip peered over the edge of the boat like he might swim after them.

I studied the sea on the other side and thought about how it looked the same from a plane and a boat, just on a different scale. Each wave was chipped at like a Stone Age spearhead, a thousand other waves inside it. Zoom out, zoom in, and there we were, the three of us, bobbing up and down near an orange dot. It was our table, but at sea.

The boat was suddenly too small and still. Sofi jumped up. 'Fuck this waiting,' she said. 'Feminism!' She zipped up her lifejacket and grabbed the wheel. She fiddled for a second, metal on metal, a tuk-tuk noise. Then there was a roar and we started moving. Jerkily, then incredibly fast. She screamed a 'fuck' which rose in the air like the boat: with me and Pip sat at the back, it reared, violently, as if on its hind-legs. We were going unbelievably fast, and doing a boat wheelie.

It's funny where your mind goes at moments like that. I remember thinking, *This is where I die, this is where it happens.* And then this other thought, *Somehow I don't mind because here I am with you, by the sea, and we're together.*

The problem was none of us could see where we were going. Sofi had abandoned the wheel, flinging her body across the bow to weigh it down. And I could see, our captain's eyes were closed.

That was when we flew over the biggest wave. Pip grabbed my jacket to keep me in the boat and Sofi gripped the rope on the bow so hard that later we saw she'd cut her hands. The wave threw us high into the air – so high we were flying – and the boat leapt out of the water like a fish. That realization that I was going to die tucked itself in again, calmly, lightly, as if it were a napkin.

But we landed with a bump (more than a bump, a bone-shaking slapdown, blue-brown bruises for weeks) and then kind of stopped. I could feel my heartbeat through my life jacket; it made the material move.

'I forgot you could brake,' Sofi said. She turned around to us. Pip was still holding onto my jacket. 'Forgot there was a brake. Soz. Sorry. Do you want a go?'

We were silent. Eventually I said I didn't know how.

'So? Did it look like I did? Just *do* it.'

I got up and my legs felt like ropes. I went so slowly at first, the waves moved us more than the engines. I made us go in spurts, letting go of the accelerator every time I felt it work. Pip and Sofi were both sitting at the back now, looking at me. So I thought, fuck it, just *go*, chump. And that was when we nearly crashed into the ferry.

Sofi took the wheel back after that and we skittered like a stone thrown across the water, less vertically now, because, as with a lot of this, we'd worked out who had to go where for things to work.

By this time we'd been at sea for a while, and I hadn't been to the loo before we left. I shouldn't have mentioned it, because Sofi started singing 'Let it flow like a river'. In the end I had to wee in an ice-cream tub which was kept in the boat for shovelling out water. Carte D'Or. But we said that 'what goes on in the boat, stays in the boat', so Sofi peed in my pot afterwards. We offered it to Pip as well, but he said ice cream was a girls' thing. He held the Captain's wheel with one hand and peed off the stern, checking the direction of the wind, and checking to see if we were looking.

My hands got cold because I tried to wash them in the sea and the wind chews wet fingers. Sofi gave me some spare socks she had in her pockets to wear as gloves. We kept the boat away from the buoy so we didn't catch the Czech boys in our blades, and we drove in a tight little circle, round and round, because it made the sea go strange in the middle, like a flat and rippling jellyfish back.

'Are they still cold?' Pip asked me. 'Your fingers? Because I'll

blow on them.' But just then the orange buoy ducked underwater, and seconds later Vaclav's head popped up.

They hadn't died either. All of us, I thought, we keep on not
dying.

Vaclav rolled over the side, into the dory. He spat out his
snorkel, grabbed Sofi, and kissed her between her nose and her
cheek. He held her face for so long, he held his kiss. That happens when you don't die – you feel chosen; you want to talk a
lot and touch people.

'Fifties! Hundreds!' he shouted. 'Look at all this fucking fish!'

Pip helped Armin heave up a net bag full of dirty white
shells, chinking like china. The Czech boys undid the screws on
their tanks and let out the rest of their air with a hiss.

We couldn't go back to Creux harbour, because there were
fishermen sitting on the wall. We had too many scallops to
sneak them up the stairs in our pockets, and it wasn't scallop
season. Like Pip had said, it was illegal and we'd have been
reported. We saw the fishermen from a distance – scallops
themselves in beige and orange oilskins – and backtracked to
Dixcart. Sofi was put on the bow, a golden figurehead, and I sat
to the side, freezing cold with her socks on my hands.

Vaclav dropped us off when the water was knee-height. Pip
carried the scallop bag from underneath, like a huge, breakable
baby, and an air tank under the other arm. He asked if I wanted
a piggyback.

'You're light,' he said. 'I could take you.'

But I said I'd be fine and waded through the water and up
the beach. I was so cold I could only look at Pip's feet in front
of mine and follow them. My toes were hard, squeaking

together like marbles. All I remember is cold, wet salt. You always associate salt with dry, but it can be the wettest thing too.

We got to the boys' field and drank tea outside their tents with our salty lips, which changed the beginning and the end of each mouthful. My lips and knees were blue. My bikini top was still wet. I was trying to put myself in the sun, but it wasn't getting through. I shut my eyes and saw filaments, a leaf that's gone like lace, and willed the sun to warm me.

My fingers felt bigger from holding my tea so tightly. The others didn't seem to be cold; they were talking, and eating Penguin biscuits. Sofi was playing with Vaclav's feet, even though his toes were hairy, and he was telling us more anecdotes about the Farquarts.

'They are putting big family crest on everything. On plates, on helipad, on knob on the door.'

They also wanted their cooks to prepare all their food (smuggled scallops, Jersey beef) in a gorse-burning oven, but the chef couldn't get it any hotter than seventy degrees, so he'd bought a secret Calor gas stove, which he hid behind a sack of potatoes.

'They say is traditional, but it fucking stink, this gorse fire,' Armin said. 'We say no for us thank you, no no. Calor gas please. Or microwave oven.'

Vaclav said they got paid £100 a week. If I hadn't been so cold I would have laughed but he wasn't joking. At least they were getting full board.

'Full board. They are laughing. What is this? Not even cardboard.'

'It's shit, man,' said Pip, and then, quickly, 'not your tent, I don't mean your tent, just the situation. The situation's shit.' And he went back to doodling in his notebook.

I wanted to say, 'You never swear, Pip; you don't say man', but I was too cold. Even though the sun was on us, I had goosebumps all down my arms, and tiny little hairs, standing up and beckoning.

Vaclav and Armin were making wicker baskets to sell on the Avenue, and with the leftover willow they made twisted crowns for the three of us. Mine was too big, so Pip swapped.

'Have mine,' he said, coming over and putting it on my head. 'Coronation on a campsite.'

Sofi's was too big too, and kept on slipping down over her eyes. She couldn't stop laughing. I didn't really understand, but it was something to do with Armin's cowlick. She said she'd never heard that word before.

Finally, she noticed that I wasn't saying anything. She touched my hand and said how cold it was, then asked if I wanted to go home. I said I was OK, unconvincingly, meaning to be unconvincing, rubbing my hands together; Russian winter. When we left, the boys gave us a plastic bag full of scallops.

The walk back felt very long. I shuffled it, jaw locked. At one point Sofi put her arm around my shoulders and told Pip to do the same. They cocooned me, but as a kind of a joke rather than a 'this is necessary', and after five steps they broke away.

I ran the shower boiling before I could bear to take off my clothes. I got in with toes like rocks and when the water hit them it felt like dropping ice-cubes into a hot drink. I let the water run over me, arms crossed over my chest, and still felt cold. I thought of school trips to swimming pools; of the wind when we were on the boat with the engine off. I thought of Sofi touching Vaclav's feet.

It was as soon as the cold set in, sitting on the boat with socks on my hands, that I had remembered. Eddy was back tomorrow, and in three days I'd be leaving.

I turned the shower up as far as it would go, and let the water run all that away. It took nearly twenty minutes until I felt that my body was all in one piece, and could move again.

15

When I came out of the bathroom, Pip and Sofi were doing something to the scallops on the kitchen table. 'It's called shucking,' she said, 'I read about it.' She was using scissors again.

'It's my first time.' A shell broke open like a cracked tooth. 'Fuck, there's a *load* of skank in that one. Worst so far. Look, Pip.'

He peered in. He was holding loo paper over his hand. 'Cut myself on the first one,' he explained.

My face felt too clean, as if all the makeup I'd ever worn had gone. I was worried I looked very young, but at least I wasn't cold, so I asked to open the last one.

'You sure, Judy?' she asked. And I told her to shut up, rat, and give me the scissors.

We were no good at shucking. Sofi asked me if we were supposed to keep the orange bits or ditch them. I had no idea, so I said the orange was the best bit. I was about to say something about Pip being all punchy-army with the Czech boys, and to be girls v. boy for a bit, but then he said thank you.

'For letting me come. It was cool . . .' He started a few sentences, but didn't finish any of them. 'I had a cool time. Those boys are nice. I don't know many boys, actually. So thank you for letting me come.' He was still wearing his wicker crown.

Sofi took him into a headlock hug and said something about the word cool not being cool if you say it eight times but apart from that he was a lovely boy. The table was a jigsaw of shell shards and mangled scallops, a slop of orange, a slop of cream. I asked what we were having for dinner.

'Not *them* bastards,' she said. 'The sea-snot's butters.'

Pip asked what 'butters' meant.

She told him that when he got to his new school, and people said words he didn't know, he couldn't ask. 'You just have to start saying it yourself. Act, mate. You've got to *act*.'

'Potato smileys and baked beans,' Sofi said then. Twice, an incantation that might make them appear. Kids' food, she said; we were kids and we were going to have kids' food. Teacher, cook, we were all acting.

'We don't have that kind of stuff,' Pip said.

'*I* do,' she said. 'Secret supplies.'

She added extra oil to the tray she baked the smileys on, and cooked the beans until they were dry. We sat down at the table. Not in Sofi's kitchen, but at Eddy's table, the adult one. All three of us and just the three of us, with polystyrene plates and a proper fork each.

'Fuck – *me*,' Sofi said after her first bite. Each word sounded like scooping out ice cream. 'Stodge. I love stodge.'

She was sitting at the top of the table, in Eddy's seat, just that bit higher than anyone else's. 'It suits me up here. What do you think, Pip?' No reply. She was wearing a potato smiley as a ring, her little finger through the eyehole. 'Ketchup?' she asked, holding the bottle up and Jackson Pollock-ing her plate.

After dinner, we had choc-ices. They were more ice than choc, the paper-wrapper wet and see-through, but Pip finished mine, and after that there were Maltesers. We aimed them into one another's mouths. Sofi lay back on the table, feet on Eddy's throne, and blew Maltesers up from her lips so it looked like they were levitating.

I'm not sure why I decided to go to the bathroom upstairs, but for some reason I did, and I ran up there, light on my feet. Sofi was doing a back crab on the table now, with just her right hand, and then just her left, and I could hear Pip laughing.

I washed my hands and looked in the mirror. All my makeup gone – young, yes, but that was fine, tonight. I remembered what Sofi had said about guitars and pianos and so I put my hair down, and started back to the dining room.

The door was too easy to open. Another hand had pulled it from outside: I walked out of the bathroom and straight into Esmé. People say this too often, but it was like seeing a ghost. We both started, our faces fell, we backed away, and in exactly the same way. We mirrored each other like inkblot butterflies.

'*Sorry*,' I said, so English, eyes falling flat to the floor, and skirting past her to get out of her way. Both of us were still for a second. Downstairs, Sofi was singing Sisqo's 'Thong Song', and Pip was still laughing, and you could hear them, clear as day, from Esmé's corridor. 'Sorry,' I said, a second time.

Esmé went into the bathroom and clicked the door shut behind her.

I ran down the stairs, back to our table.

'I just *saw* her.'

'*Shit*,' said Sofi, and froze. She'd decided to smoke inside tonight as a special treat. She was perched on the edge of Eddy's chair, flicking her ash in his christening cup. 'She's not coming down, is she?'

Pip walked over to the stairs to look up.

'She's so thin,' I whispered to Sofi.

She looked at me. 'You're not exactly Pie-man.'

'She'll *ill*,' I said. 'I'm not ill.'

'But is she coming down?'

I said I didn't think so, she looked like she'd been in bed. But then, because of the ash, and because of Esmé, Sofi remembered Eddy was coming home. She swung down, feet slapping to the floor, said 'Ballsacks' and covered her face.

'Tomorrow. He's coming back tomorrow.'

She stabbed her fork through her polystyrene plate. Pip started picking up empty Malteser packets from the table. He crushed them in his hand. None of us said anything for a moment.

'Do you – do you girls want to stay here tonight?' He couldn't look at us. 'Last night before he's back, and everything.'

'I don't know,' I said. 'I think Sofi's tired,' which wasn't a lie, because she'd just flopped her head onto my shoulder. I tried to hold it stiff, higher than it normally was, so I'd be good to lean on.

'Tired,' she repeated, a sad, single note, then lifted her head off me. She said she was going to the loo. While she was gone, Pip found one last Malteser in a bag. 'There was one left behind,' he said and he offered it to me. It had melted slightly in his palm, so it'd lost its shine and stuck rather than rolled.

'You have it,' I told him.

We left Pip – did we leave him with the washing up? The burnt baked-bean pan, I think we did – and walked with arms round each other to the bikes, our hips banging like bottles in a bag. 'Cycle for me?' she asked, but then she got on, pedalling more slowly than usual, but still in front, following long lemon curves with the moon on her back.

16

When we got to Bonita's, Sofi sat motionless on her bike. She said she couldn't be bothered to get off. We both sat there for a second, in a two-girl bicycle queue, in the dark, on tiptoes in our seats. What was it? The sun, the wind; the water, being scared, cold, Eddy, that all this would end. These things were heavy on us.

Then Sofi said 'Blackberry' and reached out for one in Bonita's bush. And with that, she toppled over: very slowly, entirely complicit, like we were watching ourselves in a short film with an inescapable ending. When I helped her up, she kicked the bush for making her fall, and then the bike, and then held her hand out to me, fingers lightly spread, so I could hold it. We wandered up the garden path, past the sunlounger she sometimes slept in, past the gnomes.

Bonita was asleep on the sofa. Her head had slunk to one side, and her cheek was resting on multiple chins. We slap-footed into our tiny bedroom and flopped onto my bed.

'*Every* time. Every time I forget how hard these things are,' she said. We didn't move for a while, we just lay there, flat on our backs; knees hooked over the edge, our sides next to each other, like two tectonic plates.

I was looking up at the ceiling, but I realized, out of the corner of my eye, that Sofi was looking at me. At least I thought she was. You think you can tell when someone is look-ing at you, but it's so easy to imagine it. I tried to see if I was right without turning my head, but it hurt and my nose got in the way. She was definitely looking at me.

'You have *dan*druff,' she said. What was weird was she said it so softly, and kindly, as if she was telling me she liked the shape of my eyes.

I put my hands to my head as quickly as I could, and told her she wasn't allowed to look at me.

'Don't be crazy!' she said, trying to pull my hands away. 'It's dandruff.'

I'd curled into a ball by then and Sofi was genuinely fight-ing me, peeling at my fingers. She made a grab at a bit of hair just above my ear.

She said she'd got some, and inspected it on her finger. I tried to slap it out of her hand, but she stuck her finger in her mouth.

'I don't care – it's normal, it's dandruff. I don't think it's dis-gusting. It's from you. How can it be disgusting if it's from you?'

I put my hood up and did up the drawstrings so all you could see of my head was from my eyes down.

She said she was only looking at my hair because she wanted

me to cut hers. She pulled her fringe down, almost to her nostrils. 'It's ratty. I thought we could have a beauty evening.'

I said dandruff wasn't beauty, and at exactly the same time, she said she meant cucumbers on the eyes.

'We don't have any cucumbers.'

'You know what I mean. A beauty evening. *Moisturizer.* Like girls are supposed to do.'

'Like apes? Picking fleas off each other?'

She wanted to do her nails. I looked at her. She was not the manicure type. Her nails had a black hedgerow of dirt. She held her hands up to the light. It looked like she'd been digging without a spade. Then she folded her fingers into her palms, like she didn't want either of us to see them any more.

I demanded that we do it on her bed, because even though she tried to catch the bits of nail, each curve pinged off and got lost in the duvet. Peanuts were fine, I said, but not fingernails.

'Yellow,' she said. 'Smoking. Terrible. Wait. Do it again. Listen . . . *listen*,' she said, eyes wide, 'every time you do it, it sounds like someone opening a Tupperware box.' It was true, there was this quiet hiss when you cut them. Her nails felt soft and air-pocketed under scissors, but they flew off hard, like bone boomerangs. When I'd finished, she ran her fingers over my face to show they didn't scratch.

Then I cut her fringe. She crossed her eyes, trying to see what I was doing. I thought about her forehead, the lightest lines across it, that it was frowning and that I could smooth it, but I just cut and caught the hair that fell in the palm of my hand. She asked if I wanted to keep a bit of it, to put in a locket. She told me I was cutting it wonky. She looked through her hair at me and said she was counting my eyelashes. I wondered if someone letting you touch their head means that you have got close to them. I wondered what any of it meant, or if it meant anything at all.

After that, she stood in front of the mirror, dusting her fringe from left to right and seeing if she liked it. I looked at her in the mirror and she looked at me. We both looked different backwards; I was about to say that I liked having two of her, but she said, 'Oh *no* you look all skewiffy,' and that I was better in the flesh. She put her hands on my waist and turned me to her.

'Better face to face.' We stood there for a second. It was just a second.

'Daddy-long-legs,' I said, and leaned out of her hands to scoot one out of the window.

A bit after that, I came back from the bathroom in a thin tank top and pants, rather than pyjamas. I stood in the narrow alley between our beds, taking longer than necessary to set the alarm on my phone, not wanting her to look, but not wanting her not to see. And then, from behind me, from her bed, she said not to move.

'Your legs,' she said.

I had my back to her, and for a terrible moment, I thought she was going to reach out and touch me.

She didn't though, and I finished setting the alarm, and climbed under the sheet. She stretched out her hand towards me, nails neat now, and turned off the light. Some time between the first night and that night, no light no longer meant silence.

There's something about people lying together in the dark.

It fills in the lulls, colours in the gaps. Other things do too; background television, cutting carrots, a third person. But lying in the dark at night is the best. Everything you say could be said quicker in the light, where you are not allowed to look away and think about something else, or be quiet. But in the dark, there is so much to say. You talk all night. You can't see dandruff or chipped teeth or dappled skin. The camera is soft focus.

We talked the moon across the sky, in steep slopes and plateaux and stumbles. Then we slept. I'm not sure which one of us fell first.

17

I woke up in that way where your eyes are awake before you, and they are ready. I woke up to sun, because we hadn't shut the curtains. There was Sofi, naked, sheet off, face flat down on the pillow. The gilt square of the window broke on her pillow and spilt onto her shoulder. If I'd wanted to go from flat to standing, I could have done it in a single movement. I lay there, light.

Sofi woke with a 'fuck'. And then yes, I remembered too, he was back today. A ball bearing rolled around the bottom of my belly.

'And fuck – *fuck.*' She smacked her mattress. 'I forgot to defrost the Chateaubriand. He told me Chateaubriand.' She rolled over, and buried her face in the pillow. 'I'm going to have to put it in the microwave. *Fuck.*'

Sofi brushed her teeth with her finger, and I got changed on my bed. We cycled fast to Eddy's and Sofi didn't sing. When we got there, Pip had cleared all of the kitchen surfaces and said he wanted to make us eggs. 'No time, no time for eggs,' Sofi said, reaching up to touch his face as she made her way past him to the vacuum cleaner. He turned to me, 'Eggs?'

'Report cards.'

The agency had asked me to fill in weekly progress reports. I hadn't done a single one; they were hidden in the drawer with my ticket home. We took all of it out. Pip had things to fill in too. He was supposed to give me marks out of five for competence and professionalism. We filled them in at the table as Sofi hoovered around our feet in odd patches, just the bits that looked messy. When Pip was finished, he pushed the papers over to me and got up to get a glass of milk. He'd given me fives for everything.

Sofi had decided to leave the Chateaubriand out in the sun rather than microwave it so she'd hidden it behind the shed, perched on an old bird bath. I was sent to go and turn it.

'If it looks like it's cooking,' she shouted as I left the house, 'if it's going grey-y, Jude, whack it under a bush.'

The meat was fine, hard as ice and just as cold, though beads of water rolled off the vacuum pack.

Next to the stone bath, though, there was a bird, the colour of suede shoes, but softer, tiny. It was completely tame and it looked up at me. I started whistling the Carpenters' 'Why – do – birds', then called for Sofi, who ran out, thinking it was about the beef.

'It must be an island thing, Sof. Come, look how tame it is.' She got down onto her knees, then got really close. 'Beautiful baby,' she said, then stage-whispered for Pip.

He came out slicking his hair with water in that way of his.

He knelt right in between us, and then, without even looking properly, he said it was dying.

'No it's not,' I said, joining them on the ground. 'It's . . .'

'Dying.' (This was Sofi.) 'Fuck, man.'

'No,' I said. I wanted to say we could feed it water or worms, that it wasn't too late, but Pip had gone to find a spade.

They did it together, and put it in a bag, with the rubbish, by the porch.

Pip came to find me after it was done. He said that I knew about science, that you had to when it's like that. He said that line about stopping it from suffering. And then he did this half-hug thing – it was more him draping a bit of his shoulder near mine – and said he was sorry. He looked at my hair like he was tucking it behind my ear for me, and said he really was sorry.

Just then Sofi came in to wash her hands. 'He smacked it on the head,' she said. 'Ka-pow. Out like a light. Stone cold soldier-boy this one.'

18

We saw them first from the window. They'd taken the Toast Rack up from the harbour, and now they were walking up the garden path.

I don't actually think they were wearing dark colours – the boys at least were in bright beach shorts – but when I think back, I see them in black or brown. I also think I can remember hearing them through the windows, and that their voices were loud and in chorus. And I don't think that can be true either, because the windows were closed, and you could never hear anything through them.

But when I think back, it's *Lord of the Flies* again. I see a choir in black and hear a chant that cut through our kitchen glass. That's not what happened. I went out to meet them and say hello. I shook everyone by the hand, kissed the most important cheeks, and, just like that first day, I spoke in my voice for friends' parents, and parents' friends.

The pack poured into the kitchen. The office, the kingdom, overtaken.

Sofi was introduced once by name, and her name was said quickly: 'Say-fay'. She was prepping the dessert for that evening, so she threaded through the crowd, excuse me, head down, shorter than I thought she was.

'This is my brother,' Eddy said. He was called Caleb and he was Eddy again, but bigger; the kind of man it's impossible to imagine in a caravan or loo or anywhere small, because he seemed so big. He wasn't fat, but his presence wasn't a vague thing. It was hard and unbending, a huge blocky coat. There were also his four boys, an arpeggio of ages from about thirteen to seventeen. They were so different to Pip, with their bulgy faces and big, blunt bodies. Pip was taller than them though, and everyone kept on saying how much he'd grown.

It was definitely a situation where you hear names but they fall through your ears. Who were these boys, so much less graceful than Pip, touching things in the kitchen and opening cupboards? They were octopus-like: flailing, sprawling, impossible to see what all their trunky arms were doing.

I could tell Sofi was unhappy by the way she was pushing her pastry into the ruts of the baking tin. Her fingers were hard; she'd left nail marks in the base. I saw her think that it was her kitchen and there was no room for these new people here. I thought it too. But I went to offer Eddy's brother one of Sofi's shortbreads.

'Call yourself a brother,' Caleb said. 'Drink on arrival's not much to ask, fuck. Oh, sorry boys.' Then he did this face like a wisp of smoke coming out of a lamp: one must go through the motions.

Eddy told Sofi to run and fetch a nice little bottle from the cellar. He always used diminutives when things were particularly expensive.

'Rosé – yes, that *is* the pink one – Monte Fiorucci, lots of gold on the label. And beers for the boys.'

When she came back, two bottles under one armpit, her other hand pulling out her skirt to turn it into a cradle for the cans, Caleb asked if us girls wanted to join them. He moved his eyes down Sofi's back like a zip. She didn't turn around.

'It's rosé,' Caleb said. 'Practically fruit juice.'

Because it was sunny, and I thought Sofi would say yes, I said OK, just an inch.

'An inch from the top,' Caleb said, then, 'Sarah?'

He had one of those Dickensian mouths, like an oyster left out in the sun. One side of his lip arched more than the other, like even his lips looked down on you too.

'It's Sofi,' she said, and said no. The men and boys made their way to the door, apart from Pip, who stayed sitting at our table.

'Pip,' said Eddy, gesturing with his head to make his son stand up. Pip rose – taller than his father now – hands in his pockets.

'Sofi,' Eddy said. 'Where's the beer for my one?'

She asked Pip if that's what he wanted. He said no, and could he have a can of Minute Maid, please. Then he followed his father to the gazebo in the garden, as slowly as I've ever seen a person walk.

19

After lunch, I found Sofi behind the shed, smoking a cigarette.

She stubbed it out into the vegetable patch and said she was keeping an eye on the meat.

'Fark? It's *fuck*. Ff – uh – cuh. Fuck. It shouldn't rhyme with Sark.'

'He's just one of those men, Sof. You should have come and had wine, it was nice in the sun.'

She said she didn't know 'those' men. I said she did. Friends' dads; rich, bit pervy, harmless really.

'The dads I know aren't like that.' She lit another cigarette.

'Oh come on. Men are men. You know men. You smile, they like it. It's just men, Sofi. If anyone knows men, it's you.' I said 'men' many times.

'What's that supposed to mean?'

'That you're so . . . easy . . .'

'Fucking *hell*.'

'Not like that. You know what I mean. Easy, meaning – relaxed. Meaning, not like me.'

'You seemed OK in there, just then.'

I took the cigarette out of her hand, had a drag, then felt like I'd stood up too fast.

She said she needed to get out of the house. 'Can we go? Bring Pip. Tell Eddy you're going to teach him about the sea, whatever, I just need to go.'

When I got back to the gazebo, the men were opening their third bottle and talking about Caleb's third wife.

'Sorry to bother you, gents,' I said, shifting my top slightly, smiling, 'but Eddy, shall I take Pip to the study now, or . . . ?' And I left the 'or' high in the air, for him to take it.

'Inside?' Caleb barked. 'Sunny day! Young boys shouldn't be inside on a sunny day!' He stretched out his arms, leaning back in his chair.

Eddy looked at all the cousins, the middle two chiselling a ball at each other, the oldest giving the youngest nuggies. Eddy told me to run along. 'No school today,' he said, 'the boys'll play rugby.' Caleb yawned, 'Good man,' and curled his big arms back in, bottle in hand.

I told them to enjoy their wine and the sun and their sons, and walked away. I'd almost got back to Sofi when Pip came out from inside, hair slicked back with water.

'I was looking for you,' he said. 'The kitchen's not safe. Can we go to the study? Those boys . . . where do they *come* from?'

I said Warwickshire, but I knew that wasn't what he meant. Then I said no to the study.

'Sorry. It's just that dads want sons to play rugby.'

'But I don't play rugby. I've never played rugby.'

'They're your cousins.'

'I hardly know them at all.'

'I'm sure they'll play nicely,' I said. I couldn't look him in the eye when I said that.

'Where are you going?'

'Nowhere. We're just going to cycle for a bit. Give you family time.'

'You and Sofi?'

I nodded.

'Can't I come with you?' (I looked away. Sofi would be waiting. I hoped she'd waited.) 'Please?'

Maybe he could have, if we'd asked. He probably could have. But I said no, and never told Sofi he wanted to come too, and we left, and left him behind again.

20

Neither of us planned on going to the sea, but on an island, if you don't fancy cycling uphill that's where you end up.

Sofi seemed her right size again, once we were out of the house. She slowed up and let me cycle beside her for once. 'Fuck! As soon as I'm out – bam! – I'm fucking fine again.' Then 'Fuck!', a bookend, and she sped off into the lead.

That afternoon, there seemed to be no one else on the paths. I didn't look left, I didn't look right. I looked at Sofi from behind, followed her path exactly and made my legs move at the same time. I looked at her and looked at her, because she couldn't see me, so I was allowed to.

When we came out onto the beach, the sea was beaten metal and we walked towards it. The sun was so strong. It hadn't been so hot before, and it wasn't so hot after, but for about twenty minutes, it was the kind of heat that won't let you talk about anything else. Sofi said it was because I was still wearing jeans.

We were lying on the sand. The light bounced off pools of water on the beach and left sun scars in my sight. I tried to look at them, dancing blotches, bigger then smaller, yellow, red.

Sofi pulled my hand to her face; feel this. She had a dry patch on the peach of her cheek, and she looked into my eyes as she held my hand to her face, trying to read what I was thinking.

'What's it from, do you think? Will it go away?'

How was I supposed to know? I told her that seawater would be good for it.

'We're going to swim then?'

'No,' I said, 'we can't, we don't have our things.'

But she said we had the sun; come, I should come.

And because it was so hot, and because the rosé made everything less hard, and because, still, she was holding my hand to her face, I said OK.

It was hard to get my jeans off. Sofi, bra undone at the back, grabbed the hem round the ankles and yanked them. She fell backwards, and pulled me a metre down the beach. I grazed my back on stones, but I didn't realize it at the time. Sofi stood either side of my ankles and pulled a necklace off over her head. She told me to give her my top and then she weighed it down, next to hers, with a rock.

'Bra!' she said, her own flung behind her, somewhere near her shoes. She was running down towards the sea in high, light, half-stride tiptoes, the way you do, with the ball of your foot to the beach, because that's how the stones hurt least.

When Sofi reached the edge of the sea, she looked back over

her shoulder at me. Her hair was stuck to her lips and caught in her smile, and I wish I could have taken a picture of that, just then. I don't know what it is about someone looking back over their shoulder at you; even if they're smiling, there's something sad about it. I think it says goodbye. And I wish I had a photograph, because all of summer could have been in that shot.

Then the sea came over her feet and she did a silent scream, arms over breasts, elbows over nipples. She said it was freezing. She waited until I was standing beside her. I did the same thing with my arms over my breasts, because it kept you warm where your heart is, and it's what your arms do when you're cold and naked and a girl.

She asked me if I was ready, took my left hand off my chest, held it in her right, and then she ran.

We ran as fast as we could, but it got deep slowly and our torsos moved much faster than our legs. We got stuck in seaweed and trod on sharp rocks, both of us making a noise that was somewhere between screaming and laughing.

When the sea got up to our pants, we stopped and faced each other. And then I realized that her breasts were right there and my breasts were right there and so I turned out to sea and dived in.

You feel it on your head first, like a vice. And your teeth are tight and your tummy feels empty and icy and you have to make a noise when you come up, you have to.

I turned back to Sofi, safe underwater now, and shouted that it was warm once you were in. She wasn't used to being second; she dived in deeper than I had, and stayed down longer. I didn't know where she would come up. My head felt like a magnet for the wind. Sofi found my legs underwater and pulled herself up to the surface.

It's true though, that it's fine, once you're in. She splashed my face and I splashed her in return and we swam in semicircles, through pools of warmer water and rushes of cold. We swam out till it was deep and dark, and then back to where it was shallow and we could do handstands.

Sofi got out first. She held her hands up to the sky, making a Y, and said, to the world I think, that it was beautiful. And then she walked slowly to shore, diagonally, so her face and hands were pointed straight at the sun.

Your body feels hard when you come out of the sea, like your skin's been pulled tight. Skin of a drum. I had goose pimples all over, my breasts almost hurt. I looked down at my feet and I looked up to the sky. The wind blew the heat of the sun off us, but it couldn't blow away the light.

Sofi was lying flat on her back with her eyes shut and her wet head on my T-shirt. I lay down next to her, our damp heads touching. She opened one eye, said 'hello', then shut it again, and said she just needed one moment to make sure she was going to stay alive and then we could talk. We lay silent and concentrated on letting the sun dry us.

She turned onto her side and faced me. Her waist dipped deep like a hammock, and she put one knee towards me, recovery position, to balance herself.

She looked me up and down – or left to right, rather, because we were lying down. I flicked a puddle of water out of my bellybutton, rested a hand there, and looked away.

She touched my hipbone and said, 'Cold. You must be even colder than me.'

She licked her finger and ran it over her thigh then licked it again. 'Salty. I think the sea is saltier here. It's drawn on me.' We were both scribbled with salt, but it showed up more on Sofi because she was darker.

She rolled in my direction onto her front. 'So brown now. Look, when I lift up my arm, this bit' (it was her shoulder) 'this bit turns to crêpe paper. I like that I've made my skin different.' She stretched both arms out in a dive and shut her eyes. I could feel her breathing. The beach was made of tiny, tiny, flinty stones. They'd stuck to the backs of her arms and legs and purpled like petrol in the light. Like scales. I told her that she looked like a mermaid, but I don't think she heard. She moved a tiny bit closer, said 'Body heat,' and we lay next to each other, one face up, one face down, stone mermaids in the sun, breathing nearly at the same time.

I don't know if we fell asleep exactly, but time passed. I remember suddenly noticing my pants were wet, and my hair. The sun had gone in. Cold again. I dusted stones off Sofi's back to wake her up.

She turned over, and for a moment, both of us were too cold to put our clothes on. We leaned back on our elbows and watched the weather change. We saw it first over the sea, the rain. A paused, powdery curve, the air darker around it. If we'd stood up and watched, we would have seen it run towards us like a tiny, invisible army. But we both realized at the same moment how undressed we were, and reached for our clothes.

The rain had nearly reached the sand by the time we had our

jeans on. We ran to the trees with our buttons undone, then ran through the woods, up to the bikes. The drops were so heavy it sounded like fingers were drumming a beat on the leaves.

What was amazing was that up where the bikes were, it wasn't raining yet. When we cycled up even higher, we saw that two different skies were tussling. I thought about flying over Sark on that first day, and how the sea on one side was black, and on the other pink-blue. I thought that's how it would look today, on one of my last days, too.

We turned away from the rain and cycled to the sun. It was right at eye-line, and we cycled into it. It pushed back towards us through leaves and trees and fences, making them look like they were burning. I wanted to say that this was the most beautiful time of day, and that I did, I did know what she meant about your soul feeling big, but Sofi said it first and so she said it for me.

When we were round the corner from the house, she stopped and told me she didn't want to go back. She didn't want to go back to the men and those boys and the salty, salty sauce she'd made, and she asked if we should run away. I wanted to say yes, but my head suddenly felt cold again, and I looked towards the house and saw the light of the kitchen through the window. I knew it would be warm there and easier. 'Come,' I said and cycled off ahead of her into the drive.

Pip was alone in the kitchen, holding a bag of frozen bolognese sauce up to his eye.

'Middle one's elbow. Right in the . . .' He stopped and shut his good eye, his nose crinkling as if it stung . . . 'face.'

Sofi peeled away the bag. His eye-socket was purple, but maybe that was the cold. She padded her fingers over her own cheekbone, as if she'd be able to feel if it hurt on herself.

'I can't play rugby,' he said, but he didn't look at me.

Sofi kissed it better and told him to put the frozen bolognese in a tea towel. I asked him where the men were.

'The men,' he said. 'The men have gone to the pub.'

He looked at me, and I felt the shoulder hit his face. His cheekbone was so close to the skin. I wanted to touch it because that's instinct, isn't it, but I asked what time the others would be back, and went to lay the table in the dining room.

I was putting out the napkins when the youngest of Caleb's knobbly celeriac sons walked in. Jared, Jake, something that began with a J. He shook off his raincoat onto the floor.

'Why are *you* doing the table?' he said. Such a gormless face. 'Isn't that what the Polish girl's for?'

His lips were fat as pillows; wet and meaty. He walked past me and thumped himself onto the sofa, flicking on the TV in a single movement.

I put down the rest of the napkins and went to tell Sofi that they were back. Pip was stirring her sauce with one hand and using the other to hold the bolognese bag up to his eye. It was melting now, and water was dripping onto the floor. I thought of the brine from the olives on the first night, and even though it had started so thornily, I wished I could do it all again.

'Did you two have fun?' Pip asked, and not even unkindly.

'Yeah, it was nice. Got cold though.'

Just then the lighthouse siren sounded, and aftershave and male voices, all of it fighting, filled the house.

21

The first thing Eddy did when he came back from the Bel Air was tell his son to get out of the kitchen and get changed. Pip was still wearing his rugby clothes: shorts meant for a child and one of his dad's Hong Kong 7s T-shirts. There was mud on his legs but mostly they were blotchy from the cold (that was another thing about Pip: he never noticed if he was cold, hot, hungry or sitting in a way which would cut off his circulation unless you told him).

Eddy peered into the pan that Pip had been stirring, moving the spatula to one side as if it were a lid. His nose curdled, then he picked up the melting bag of bolognese.

'And what the hell is this?' he said to me. 'Get Sofi to deal with it. We have *people* here.' He went to the cellar to get wine for his carafes.

Sofi came back from the loo and I told her Eddy said she had to move Pip's eye-meat.

She looked at me like I was joking. 'Why don't *you* do it? Shove it back in the freezer, it'll be fine.'

I told her I wanted to get changed for dinner. I was happy after our day by the sea; I had spare clothes in my bag, I wanted to look nice. It's strange how being happy can make you more obnoxious than almost any other feeling.

I came back down in a red dress. Eddy was lighting a fire using a whole pack of firelighters and one of the Farquart newsletters, and Caleb was talking about the new rugby pitch at Sherborne. Eddy was saying 'Yah, yah,' a stroke for every sentence. It took him so long to light that fire.

I pretended to look at the books on the bookshelf, until Caleb tipped his oyster mouth in my direction.

'Like the dress. Where did *you* school, Jude?'

I said it was just a small day school, Dad hadn't been a fan of boarding himself, but that one of my best friends at St Andrews ('Oh, of *course*. Stellar university') had been at Sherborne and had played for the first fifteen. Caleb asked for a name. Then he did his own 'yahs', said he knew the family and poured me some wine.

Sofi brought in some puff pastry balls. She held out the plate and Caleb's boys took huge handfuls. I tried to catch her eye but she kept it on the crumbs. She looked like a quiet girl. I went to take another sip of my wine and realized I'd finished it.

The youngest cousin was sent to the cellar to get all the other boys beers. Pip asked for another Minute Maid, and Eddy told him, for fuck's sake, to have a beer. I thought about Sofi, and how differently people can say 'fuck'. I'd had two glasses of wine by then and the men had had three since I'd been there. There were six bottles lined up on the mantelpiece.

'Esmé coming down?' Caleb asked.

Eddy shook his head, mostly with his jaw, don't talk about it.

'Lads' dinner,' Caleb said then, looking at the wine. 'Cheers to Sark.'

We all chinked our glasses. I looked to see if Sofi saw.

Pip had a beer in his hand but he hadn't opened the ring-pull. He asked me why the table was only set for eight. I told him Sofi wasn't eating with us obviously, peeling my little finger off my wine glass to point at Caleb and Eddy. They were talking business by the fire, glasses close.

Pip was silent for a second, then said, 'Well, I'm going to help her bring stuff out.'

I said it was best not to, and that he should open his beer before his dad saw. I had a vol-au-vent and then another one, so I could tell Sofi I liked them.

We sat down – Caleb clicked his fingers until napkins were on laps – and Sofi brought out dinner. She hadn't warmed the plates. Eddy felt the rim then cracked his knuckles. The men were served first. Sofi gave me fewer carrots than anyone else and too much béarnaise, even though she knew I didn't like it. The boys got served last, piles of potatoes, and the J child scraped his sauce off with his fork.

'Start before it's cold, boys,' Eddy said, finger back testing the rim. 'Sofi, the red on the left please.'

The Chateaubriand was overdone. The boy who didn't want the sauce held his beef up on his fork and said his knife wouldn't cut it. Sofi was sent for sharper ones.

I wasn't used to red. Boys drank red. I could feel it in my head, thicker, heavier, downwards rather than up. I kept on remembering that I was leaving – soon, so soon I would be leaving. I let them fill my glass. Each new bottle meant a swirl and a sniff. I followed suit. I remember one in particular – the fourth I think – that got caught in my throat.

'Fourteen percenter. Lovely little Chilean.' Eddy passed the bottle to Caleb who looked at the label and stroked the shoulder of the bottle like it was a body.

There were pools of conversation. The younger boys down one end, talking about a girl called Possum. Eddy and Caleb, sparring over coalition governments and fees for school ski trips. Pip in the middle. The dads asked me questions about interviews for Oxford, and exeat weekends. We drank more, and more, and more.

I do remember most of it, but it did become sticky. Some bits of that meal clot together and I can't pull them apart and say exactly which order they happened in. But at the same time, everything was slowed down. When Sofi came in to clear the plates, they – we? I don't know – looked her up and down, the movement of our eyes stuttering like the motion in a flick-book. A steak knife slid off a plate and clattered to the floor and Pip tried to get it for her. Caleb stopped him with a hand on his shoulder. Sofi bent down, skirt tight, and Caleb breathed in like he'd taken enough air for everyone. He had his hand on the wine bottle again.

'It must be hard,' he said to Eddy, filling up his own glass, 'to control yourself with something like that around.'

Pip looked at me, his eye itself bruised now, but I looked

down to the tablecloth, and took my dessert spoon in my hand, like a kind of talisman. Let it wash over you, I wanted to say to him, why can't you ever let things wash over you?

A bit later, Sofi brought out strudel. That hadn't worked either. Burnt top, soggy bottom, and whatever knife she'd used had broken it up rather than sliced it into pieces. She served the younger boys first; she poured their cream for them. She didn't want to come up to our end of the table, you could tell. When she put the last bowl down in front of Caleb, he held his heavy fingers over hers.

'Absolutely delicious,' he said, looking at her, each syllable lasting too long. She pulled her hand away and we started eating.

It was the wine, or madness – both – but somehow, I thought it was going OK. It was a Saturday, I was still imagining we'd go to the Mermaid. I ate the appley bits of the strudel, left my pastry. Sofi, Sofi. I said I was going to the loo so I could find her.

The rain had eased off for a moment, and she was sitting on her smoking step in the garden.

When I got close, she told me my teeth were purple. She stubbed out her cigarette before it was finished so I couldn't have a drag.

'Can I sit?' I said.

'It's dirty. You'll get shit on your nice clean skirt.' She was wearing the same clothes, damp still, that she'd worn to the beach.

'Dinner was nice.'

'It was shit, Jude. The whole thing was shit.'

'I liked the vol-au-vents.'

'Really?'

'They were nice.'

'Really? Are you *really* going to come out here like all that shit is OK?'

I told her to stop saying shit.

'I live in Ealing. I just didn't think these – *things* existed any more.'

I wanted to change the subject so I said she smelt of Grand Marnier.

'Oh fuck off, Jude, with your wine-face teeth. You were ...' She didn't know what word to use so she tensed up all her fingers. 'You're someone else with them.'

I started to feel something in the pit of my stomach then. It was the wine, but more than that.

'Fucking *private* schools.'

'Public schools.'

'I don't *give* a shit. I know you'll think I'm even *stupider* but I didn't know it was like that. That you all knew each other and had these words and are just so fucking *different*.'

'You're not stupid,' I said, 'just exaggerating.'

'You can't even see it because you're there, talking about your exxy-ats. I did an interview for college too, you know.' She started talking about it being a secret organism.

I said this was conspiracy theory stuff. I told her to stop it, that it was too much. She took a swig from the bottle of Grand Marnier and told me I wasn't (fucking) listening. She kept going. On and on.

It was when she said that I could 'turn it on and off' that I had to stop her, because that wasn't true.

I took the bottle from her hands, and said, no, that's you. 'That's you. That's *you*. And you love it, Sofi. You love the power you have.'

She had her hands up by her fringe. She was trying to smooth it down over her eyes so I couldn't see them, but it was too short now.

'But you *do*, Sofi. You do it to all of us. Pip, Eddy, Vaclav, the guys at the Mermaid . . . me . . . ' When I said 'me' she stopped touching her face, so I said, 'Caleb. You were definitely flirting with Caleb.'

She was shaking her head and then she said, 'Do you think I liked that? The way you all looked at me when I came in? I never asked for that. I've never . . . ' Whatever she wanted to say was in her hands. She was looking into her palms and I thought she was going to cry. 'I'm not like you or Pip, Jude, I don't have the words.'

I had never seen her cry before. There hadn't been any reason to cry. They say this about people with blue eyes but this was the first time I saw it. The blue went brighter. Brighter, unbearable blue.

She said she had to make the coffees, and left me. I looked at her cigarette stubs in the bird bath; I looked at the Grand Marnier. All of it was finished.

22

I went back to the dining room and the men filled up my glass. I drank it because my mouth felt dry as wood.

By then the younger boys were on the sofa, watching a film with lots of shouting and shooting. Caleb's eldest had moved closer to his dad, his beer glass full of red wine now. Eddy was telling a story about joy-riding a tractor, drunk, off a friend's bridge. Caleb was laughing much too loudly and his lips were so wine-soaked he looked like he'd been sucking on a leaking biro. Eddy had almost got to the end of his story, when Pip stood up and started dusting flicked bits of carrots and pastry crumbs into his palm. Eddy asked what he was doing.

'Clearing the table a bit. For Sofi.'

Caleb leaned back onto the hind legs of his chair. 'Fuck,' he said. I wondered if the legs would break. 'Fuck!' Another inky laugh. 'You're not fucking her, are you?'

Everyone went quiet. That's when I stood up. I didn't mean to stand up; it just happened.

'No,' I said, and everyone stared at me. For a second, Pip looked so grateful.

'No,' I repeated. Did I nearly laugh? '*No*. Of course not. I mean – he's just a boy.'

Pip's face fell. And that was when Sofi came in with the coffee. I looked at her, and then at Pip. 'You're just a boy,' I said it like a question. I was asking him to agree.

But he shook his head. 'I'm not a boy.' Pip looked at all of us. 'I'm not just some boy.'

There was a second of silence and then Caleb burst into laughter. Right into his wine glass, red waves crashing up the side, and slopping down his chin.

'Look at her,' he said, and he turned to Sofi. 'Surely she'd rather fuck a real man?'

'*Fuck* you,' Pip said, and took a step towards him. Eddy put a hand out to get in his way.

Sofi looked at me. Unbearable blue. She looked for help, and I looked away. Caleb was still leaning back in his chair. I stared at the legs, willing him to fall.

'Sofi, we're going,' Pip said, and he pushed his father out of the way to get to her.

She still had the coffee in her hand. She banged it down on Eddy's sailing charts. It spilt black.

'It's instant,' she said, blunt as stone. And then they left together, and Pip put his arm around her.

Caleb tried to fill the space where they'd stood with laughter, but no one else was laughing. His oldest son got up to watch the film, leaving dregs of wine like blood at the bottom of his pint glass.

It was only adults left at the table. I stayed because I had nowhere else to go.

23

I don't know how long it was before I stumbled into the kitchen. Our round table was empty, of course.

Of course. Those were the words I heard again and again. I thought of Sofi touching his lips with her Vaseline, and the way Pip would lean, close, into her to see what she was cooking.

I went to look for them in Pip's bedroom. No one, just blue walls and books for a boy much younger. I was about to leave when I saw my orange Hemingway on his desk. I suddenly felt that he couldn't have everything, and went to take it back.

Underneath it, exactly the same size, was his leather notebook. I knew I shouldn't, and that I would. I opened it on the first page and saw writing: spider small, leaning backwards, the nib of the pen never thin enough. I skimmed the lines and saw a time before us; the mention of a jumper, winter. I skipped forward. I looked for Sofi. All I wanted was to find Sofi.

I turned, until I saw, darker than the writing, taking up a

whole page, across the lines, a drawing of a girl. Sofi? I thought. But it wasn't her.

It must have been Esmé when she was younger; dark hair, almond eyes, a sadness that came off the page. She was even more beautiful when she was young; I wondered what she had to be so sad about.

And then I realized that the girl was me.

They were my eyes and my lips. My sadness. It must have been from the start of summer, because Pip had put me in the study. I had my hair tied back. I looked so worried; how had he done that in biro? But the curtains: he'd drawn them open. I ran my finger over the page, felt how his pen had changed the paper.

It was mostly writing, but there were one or two other sketches. One of three backs, a boy-sized one in the middle, sitting on the harbour wall. One of the Coupée, imagined from above. One of me, lying down – thin, too thin maybe, light little lines for my ribs – on our flint rock on Little Sark.

It was only on the very last page that I found Sofi. But it was Sofi and me. Together, heads touching. He'd drawn us in our wicker crowns, except he had put flowers in mine.

Together, touching. It had been us, and now it was them.

I cycled back to Bonita's alone, and there was no moon. Somehow my body remembered when to turn left and right, and that I had to keep moving my legs to go forward. All of me felt heavy, wet wool on a coat hanger. I got back to Bonita's and took a handful of her nuts for the birds, because that's what Sofi would have done.

I lay on my bed and held the stupid nuts in my hand and I

wanted to cry but nothing would come out. I kept on looking at my phone, locking and unlocking it to see if anything changed. I didn't have Sofi's number, because I'd never needed it. We'd been together the whole summer. Still, I wrote texts I couldn't send. And what I said changed. I looked at her empty bed, and thought of another bed somewhere that would be full. Pip and Sofi, together. Behind my eyes and nose, it burned sharp and black.

24

In the morning, I knew before I opened my eyes that the world was wrong. I kept my eyes shut. Hayfever head, thick with wine and over-breathed air. Blur. For the meaning, for the sound. The night came back in beats, each one bad. I decided I would never open my eyes again.

Then I heard a noise. I was not alone. Someone was in Sofi's bed. I looked through locked lashes. Sofi was in Sofi's bed. She was wearing pyjamas for the first time that summer, but she was here.

'I know you're awake,' she said. I made sure none of my body moved. I stopped breathing.

'It's OK,' she said then. 'It's OK.' Long breath out. She was smoking. It was freshly lit. 'It has to be, you're leaving tomorrow. Hey, look at me.' I couldn't.

'Pip?' I said, eyes shut.

'Yeah?'

'Did you—?'

'We went to see the Czech boys.'

'But you didn't—?'

'Didn't what, Jude?' She stopped. 'After a while he said we had to go back for you. I came here and found you passed out in a pile of peanuts.'

I didn't know if I wanted to say sorry, or thank you. It was right at the back of my throat, but there was so much of it there it got stuck.

'You can open your eyes now,' she said. 'It's OK. It's your last day, it has to be OK.'

It was the third Sunday of August, and that morning, my last morning, it was the annual Service on the Sea. There'd been posters everywhere. We'd said we'd go. The two churches on Sark would come together, and everyone would be there.

Everyone would be there, but I couldn't go now: Pip would be there.

Pip. He had given me flowers in my crown, and what had I given him? When he needed me, I had given him nothing.

'Just *move* it, Judas,' Sofi said, ripping off my sheets. 'We're not going to be late for church.'

We played tug of war with my sheets, but there was still enough wine in my blood to let her take me. I saw the world through the glass I'd drunk from. Softer edges, separate, still slightly more shine than there should be.

It was raining, but even so there must have been about two hundred people down at the harbour. Half the island, in coloured raincoats or under umbrellas. I saw the woman from the shop, with a baby I thought she'd be too old to have; men who'd said hello to us from ladders; young girls in baggy leggings who'd plaited Sofi's hair. Up at the front, DJ Roger, ringed fingers on his song sheet, and behind him, Bonita, in a huge blue hat. Up high on a ledge at the back, the Barclay brothers, who we recognised, and a few of the Farquarts, who we didn't. A hymn was just starting. It was 'Great is thy faithfulness'. I knew it from school but I couldn't sing.

Further along the harbour wall from us, I saw them. The men and the cousins, in a black line, practically in height order. A little bit away from them stood Esmé, tiny. Even Esmé was here. And next to her, arm around her shoulders, Pip leant down to kiss her head.

I felt a seam of pins and needles prickle round the back of my neck.

Caleb saw me and tipped an imaginary hat, as if nothing had happened. Perhaps he didn't remember. I pretended I hadn't seen. I looked at the vicar, tried to look at every single thing about him so my mind had something to do. I tensed my ears to fill them with white noise, but I could hear the sea slap at the harbour wall. It was that or my heartbeat, I'm not sure, but it was faster than normal.

When Sofi saw Pip, she touched my arm. 'It's his new suit for school. Fuck, he looks handsome; doesn't he look handsome?'

The rain ran fast. The birds chattered louder behind the Salvation Army band. A trumpeter with a purple nose stopped playing so he could wipe his glasses.

The sermon started. It was the vicar's last service. He was talking about leaving Sark for a different parish.

'Like you and me,' Sofi said. And I said, 'Like Pip.'

He was holding Esmé's umbrella for her, her bag, her song sheet. She was holding onto him. I reached for Sofi's hand, hers hot, mine cold. We all held onto something.

By the time the service ended it was raining so hard it made the stone harbour floor bounce and pixelate.

It shouldn't have been, but in the end it was Pip who came to us.

'Sorry,' he said, and so he said it for me. 'We shouldn't have left you.' There was rain on his eyelashes.

I suddenly didn't want him to look at me, I couldn't disappoint him again, and so I buried my face in his shoulder. Sofi still had my hand and ran a finger over the veins on my wrist. Then she reached up and touched Pip's tie. 'Let's go home,' she said. 'We'll make a goodbye cake.'

Summer would end in Sofi's kitchen.

25

B ut there was never any cake.

The wind and the rain. The dirt path home from the harbour had turned to paint. By the time we got back, Pip's new suit shrink-wrapped his arms. Eddy was in the kitchen; it had been cleaned. He avoided our eyes, fiddling with his barometer and looking out of the window. 'Bad one,' he kept saying, 'I can tell a bad one.' He went into his study to make a call. Sofi got out the flour and the scales. Pip had taken off his suit and was drying himself off with a towel, in his boxers.

When Eddy came back out, he said he was sorry to break up the party. He'd just spoken to Tom at Le Maseline harbour – he was saying this to me rather than the other two. 'I was right,' he said. 'They're saying it's going to be a bad one. Force 4 on Alderney apparently.'

Then he asked if my flight from Guernsey was in the morning.

'Yes,' I said. As soon as I said it, I wished I hadn't. 'At 11.15.'

He said he thought tomorrow's ferries would be cancelled, that the last sailing they were definitely letting leave was the next one, in an hour.

It happened that fast. Eddy said I had to go; that it was now or never.

26

I cycled back to Bonita's alone, again. That journey is a blur. Maybe there were still the echoes of drunkenness, but I couldn't tell you whether it was raining or not; I couldn't feel anything. It should have been my last day, then my last night. There had been plans. The Venus Caves again, and Port Gorey. Sofi had still never been to the Window in the Rock. We were supposed to go to the Mermaid, we would have said things to each other. You're allowed to, at the end. You imagine that you will be given the chance to join up the dots, and say goodbye. You always think that a last day will be longer than it is.

I tried to pack my things, but kept looking at Sofi's. They were draped in thick piles over backs of chairs, screwed up and strewn around her suitcase. She'd laid down her coat like a lily pad for us to tread on. There were so many more colours on her side. In each of her tops, I saw the day she'd worn them. All of summer was there.

I picked up a cardigan, white, beigeish round the cuffs. It was soft in the way that meant it hadn't been washed for a long time. No starchiness. It smelt of her perfume, sprayed over a week or two. And deodorant, and maybe something more complicated and earthy, lightly in the stitches. It smelt like a whole day, nothing bad.

I got my things from the bathroom; could I take her shampoo, no. I looked at myself in the mirror and saw things I hadn't seen before. One more mole, footsteps of freckles, too much light; were those smile lines? I'd spent all summer glad I was older. But I didn't want to be older any more. I didn't want to change, I didn't want to leave.

When I got back to the house, it was just Eddy in the kitchen, sitting on Sofi's stool, a glass of nearly-black red wine on the cutting board.

'Sorry about last night,' he said to the window. 'Caleb can knock it back.'

He said the agency would pay me by bank transfer, and then he handed me a ₡00 bill as a tip. It was green, with a tunnel on it. No Queen looking younger. 'Not really the right currency for either of our countries, but it's the only cash I've got.'

I said I couldn't take it, but he said I had to. Before I put it in my pocket, he made me take another one. I didn't want money. He saw me look into the next room to see if they were there. No one.

He nearly let me leave before he chewed my name for the last time. 'They've gone to pick you flowers, I'm told.'

'Sofi?'

'Sofi and Pip. They're going with you, apparently.'

All through life? was what I thought for a second. All of life, would they come with me for all of it?

'To Guernsey with you, to say goodbye.'

I tried to say thank you, but he shook his head.

'It's Esmé you have to thank. She can be very insistent. She said you worked hard while I was away.'

I looked down at my watch; the ferry was in five minutes.

'Everything. We had everything when we were young like you.' I heard him put his glass down, but I couldn't turn around.

I pulled my suitcase over the grate, heavier than it had seemed when I arrived, and shut the door to our kitchen behind me.

They found me halfway down to the harbour. Pip took my bag, throwing it up on his shoulder, and Sofi took my hand. They'd picked me flowers in the rain: yellow, blue, purple-pink, fine petals, thick leaves. Sofi had put a lot of dandelions in her bunch. Pip said that if I threw them off the boat when we pulled out of the harbour, that meant I would come back. 'It's a tradition,' Pip said. 'You will come back, won't you?' I kept on wanting to cry. It came in waves, and waves, and waves. We stood on the stern of the *Sark Venture*, and the three of us waited to leave.

When we pushed off from the wall and pulled out of the harbour, I threw my flowers. They fell in an arc, a tiny rainbow. They fell at different speeds, falling apart.

The rain was slowing down, dotting, but stopping, and we stayed on deck. We passed our scalloping ground. I asked them to say goodbye to the Czech boys for me. We got further away from the island and saw the Farquart castle from a new side. I tried to take a picture on my phone but it didn't come out. I looked at my camera and I only had three photos. It was too late to take them now.

The trip to Guernsey only took fifty minutes, but by the time we'd got there, the rain had stopped. I was the only one with a bag and Pip and Sofi walked off in front. For a second I stood still because I felt I should let them go.

But Sofi turned around. 'Keep up, for once. We're all going to have a cigarette on this bench. And no, Jude, you are not just having drags of mine. It still counts. It's just more annoying.' She'd bought the same brand as DJ Roger. Royals, the island cigarette. We took one each. She lit hers then swapped it with Pip's, who looked at the burning end the whole time he smoked it.

'Finally,' Sofi said, 'fresh air.'

27

It was exactly midday. The sun had won and was a perfect circle right above us in the sky. Sofi wanted to have lunch in a small café which did 'compose your own' baked potatoes. It took me a long time to order. Sofi said if I didn't make a decision in five seconds she'd have a stroke.

When hers came, she said she might have got a bit over-excited. Prawns, baked beans, green olives, and on top of that, chilli con carne. 'Not as bad as it looks, though. Want some?' she said, fork near my face. I felt in my back pocket to see if Eddy's money was still there and I said this was on me, all of this was on me. All I wanted was that, right at the end, everything would be golden again.

We needed a hotel. Esmé had made Eddy give Pip his credit card. It was Coutts, but Eddy wrapped it in a piece of paper which said 'Do not go crazy'. We saw a B&B up a side street which had twins for £64 a night, triples for a tenner more. We decided to go for a twin. It was mostly Sofi's idea.

'One of us'll just sneak in. This is what everyone does, trust.'
I remembered Sofi telling me Bonita's was the first hotel she'd
stayed in.

Sofi was smoking, so Pip and I went in. The lady at the desk
was reading *Chat* magazine, which was open on some story
about a man who ate his girlfriend's budgie. (Pip saw; I was
trying to be relaxed, catch the woman's eye, be normal.)

She asked if we wanted a double, and I said no, a twin.

'Only got doubles I'm afraid. Will that be OK for you and
your . . .'

I looked at him, ' . . . brother? My brother?'

He looked back at me. 'It's up to you,' he said.

We took the key and went up to the room to drop my bags.
The room was a huge assortment of patterns, on the quilts, curtains, bath mat.

'Doesn't smell as bad as it looks,' Pip said, peeling back the
duvet suspiciously and peering at the sheets.

After I'd dropped my bags, we went to find Sofi, and then
the beach. We sat on the sand drinking Strongbow in warm
cans. Sofi had appropriated one of Eddy's jumpers and was
stretching it over her knees. I saw Pip notice for a second, and
then just let his face relax. He drank, can held high as a tele-
scope, then lay back on the sand, face angled at the sun.

'Fuck all of it,' he said. 'Sun: burn my eyes.'

Sometimes, there was something so beautiful about that boy.
He was perfectly symmetrical. There were so many ways you
could imagine following his face with your fingers. I watched
the waves crash up the beach and then slide back down again.
The cider turned us into waves too. We fell gently backwards;

were caught. We were getting our last day of summer. We lay on that beach and I tried to take in every little thing.

There was water from a big pipe flowing down over the sand. It ran in ribbons, flaring, tapering, ribbed like unwrapped muscles. In the wind came different smells. Salt and vinegar, which I'd never understood on crisps, but did on that beach. Weed (not ours, though two twelve-year-olds in Ferrari T-shirts gave Sofi a drag), and also seaweed, green, sweet, sandy.

There was a handsome, cross-eyed boy in yellow shorts, and lots of fat girls, fully clothed, one like a jellyfish, or melting ice cream, thick ankles poking out of a play tent. There were ribby children, and a family in black sitting at a fold-out table reading Terry Pratchett books. So much of life was there, and we wrote their stories, whole worlds for each of them.

Sofi said if she could write like anyone, she'd write like Hemingway. The way I said 'What?' sounded snotty.

'Pip said it was your favourite, Jew; he let me borrow. I read it when I couldn't sleep. Laptop as a light. What did you think I was doing in Bonita's garden?'

I flicked the sand. I really had got most things wrong.

We had dinner at a Chinese restaurant because it was the only one that would serve us alcohol. Pip wasn't good at hiding his sips, and we'd already been kicked out of a Bella Italia and a bar which had icy crates of oysters at the front. The lady in the Chinese restaurant looked at us suspiciously then said, 'Want beer?' When we said yes, she sent us 'upstair', singular.

The light was very bright, and there was still tinsel up from Christmas, red as nail varnish. The only other people there were a silent couple, and two women with choppy hair and going-out tops, but the waiter's face shone and bubbled with sweat.

'Real-life Chinese though,' Sofi said, pointing to one man in the corner. 'Why do they have *Braille* on the edge of serviettes?'

'They're called *napkins*,' I said, and she told me to rod off.

The wine only came in litre pitchers. It was bright red, fridge-fresh, and the label was in Chinese. I'd never had Chinese wine before. Cheers. We looked at each other, each one, straight in the eye. Sofi reminded us that it was that, or seven years bad sex luck.

I can tell you about what we ate. Crispy stuff, salty stuff, parcels, balls and sticky rice which held the shape of the bowls when you tipped it out. Sofi ordered far too much, but still ate her prawn tails. I hoped wine got on my lips and made them redder. We had scallops, so much smaller than the ones we'd smuggled. Pip finger-painted our initials on the window, which had fogged because of our heat. J + S + P, and then Sofi drew a heart around us.

She couldn't work out whether she liked someone else serving her, or not. She smiled a lot at the sweaty waiter and made me leave more of a tip than I had meant to. It was still light when we left the restaurant. It should have been dark, considering how much we'd drunk, and because sometimes it seems like you have to wait for the dark for things to happen.

It was definitely too light for Pip to be sick. He said 'just a second' then ran to some railings. He tried to keep us away with one hand, and it came in three hot bursts. I touched his back, stroked it even, partly because I was glad it wasn't me. He kept on saying he was sorry, and that he didn't want to go home yet.

'Don't be a FLID,' Sofi shouted. She really did shout it. 'The night is young. *Young*, Pip. There will be no flagging.' She handed him three bits of chewing gum.

'You don't get it,' he said, holding onto the railings like he might drop to his knees. 'I fucked myself.'

Sofi turned to me, disappointment in her eyes: 'Why does he *still* not know how to swear?'

'No, I'm fucked,' he said. 'I *am* fucked. I fucked myself.'

'You're fine,' I told him. 'Just drunk.'

'No. No.' He was shaking his head. He took his hands off the metal bars and put his fingers in his ears as if to stop sounds from coming in and then brought his hands up to the inner corners of his eyes and pressed. 'I've done something terrible.'

'It's Strongbow,' said Sofi. 'It couldn't harm a baby, honest.'

'The exams. I fucked the GCSEs up and I see it now.'

'Pip,' I said. I'd never met anyone as clever as him. 'You really don't have to worry.'

'No, you don't understand. I did it on purpose. I didn't want to leave her.'

Neither Sofi nor I said anything.

'My mum. I didn't want to leave her,' he said again. 'So I deliberately wrote rubbish. In the exams. I wrote all this rubbish. So Eddy couldn't make me leave.' His voice stopped working halfway through.

Normally in life you can say it's OK. You can say it's OK and mean it. What do you say to someone when it's not? Neither of us said anything.

'I didn't want to leave her,' he said again, taking his hands away from his eyes. When he said, 'But now I think . . . now I think it would be good,' he sounded exactly like a child.

In my head, I heard the sentence he'd said to me on the first day in the study, and I heard it differently: There is no point in you doing this.

'It *will* be OK,' I said. I pushed the future tense at him. I thought if we both believed it – if we all believed it – it would be true. 'It *will* be. It has to be. There are ways.' I looked to Sofi because I wanted to see her nod, and she said what we needed was more cider.

Young Pip. He waited outside when we got more Strongbow from a newsagent. He took a swig, gargled with it, then spat it into a rubbish bin. He asked if it would stop him from thinking, and we said yes. We drank the rest on a bench underneath a street light, until we got too cold and went to heat up in an arcade. We shared the last cigarette outside a fish and chip shop, and said we'd smoke our next one together in Paris. We will, we said. We had tequila shots with slices of orange and coffee in a bar where the drinks were blue. Everybody looked at Sofi. 'And you,' Pip said. It was true; they looked at all of us. It was as if the light was shining on us, and only on us. Or maybe we were the light.

Pip said we shouldn't worry, that he'd fight for us if we needed him. We had another tequila, and then one more. I paid with the green note. We realized it was a full moon. And we played bingo, didn't we? I remember coloured balls, twangly music, being the only people shouting (all the time, for every number). We didn't win, but the others danced. No, I did too. We were definitely dancing. Someone took my picture.

We walked back to the hotel as one person, bumping legs, arms round one another. Sofi sang 'I know who I want to take me home' – just that line, badly, but again and again.

We fell into the room making noise. But it was so much stiller in there than it had been on the streets that we fell silent.

I never thought it would be me who went first. But Pip, he turned to me in the sudden nothing after all the lights, and said, 'Jude?

'Jude. When it's over – when the summer's over – can I go? Will she . . . will she be OK if I leave her?'

I had spent the whole summer pretending I had the answer. I didn't have any answer. But he looked to me, again. And so I kissed him.

He almost pulled away – I felt it in his face – but then he didn't. His lips didn't move at all at first, like they were in shock. And then he kissed me back. As I turned my face to find Sofi, his lips left a line across my cheek.

She was still there. She looked at my lips, his lips, then eyes, lips, eyes, like she'd done a thousand times. I told her to come. I fell away from Pip to make space and leant against the wall. I held my hands out, my palms up.

She took them, and held them either side of me. Lips, eyes, lips; a decision and then she made it. She kissed me and I felt it behind my belly button. She let go of my hands and looked at hers. They were shaking. Mine stayed where she left them and I could feel my heartbeat in my fingers.

We needed Pip, so that it was all of us. We came back together. We kissed in a circle, one way, then the other. Then together, a tangle in the middle. Someone laughed. But it wasn't a laugh which said that it was funny and now the joke is over. We laughed and then the only thing we stopped was laughing.

Sofi crossed her arms down over her body and pulled off her top. She was wearing the same black bra she'd worn the night I arrived. She took my hand – my heartbeat in it, my whole heart in it – and put it to her. I pulled Pip with me. The lace on her bra was so thin. I looked at it, underneath it, felt it on my fingers and then felt her start to undo my jeans.

I wasn't thinking. What my lips were doing, where my hands were, I wasn't thinking. Pip was looking at my hand there, her hand here. We saw him swallow. Then Sofi started kissing him, and then I did, and with his own hands, he started undoing his shirt. I remember the sound of breathing – in-breaths, out-breaths, broken, louder. I remember finding sand, because it hides on you, and you find it later, when the sea is nowhere near.

Pip was still in his socks. We pulled them off, one each, then he pulled us both back to him, scared for a second that he had lost us. We took him back between us, we kissed him, we held tight.

I had seen these bodies before. But bodies are so different when you are allowed to touch them. Bodies are so different. Adam's apple, hard breasts and scars on hands. Pip had stubble. His body was harder; his shoulders smelled like milk and new shoes.

We had never seen Sofi blush before. But all across her cheeks she was rose-gold and we kissed her hard to make it last. She said things out loud, and she was the only one. She said sentences for both of us, and for all of us, and she was the one who had the words.

One or two I said back in a whisper, into her hair and into his neck. I pushed her hair aside to kiss her beneath her ear. There was the fruit and clean of shampoo, and salt, and I kissed them and said things into their skin.

So much skin, planes of it. Pip's white and taut as a sail, Sofi's, warmer than ours, a photograph of summer. Maybe it can never be equal. Maybe it just can't. But I do – even with everything – I do think it was. All this skin was ours and no one else's. We shared everything we had, and we all felt like the one being kissed.

28

We woke up in a hot, melted knot. But it wasn't uncomfortable, it really wasn't. Until we left that bed, nothing could be wrong. I tried to work out whose body was whose; whether it was a back against mine or a chest; if it was Sofi, or if it was Pip. Things we had done played against the inside of my eyelids. My legs off the edge of the bed, Pip behind Sofi, the tip of a tongue painting a line down the side of my neck, hands, so many hands. Flashes, sunspots. But when I looked straight at them, they disappeared.

We all woke up at the same time – or did I wake up last? It felt like we woke up at exactly the same time. Someone moves, imperceptibly, but the stick of sweat means you feel it. Someone thinks of your body, and you, and that also wakes you up. There are many forces at work the next morning.

All of me felt touched. Nothing that would ever show, but as though if I pressed myself I could feel where hands had been.

The skin on my collarbone smelt of olives, from where kisses had dried.

Beautiful, fragile grace period. Even though the curtains were open and it was light by then, it would be night until it was broken by clothes or food or other people. We stayed under the covers, and arms and heads were kissed and circles drawn with fingertips. Sofi said good morning, a croak on the 'morn', and then laughed. Pip's chest raised like it was laughing (my head was against it) but he didn't make a noise and then we were quiet again. His was a hard chest to lie on, and when it moved, it moved in bones. Our fingers walked around one another's bodies to say we hadn't done a bad thing. Be grateful for the grace period. You can tell yourself you kissed in daylight too.

I remember putting my hand on Sofi's stomach. I held it there. And I don't know why but I thought of the babies she would have. I held my hand over her stomach, and thought of all the other hands that would touch her, and Pip, I felt his hand on me.

Before we left the bed, we hugged like muscles in a heart.

29

My flight home to England was at 11.15. It was difficult to imagine times like that existed. Fifteen minutes past; there was no point in anything apart from what had just happened.

I was the one who left the bed and broke the spell. I got dressed in the bathroom and I couldn't look in the mirror. When I came out they were sitting on the bed. They stood up together, bed sheets like loose togas. I kissed them goodbye. I pushed so hard into that kiss. I pushed sorry, goodbye and everything into that kiss. I wanted them to feel it when I had gone.

I left the hotel. I can't say I was walking because it wasn't walking, it was floating, or falling, not walking. The wind hit me. I could feel where the wind started and I stopped.

Then somehow I was in a taxi. Again, I wanted red lights, zebra crossings, things that get in the way. I thought of fog and faulty engines. I was sure that something would happen. God would intervene; I'd held my hands to God.

Right until the moment when I felt the wheels of the plane start to pick up speed on the tarmac, I believed I would not leave them.

But I left the island on a normal plane, blue seats, not leather, no kisses; just stewards selling scratch cards. What I found so hard was that there were all these people, all these other people, who didn't know any of the things that had happened. Men with shaven heads, kids with colouring-in kits, and no one understood that the world had changed.

A young boy in the seat next to me tugged at his belt to look out of the window. I looked over his shoulder and there she was, Sark. I saw it – her – from above, as Sofi had. I saw it all, swollen green in a sea of gold.

I did not know when we would go back there. Or if, when Pip did, he would ever leave.

Maybe it doesn't matter. As long as it ends where it began, with leaves, and light coming through them. With the sun. Sun on Pip, and sun on Sofi. The sun on all of us, when we were young, when we were kings.

2

Then he would reflect that reality does
not tend to coincide with forecasts about it.
With perverse logic he inferred that to
foresee a circumstantial detail is to prevent
its happening. Faithful to this feeble magic,
he would invent
so that they might not happen, the most
atrocious particulars.

Borges, from 'El Milagro Secreto'

Beni and the Kids

Benigno Ciampa was like a fat Fagin. Except he wasn't Jewish. He was half-Italian, half-Indian, a third Scottish and a quarter Kilburn. That added up to more than one person, but, like he said himself, he had enough room.

Sofi met him in a midnight-blue restaurant. She hadn't been in the city long. She'd met a man in a park and he'd invited her for dinner, but when she turned up at the restaurant there was this fat guy at the table too. He had a huge veal escalope on his fork, and he talked to her in French. Sofi couldn't look him in the eye. It wasn't just that he was fat, he had a hole in his cashmere. It was one or the other, she thought, you can't do both.

She apologized for her French. 'Oh no,' she said. 'No. *Moi, je parle pas. C'est un peu* ... shit.'

'You're Scandi,' he said.

'No, just blonde.'

'Too pretty to be English.' His eyebrows – both of them – rose when he smiled.

'NHS dentists are good now,' Sofi said. She shook her hair out of a ponytail. 'Poland,' she conceded. 'By way of Ealing.'

He told her he was from Kilburn, a bus ride away. 'Same difference though,' he said. 'North London. High street. Both of them the whole world in mini.' He had a bit of crumb on his beard.

'True,' said Sofi and she told him about a fight she'd seen in Benny Dee. 'That was like a world war.' She thought for a second. 'Actually, that time they were mainly Irish. But I think *I* started it.'

Beni laughed and swallowed the last, heart-shaped bite of his escalope. 'I liked Kilburn.'

'Why did you leave?' she asked him. 'Why did you come here?'

'This place. This is mine. Restaurants.' And he called out for cheese. '*Mais pas de bleu!*' he shouted, then turned back to her, patting his belly. 'I find it a bit rich.'

Sofi was twenty-one then, just turned. The money she'd earned from Sark had long run out. She'd worked for a while at JJB Sports but got fired when she did a handstand and landed on a customer. 'Normally it's *fine*,' she told her parents. 'Promise. But this time, this time I hit a kid.' She told them she wanted to go to Paris. When she said she'd work at the Moulin Rouge if she had to, they finally agreed to call a second uncle who lived in Le Havre. He'd moved there after France won the World Cup. He was on his second wife, and, more importantly, his second pint when he got the call; he agreed to let Sofi stay until she found her feet. This was her second week.

'Beni,' she said to the fat man, helping herself to one of his cornichons, 'any chance I could get a job?'

*

She started the next day. Not at that navy restaurant from the night before, but up the road, a diner in a former printer's shop, white and windows, on a curved corner. 'Le Paris, it's called,' Beni had said. 'Snowdome winters, greenhouse summers. Lovely place, lovely kids. You'll never leave.'

When Sofi turned up, an Australian girl was waiting for her at a table at the back, underneath a map of the world, about to eat a burger.

'Sit down,' she told Sofi. 'Make yourself at home. Have a chip. Oh *fuck*,' she said then. 'Fuckin' igg's not cooked.'

'The what?'

'The igg. It isn't cooked.' She opened her burger and hooked some albumen over one tine of her fork. It rose – slick, translucent. 'Sri Lankans can't cook iggs.'

'I can cook,' said Sofi. 'I've been a cook.' She'd been expecting something like an interview and wanted to use some of her answers.

But the Australian laughed and said, 'D'you speak Tamil? You don't wanna go in the kitchen. It's hotter than sex and they get about two bucks an hour. Just when you're getting a burger, right? Don't go for the Sixpence. Take a nice, safe Classique.'

So Sofi ended up behind the bar, or serving tables. After a few hours she decided she liked it better than cooking. She cut her hands less, couldn't burn drinks. And she tried them all, each one of them, before they went out.

That first day, Sofi went home with six euros in fifty-centime pieces and smaller. Her hands smelt of coins, and even though it was in the wrong direction, she went back to her uncle's flat via the sea. At tea, her uncle was paint-speckled and his wife picked flicks of white off his arms with her fingernails. They asked her how it went.

'Yeah,' she said, though that didn't match the question. There were things she felt that she couldn't put into a sentence yet. Suddenly, at Beni's, she was with people who were like her – who spoke first and fast, and who touched her before she touched them – and she did not know what that meant. 'Yeah,' she said. 'It was different.'

The next day, and for many days after that, Beni came to oversee at Le Paris. He'd tuck himself into a corner, in a hat, with an English breakfast and a glass of claret. He left the beans – it was the sauce he liked, not the 'pellets' – but never the claret. He was proud of the new coffee machine, and would take time to clean it, frequently, with a paintbrush.

He introduced Sofi to everyone. 'Sheyna, this girl's a hard-worker. It's in her heritage. Look at her nails. Ground to the bone. Be like a sister to her. Treat her best. I mean it. Upset her and I'm docking your pay.' And Linus. 'Linus, tell this girl she's beautiful. She is, isn't she? Golden girl. Tell her again. Linus is going to build me a boat from the very best Norwegian wood, aren't you Linus?' Everything and everyone had something best about them.

And this is how it was: they (everyone but the Sri Lankans in the kitchen) got paid in tequila and tips and by tricking the till. They ran up and down wide spiral stairs with too-full trays, and everyone who worked there was young. There was Sam, who smiled, had eczema, drank wine until it purpled his teeth. Meryn, the Australian from the first day, rising intonation, never wore a bra, stole a potato skin each time she served a portion. She told everyone she only slept with black men, but disproved this whenever she was drunk. There was Leonardo, a beautiful Argentine revolutionary in white T-shirts, and his girlfriend Graça, so tiny they called her 'Tiny'; unreliable, aggressive to customers. She'd come here on Erasmus and wore the prettiest dresses.

There were others too, so many. Le Havre was like that. Those who stayed the longest said the rest came and went with the weather. There were dreadlocks and old denim, shared sunglasses, freckles, lots of accents, heights, smokers. There was a boy from Cornwall with a tattoo of a triangle, and he was the one Sofi liked best. He reminded her of sand and beaches. He had a broad back and a broad accent. 'Like clotted cream,' he said. His name was Arthur, after some long-ago Cornish king. He had a shaven head, but even his stubble seemed soft.

There were people who might have been rich where they came from, but for that moment, in that place, all of them were poor. They were equal. 'Onion rings,' Meryn would say, 'the great democratizer.' Ealing, and other things, felt far away. And for a while, life at Beni's was what, from the films, Sofi had imagined being this age would feel like.

Beni called them 'the kids'. He didn't have his own. 'No bother. World's got to have some only fathers, too.' Sofi sat with him when it was quiet. She'd ask him if he wanted a massage, and after the first time, he'd always say no. On YouTube, he played her Seu Jorge, and it made her nose sting. He couldn't believe she hadn't ever listened to the Beatles properly. He played her every album – 'It's like someone's having a yank on your heart.

Is it like that for you? Take all of it in. Take it into your head. How amazing to have that in your head' – and called it the 'invasion of Poland'. When she was late and he was there before her, Beni would sing 'She wakes up, she makes up,' and stop before he got to the high bit.

Beni had been paper-thin when he was younger. He only ever showed them one photo. His shirt still didn't fit him right. He had a centre-parting and his hair fountained in an M, but those who saw it – Sofi was one of them – said he could have had any girl in the world.

The trouble was, no one ever got paid properly. The money-man was Alessio, a dark grey Italian who ran the whole business from the midnight restaurant. You went to see him down in the kitchens. His office was by the big fridges, but it was always sweaty, because there was so much at stake. Alessio didn't know any of their names and whenever he spoke to Sofi, he always said, '*Et alors*, Marie . . .' even though Marie was black.

Everyone had their ways. The Nordics would storm in there, blond hair like torches, citing law textbooks, and the South Africans would get angry, although they calmed down easily, believing Alessio when he said he'd pay double if they waited a week. Arthur the Cornish boy wasn't used to fighting. He was too English about money. He asked for his apologetically, and apologized again when Alessio said there wasn't any.

Sofi didn't fare much better. She came back from the big fridges once, crying. The walk back was uphill, into the cold, and her cheeks looked like they'd been scrubbed with a Brillo pad.

'Beni, it's not fucking funny any more,' she said. She took a chip off his plate and held it to warm her fingers. 'It's all smiling and Seu Jorge and tequila here. All I eat are these fuck-ing *fatty* chips, and I've got to pay my rent tomorrow and I can't.' She wiped her nose on the sleeve of her fur coat. Someone else's fur coat. All they wore were hand-me-downs.

'I thought you lived with your uncle.'

'Twice-removed.'

'Well, what did Alessio say?'

'"No."'

'And what did you say?'

'I left and came here.'

'Why didn't you rob him? What happened to you, kid?'

'You beat me down.' Sofi felt tears start to heat her eyes but then said, 'You big *wanker*,' which somehow made both of them laugh.

'Look,' Beni said, and he looked left, then right, like he was crossing the road. This was a tic he had: he patted at his chest as if smoothing down an invisible tie, left hand, right hand, left again.

'Look,' he said, 'look at me. I promise. On my honour, kid. I promise you'll get your money. Tomorrow.' When he prom-ised like that, his eyes went slightly dewy. Sofi said 'OK', and 'yes, fine', and agreed to fetch him the ketchup.

She sat back down next to him, shook her fringe from her eyes and Beni put on the Beatles again.

'*You* only give me your funny paper,' she said.

Beni lifted the salt-shaker high above the chips so it snowed inside as well as out.

He has it all in his hands, Sofi thought. Older people always do. The weather, the whether, they have it all in their hands.

Death in Montmartre

A phone rings. It is half tucked under Jude's head, a small dark pillow. She thinks the noise is her alarm. She tries to turn it off; she answers the call instead.

'I know it's early,' a boy's voice. 'It's too early, isn't it?'

Jude presses speakerphone so she doesn't have to sit up. The voice is muffled by the mattress: 'Shit, you were sleeping, weren't you? I woke you up, didn't I?'

'No ...' Unconvincing. She has one eye open. She swallows. Cigarettes, gravel.

'It is three to be fair. But it's Sunday, it's early. I tried to wait. I waited. But I just needed to speak to someone.'

'Are you OK?'

'Speak to you. Anyone would have done, but you, I wanted to speak to you, really.'

'You're OK, though?' she asks.

'Yeah. Yes. Well ... yeah.' There's a pause. A long one. 'I've got the dead thing.'

'What do you mean?'

'It's fine. It's not a big deal. You know, when you're sure you've died. You get that, right? It's normal. Paranoia, we all get it. It's a normal thing.'

'OK.'

'But I haven't. If I'm talking to you, that means I haven't. Right?'

'You sound very alive.'

'You want to go back to sleep, don't you?'

'Maybe. For a bit. You're not dead, though. I don't think you're dead. Promise.'

'Thanks.' He slows down. 'Thank you. Appreciate it.' They are both silent for a second. 'I watched the news. It had changed. I mean, there was loads of *new* news. If you were dead, the news wouldn't change, would it?'

'You're alive.'

'Thanks.'

'You *are* alive.'

'OK.'

They say bye. Jude pushes her phone under the blanket, presses her eyes into the proper pillow, and tries to trace her steps back to sleep.

She does not make it. Black plastic shakes and rings again. She answers, phone still under the cover.

'Can I come over?' he says. 'I know I'm being mad but I just want to be sure. Can we walk? I want to walk. You should wake up anyway. It's three in the afternoon. Let's walk. Is it OK if I come over?'

She doesn't like to be alone either on days like this, so she says yes. He talks more slowly in real life than he does on the phone. It's the time pressure, the cost, the fact the other person can't see you.

He doesn't live far away, so she tells him to walk slowly. She wants to wash her hair. Head over sink: that has to be slow too. She didn't use to get hangovers quite like this. Only a summer or two ago they came with vague happiness, headachey euphoria, surprise. Now, it is less of a surprise. She folds back one panel of the blind; the sun is searing. Even though it's late, she puts on music for the morning – Chet Baker, maybe. Something jazzy. She still has to brush her teeth and put on makeup before he gets here, cover-stick the cracks.

She has a doorbell, but he knocks, eight times. She kicks last night's clothes under the sofa and opens the door; they kiss.

'You look nice,' he says. That's how he says hello.

'Liar.'

He shrugs. 'You look fine though. Normal.' He looks over her shoulder, at himself in the mirror. He presses at the skin underneath his eyes. His eyes are blue, his hair Tabasco red. It's a striking look, however much sleep he hasn't had. 'This is what I mean. This is the whole thing. After nights like that, I don't know how to feel. We could have died. We always could have died. Sometimes I think we *should* have died. So I think I have – I'm sure I have. But,' he touches her, then touches his own chest, 'we're still here. So maybe we should feel *immortal*? I just can't work it out. You're not listening, are you?'

Jude's been putting on big earrings, to compensate for feeling poisoned. 'I'm kind of ... ' (talking slowly because she's doing mascara now and has to tense her mouth) '... halfway in between. Half dead, half alive. Undead.' (Mascara done.) 'Stop touching my things. *No*, don't sit down. Stop looking around. Stop. I know it's untidy. Stop looking. Stand up. Up. Come on, come on, we're leaving.'

She ushers him out of her front door with flat palms, grabbing sunglasses, leaving the music, deciding not to take a jacket.

'Sun's bright, isn't it?' he says when they are out on the street. 'Almost too bright. Heavenly, you could say.' He has his hands up to his eyes. 'That was another thing. How *heavenly* it was when I woke up. Do you get it? Like we might be in heaven.'

'We're not dead.'

'Look at the clouds though. I mean it. *Heavenly*.'

'You're doing that thing where you italicize with your voice.' It was annoying when he did it. 'It doesn't suit you. This one?' It's not the nicest café on the street, but if they sit down he might stop talking about the sky.

Jude had known this boy, Seb, since St Andrews. The same halls in first year; a shared bathroom. The date at the Thai restaurant; the email when she was on Sark. She hadn't replied until she found out that he, too, ahead of her, was here in Paris. But they had become friends, and good ones, now they were both English people away from home.

The waiter sweeps by, polishing their table in a single circle. She wants Coke, he wants coffee.

'Are you sure you don't want decaf?' Jude says.

'Yes, I'm sure.'

'Just that you're already very intense today. You're going very fast, Rooks.' Seb's name, in Paris, has become Rookie. From *rouquin*, the French for redhead.

'Decaf's carcinogenic.'

'Yes, but you're ... getting to me. It's like the marbles in the jam jar.'

He's rubbing where a beard might be.

'When I was a kid,' she goes on, 'school took us to the swimming pool. We put marbles in a jam jar and shook them under water. You could hear it all the way over in the deep end. It was supposed to teach us about sound waves. Don't know why, but it made me feel nauseous. Ill for days. Really.'

'I'm making you feel sick?'

'Not in a bad way. It's just a bit abrasive.' She strokes his arm, and when that's not enough, she leans out of her seat and puts her lips to his temple. Recently, she's got better at touching people. 'In a nice way.'

She's also, recently, become a more committed smoker. She used to call herself a 'token toker', and steal drags only in the dark. But a friend – this friend – got annoyed and told her to buy her own. Her packet of cigarettes is on the table now, perched on top of her wallet. He's had his eye on it for quite a while.

'Just look at it,' Rookie says, 'I mean, it's ridiculous. It says, massive on the side, FUMER TUE. It fucking kills you. And it admits it. In capitals. FUMER TUE – foomay too – right on the packet.'

'Do you want one?'

'Yeah.' He flicks open the top. 'You've only got three left. Are you sure? Sure-sure? Thanks. That's not the point, though. It's ridiculous what we do to ourselves.'

They light up, three of four hands cupping the lighter to

shield it from the wind. The drinks arrive. Rookie asks for an extra sugar, so he can put three in. He drinks his coffee almost in one go, and then scrapes the syrupy sludge up with his spoon.

'Don't', she says, 'your teeth,' tapping her own. Three sugars; he will go mad. Madder. But if anything, the coffee slows him down.

He rests his head on her shoulder. 'Been thinking about life, you know. Life and death.'

'I know. You called me.'

'I don't want to die. I really don't want to die. In fact, I'm *desperate* to live – I mean, live-live – and then I make all these shitty decisions.' He sits up. 'Beer. Do you want a beer? We should get beers.'

'Carpe diem.'

'Carpe diem. It kills me.'

'It always makes me laugh. I knew these Czech boys once. One of them used to fancy my friend, and whenever we went out, he used to say "Come Sofroniska, we have Carpe Diem".'

'Is that supposed to be Czech? Sounds Bangladeshi.'

'He said it all the time. I remember thinking: seize the day right there? Who does he think he is? One day I said it wasn't polite. Turned out he thought it was Carpe DM – like Carpe Deep and Meaningful.'

Jude looks at Rookie, trying to catch him in the cup of her smile, but he's not hearing the story right. 'Carpe Deep and Meaningful,' she says, 'it's funny.'

'You don't think about death like I do. I think about it every day.'

So does she. She's young too, of course she thinks about

death every day. She turns over the bill, thin white paper in a battered burgundy dish, and says she'll pay.

Before they climb the hill, they stop for supplies at a shop that never shuts.

'Here,' Rookie says, emerging with a blue plastic bag. 'Beer. Also bought you biscuits. Out of date. Only fifty pee –' (he puts two in his mouth) ' – centimes. You know what I mean. Bit soft. Not bad. Here, go for it.'

She cracks her beer, licks its lip then her own. 'I don't eat biscuits,' she says and after saying it takes one, but eats it slowly, a bite every three steps, sucked till soft. They are walking up to the Sacré-Cœur, a Sunday pilgrimage.

They reach a plateau in the path and stop by a pink house. 'It's famous,' he says, then 'Biscuit,' dipping into the blue bag. He starts eating, but breathes in too hard mid-chew. A spluttering sound. 'My back! Hit my back – I'm choking.'

She puts her hand on his arm instead. 'Just drink. You're fine, fatty.'

He's not fat, he is fine. He says something about nearly dying and they carry on, schlepping up the hill in out-of-sync zigzags.

They have a bench they always go to in a small square, slightly Spanish looking, just next to the Dalí museum. Actually, there are two benches, but drinking men, boot-polish dark, usually take one or the other. Today they take the left: foreheads ploughed, forearms baked, trousers starched with dirt.

Rookie looks at the men, and then looks down.

'Got to start dressing better.'

'Who? *Me*?'

'No, me. Me. Although you ...' The way he shrugs his

mouth says 'you too'. But he looks back down at himself, and stretches out his sweater. 'I mean, look at this. There's no use.'

'Was thinking that. It's hot today.'

'No, I mean, what if I get run over? Who's going to save me? Who's going to save *them*?' He's dropped his volume; he points with his eyes at the boot-polish men. 'No one. But you see a man in a suit lying by the side of the road? You pick him up. It's the suit; you need the suit.'

'You're twenty-three. You can't wear a suit on a Sunday. We're eating biscuits.'

'Should always wear a suit.'

'You'll look like a Christian.'

'It's safer.'

'I won't be your friend.'

'It's safer.'

They've nearly finished their beers now, the cans are light. Rookie rings his like a bell, the dregs skitter at the bottom. But clutching empties makes them feel closer to the other bench, so they stand to go.

'Can I have your last cigarette?' he asks. 'I know it's rude. We can share.'

Jude puts it in his mouth. 'Hands,' he says, and they cup the flame.

It's downhill from here. They're not sure exactly where they're going, just downhill. Rue Chappe, Rue Berthe, the park on Rue Burq. It's Sunday, and on Sunday they walk slowly.

They are nearly at Abbesses when the money falls from the sky.

It's not exactly like that. It's something moving fast in the corner of their eyes and then a bangsmack, and a bounce on the pavement. It's a wallet that lands in front of them.

They look up before they look down, by instinct, just to make sure no more is on its way, but then pick it up. It's beige, ('pleather,' Jude says) with a zip. They open it and fill it with fingers. One note, five euros, a few coins, a small key. It's not to steal, just curiosity.

But they find no name. They walk backwards to the kerb, so they can see to the top of the building. Finally, from the fourth floor, a tiny face looks down at them. A child's face, a small girl, smiling, leaning out of the window over a flower basket.

'Did you throw this?' Rookie shouts up to her.

'She's *French*,' Jude says, 'obviously. Say it in French.'

'She's laughing. Why's she laughing?' The small girl is laughing. She's picking petals off the flowers now, and throwing them out of the window like the slowest confetti. She can't be more than six. 'What if she throws the TV?'

'Too heavy.'

'Where's her mum?'

'Bon*jour*!' Rookie shouts up to the child. 'I'm – *leaving* – the wallet on the – *roof* – of the – *car, OK*? Tell your – *mummy* – it's on the – *roof* – of this – *car*.'

The child laughs again and throws another hand-squashed rose.

'*OK?*'

She throws one last flower. The petals pull apart in the air, but before they land the wallet has been left, and Rookie and Jude walk away.

They are in Place des Abbesses now, just by the carousel. It looks nice from a distance, but up close it's horrible – spray-painted clowns and clunky lightbulbs. He is happier though, something about his walk says it. He uses one hand to leapfrog a bollard.

'You seem perkier,' she says. 'Are you proud you didn't filch that fiver?'

'*Filch*?'

'You're proud, aren't you?'

'Who says filch? No one says filch. Anyway, that's not it.' He leapfrogs another bollard, one leg higher than the other. 'I know I'm not dead now.'

'Why? Don't do another one. Seriously. You're going to crack your head, I can see it.'

He does one last leapfrog and stops, ever so slightly out of breath. 'I know we're not dead now. We've got to be alive. It's the wallet.'

'*Merde*.' Jude's looking in her bag. 'No fags.'

'Everything up till then was *normal*, you see. Me phoning, you sleeping, us walking. The bench. All this. We always do this. I could be dead and I'd still see all this, I think. I hope. But money's never fallen from the sky before. That's how I know it's not all in my head.'

'Can you think of a tabac near here?'

'The point is, we're alive, Jude.' He looks as if he is going to kiss the bollard he just jumped over.

They go home up Caulaincourt, a gentle spiral staircase, curved walls and light green leaves. Each waits for the other to suggest a final beer, on a terrasse, to say goodbye to the sun and Sunday.

They wait too long, and so they come to the fork in the road where they must separate. They hover, finish their conversation, half start a new one, hover, hover, hold hands for a moment, then say goodnight.

They sleep alone, thickly and deeply, and wake up early the next day. The mirror is kinder this morning. Their colour has come back: light spring tans, bright eyes, cheeks that look kissed. She has time for lipstick and he lifts weights. They are not dead, and somehow they will not die, either of them, for a long time.

Yes, they feel well, and they are early, and so they cycle to the places they have to go, sun in their eyes. Because they don't take the métro, they don't read the paper. And besides, the story they might have seen is only small.

There's been a death in Montmartre. A little girl has fallen from a window. There's a mention of a wallet, a phone number to call; but the story is so small, that nobody notices.

Six days later, it is Sunday again. They walk their walk, Rookie and Jude – coffee, bench, pilgrimage – and just before Abbesses, they see bouquets on the pavement.

'Magic place,' he says. 'Wallets and flowers.'

He pulls out a lily, still a bud, 'so it lasts', and he gives it to her.

Terrasse

S ummer has come in a day, in April.

    'Hell-o!' a voice calls, a voice Pip recognizes, a voice whose owner he is here to see. 'Hi! *Here!*'

But he can't find 'here'. He can't find her.

'Hii-ii,' again, louder, broken into two notes, one high then low. 'Here! Are you blind? Left! No, not left, then – *my* left, your right. Here. Right here.'

She's put her arms out in a Y to the sky, to make herself as big as she can. She waves her Y but keeps her feet still. Finally he sees her and walks towards her.

'Hello,' Pip says, and raises a hand. She's standing in shade, but when he gets there he keeps his sunglasses on.

'Hi. Oh *hi*. Hello,' she says. 'Look at you.' She does. 'It's been mountains – *moons*. Doesn't it make you want to say hello a hundred times?' She's holding his T-shirt along the sides, by the seams. She's looking all over his face, at his jeans, at his feet. '*Hi*.'

'Hello,' Pip says again. The sun has been making him frown, but it falls apart and he smiles at her. He thinks that maybe they should hug, but his hands are shaking so he keeps them in his pockets.

'Don't look away, saddo,' Sofi says. Her eyes feel like there is a pressure behind them, a tightness. 'Let me look at you.'

He looks at her in snatches, but it's harder for him. He thought he'd stopped being shy, but it comes back in one flash. It feels like mercury rushing through his forearms, his cheeks. He looks at the floor.

'Don't you want to look at me?' she asks. Her fingers fall from the looseness of his T-shirt and catch in the belt loops of his jeans.

How can he say no? That he is scared her cheeks are slightly changed, that she is not exactly as he remembered . . . That the fact – he is aware how ridiculous this is – she is not wearing exactly the same clothes as he had seen her in last, or at least the same colours, in some way makes his heart feel loose.

'Actually don't look at me,' she decides. 'I'm revolting. Last night was mental.'

'You changed your hair,' he says. His voice is loose too.

'You're supposed to say something nice to a girl when you see her. We taught you that.'

'Just it's darker,' he says. 'Your hair.'

'Winter. It goes bleachy in the sun but we've just had winter.' She runs her fingers through it, shakes her head slightly to give it more volume. Her fringe is now long enough again to tuck behind her ears. 'It was fucking freezing here. We didn't have the heaters on. Customers started leaving. I wore a fur coat when I worked. We could see our breath. Come in, come in. Follow me. This is where I work. Do you want a beer? For free?' No pause for breath. He wonders if she's breathing. 'It's so great to see you. Isn't it *great*? Was it cold where you were? Where were you?'

'I've been in Paris,' Pip said. 'I said. I've been trying to see you. I called.'

'I don't look at my English phone.'

Sofi goes behind the bar and cleans the spout which heats the milk for coffees. It makes a hissing sound. She gets out Beni's paintbrush and dusts away spilt coffee powder.

Pip sits down on a barstool and puts his sunglasses on the table. Swizzles on the seat slightly; touches limes in the fruit bowl meant for cocktail making.

'You have your French number on your voicemail. I called that.'

'I lose my phone a lot.'

'I thought you might not want to see me,' he says.

What she finds sad is that he does not say this in a way meant to guilt-trip. He says it frankly. What she finds sad is, he is right.

At the table by the kitchen, Arthur, with his shaven head and triangle tattoo, is wrapping knives and forks in red napkins. Slowly, with care, like each one is a present.

'Do you want a beer?' Sofi asks Pip.

'No.'

'A burger?'

'I ate.'

'The Classique's not bad.'

'I already ate.'

'Oh, be *friendly*. Don't be boring. Let me get you something. I feel this . . . *need* to provide you with goods.' She picks up a tequila bottle by the neck and swings it like a pendulum. 'So what is this, then? Tell me *everything*.'

Everything was so big it meant nothing.

She goes on: 'Gap year?' Pip's nodding but she can't really see him. 'Gap yah? Yeah? You escaped?' He's still nodding. She has her back to him, polishing the coffee machine she cleaned just before he arrived. She turns back to him, pulling a bit of paper out of her pocket. 'I couldn't read all the note you left. Your hand-writing's even smaller, dude. Do you have to buy special pens?'

'No. Normal pens.' His fingertips start a light drum on the zinc bar. 'I'm doing a Baccalauréat conversion, staying with my aunt and uncle. It reopens my . . . ' He raises a soft, ash-blond eyebrow. 'Eddy agreed to let me come because it opened up my "options".'

'For uni? To go to uni? I *knew* you'd go to university.' Sofi touches his hand on the bar. Stops it from tattooing a beat. 'That's so great,' she says. 'I'm glad for you. I really am. Student life, man. Baked beans and Febreze.'

Pip's head moves again. Neither of them know if he is nodding or shaking his head, the movement is so slight and means both.

'I should have been a student,' she says. 'I love baked beans. Still. Look at us. We got old. I want to buy you a drink.'

'I don't mind paying.'

'It's free anyway.' She leans into the bar to see if her cigarette packet is in her front pocket. 'We've got a terrasse here, have you seen?' A short ripple of excitement passes through her. It's duller than the ones she used to feel, but still. 'Very French, a terrasse. You'd never get that in England.'

'There's one on Sark.'

'That's not England. And it doesn't matter. I like it. I like metal chairs. We should get drunk. Get drunk and reminisk.'

'Reminisce.'

'So? Let's still get drunk.'

'I can't. I have to get back some time.'

'You just got here.'

'I got here yesterday. I left the note. I have to be back . . . '

'Ahhh,' Sofi says. She touches her nose with her index. 'Girlfriend.'

'No—'

'Don't tell me there isn't a girl.'

'*A* girl, yes. But not like that.'

'What about a cocktail?'

'It *was* like that. But not now. And it's – it's really complicated.' He looks up at her but she is running her eyes along the rows of spirits. 'No, not whisky. Honestly. Just a Coke please. Unless you have orange juice?'

'She French?'

'This is France.'

'Hardly anyone I know here is French. No one I knew in Ealing was English.'

'Yeah, she's French.' He uses his thumb to clean one of his other nails. 'And older. A little bit older.'

'Don't tell me – forty-five.'

'Twenty-one.' The tips of his lips give way to a small smile.

'You and your older women, eh? What's her name?'

'Clémence.'

'Actually don't say. I'm imagining it now.' Sofi screws up her eyes and does her taut downwards smile. 'The *act*.'

'You can be so dumb.'

Sofi opens her eyes again. 'Was she at least beautiful?'

'She's not *dead*.' Pip laughs unexpectedly, then turns it into a cough.

'Fine. *Is* she beautiful? I bet she is. You look bon too. Proper man. Seriously, you can see it in the neck. I swear before – when I first met you – if I put my hands around, my fingers would touch.'

'You never did that, did you? Try to strangle me?'

'No, but I remember. *Visually*. I've always had very good hand-eye.'

(Sofi would reflect later, as she told a friend about this encounter, that Pip's neck was so muscley and veiny, and broke out in red clouds when he was nervous, that it reminded her of a penis. The friend had laughed, and made a face like she was being sick, and Sofi felt sorry, suddenly, for having said it.)

'You're smoking loads,' Pip says not long after they move outside to the terrasse. 'More than before.'

'Don't you? We're adults now. What are you? At least six foot five. This is Paris.' She breathes in her cigarette so hard he hears the heat crackle through unburned tobacco. 'Le Paris. Whatever. Nearly the same.' She blows out in the smile she uses for serving.

Arthur has finished folding napkins and is now playing barman. Cuffed sleeves, thick arms, a matte silver ring on his middle finger. He's slightly older than them both; when he smiles you can see frown-lines on his forehead. He comes out onto the terrasse and takes away their glasses. He asks if they want another, or nachos. He touches Sofi's shoulder, then lightly tweaks her earlobes with wide thumbs. He's just smoked a joint by the extractor fan in the kitchen, so is even mellower than usual. He takes their order and goes back inside.

'Who's he?' Pip asks.

'Him?'

'Is he your boyfriend?'

'God, no. He's from *Cornwall*.'

'I think he likes you.'

'Be fair. His name's Arthur. Old man name. He's like my brother. Can I suck on one of your ice-cubes?'

He nods.

'Is she your first? This girlfriend.'

'Not my first ... y'know.' He looks at her. 'But my first actual girlfriend, I suppose so.' An in-breath takes him by surprise. (So much had taken him by surprise. That he hadn't found it hard. That skin didn't shock him. That once you saw it, it was only natural to want to see more.) 'It's just got a bit fucked. With the girl. Clem. I can't really talk about it. I don't know if – I think we might be making a big mistake.'

Sofi crunches through her third ice-cube now. She is not listening, particularly, to what he is saying.

'That's nice,' she says.

'Not really.'

When she realizes he has stopped talking and his chin is all dimpled, she strokes a finger over the bump-bone on his wrist. 'Awww,' she says. The type of noise people make about animals on the internet. 'You'll get through it. Everyone does. You're so handsome.'

The way she is touching him, calling him pet names, flattering him, it feels forced, almost formal. It is not like it used to be. It used to be as un-thought of as breathing.

Pip asks Sofi how she ended up here in Le Havre, and she mentions a Polish uncle and a man called Beni. She's vague. From what Pip gleans of the story, they're the same man. Then he asks where she's living, and whether she likes it here.

'France, *c'est pas mal*. My uncle's got a couple of builder mates, but apart from that there aren't many Polish … The French are less *Daily Mail* about us. It's the Maghrebis they hate, and the Romans.'

'Roma.'

'And?'

'But it's different, Sof.'

'You're not allowed to do that any more. Correct me. Now I've forgotten what I was saying.'

'About liking it here,' He motions with his hands in a way that means these white walls, and these windows. 'Are you happy?'

'What is this? I thought you didn't like exams.'

'No. It's not that. But … well, don't *you* have questions you want to ask?'

'Not really.' She's rubbing the ridged thumbwheel of her lighter against the corner of the table.

'I do,' he says. 'I have questions.'

'Mystery,' she says, '*mystery*.' She flares her eyes in that way she does, except that instead of looking excited she looks sad. 'Isn't mystery better? Sometimes it's good to leave things be.' Something she once heard runs through her head like a ribbon. 'You don't want them to become a photocopy. Not a bad photocopy. If something was great, sometimes you should just leave it.'

Pip tries to angle his straw to get to the last bit of brown liquid underneath the remaining ice-cubes. It makes a slurping sound. The islands of red on his neck have returned.

'I don't mean here, with you, now,' she says finally, but she looks at the clock through the bar window. Proper customers will be coming soon, then she will be busy, then he will understand – he'll have to – and go. She wills the fingers of the clock to push round faster. A greyhound skittles past their table on matchstick legs, its owner two metres behind it, pulling another dog too, a boxer with a face like a bullet.

The whisky in Sofi's lemonade is making her tongue feel heavier in her mouth. She hopes she is not slurring.

They sit in silence for a while.

'Listen, don't worry about your girlfriend. Girls are . . . All of this stuff is – I don't even know.' In the ashtray, all the filters are sticky pink. 'Sometimes I think we fall in love just to have things to talk about.'

'Talk about with friends?'

'No, with the person you're supposed to be in love with. And with friends.' A sip of her drink gives her the confirmation she wants from him. 'I think I'm delusioned.'

'Disillusioned?'

'Is that what they say? Whatever. Both.'

An African man in a pinstripe suit cycles past them, the hem of his jacket hanging over the back of his bike seat.

'Once you've said you're in love, you have that to talk about. You get to make plans. Do you know what I mean?' It's the first time she's been honest. She uses different parts of her face. It does not last long. 'Did you see that black man? He had a sandwich strapped to the back of his bike with a bungee.'

'Carry on about love,' Pip says. It comes out quietly.

'Wrapped in clingfilm. I think it was ham and lettuce.' She knocks on the window and motions to Arthur for another drink.

'I don't think it's true what you said about love,' Pip says. 'Sometimes I think you fall in love because you *can't* talk about it.'

'Is it OK to say "black man"? It's not racist is it?' She looks at the clock through the window again. 'Fuck. I really have to go back to work soon.'

'It's OK,' Pip says. 'Finish your drink. I have to go anyway.'

They go back into the bar and Pip takes his time to arrange his things: bag, jacket, sunglasses. He checks for his phone, twice maybe. He feels, somewhere at the back of his chest, as if he has lost something.

He shakes hands with the tattooed barman, says 'Thanks, man,' and goes to kiss Sofi goodbye. '*A la française,*' he says, accent still firmly British. Their faces do not touch.

'You should come back again some time,' she says, mostly because she knows he will not. 'Come back and bring your girl.'

'She's not my girl any more.' He swings his backpack onto one shoulder.

'Was it you?' Sofi asks.

'What?'

'What I was trying to say before. There's always one person who doesn't love enough.'

Pip does not say anything.

'Don't you think that's true?' she says. She looks at Pip's shoes. He's wearing Converse. The white rubber toecap makes them look too big. 'See you soon,' she says, and he does not believe her.

Pip notices, as he walks down the stairs to the door, that the bar is no longer playing music. The silence feels like people watching him. He pushes the heavy door open, and walks out onto the street. The concrete paving stones look different in the heat.

Then, 'Pip—'

Sofi calls after him. Part of her still doesn't understand why he had come. All this way. It opened too many things up again. 'Did you ever hear from her?'

Pip is standing in the middle of the road. He stops with his back to Sofi, then turns around. She's standing on the step of the bar, the arches of her feet balanced on the right angle. A moped drives between them. He shakes his head.

'You never have?' she says.

He shakes his head again.

'I thought about it all the time,' she says. 'I promise you I did. It's just I can't any more.'

He nods. 'Call me,' she says. He sees her brace herself. She tries to smile, 'If you like.'

He nods again and holds a hand up in goodbye. For a second they stay like that, and then he walks away, ignoring car horns, walks away slowly, right down the very middle of the road.

The Chaperone, the Children

The path is steeper than a ski slope, an angle that tugs at ankles. My shoes don't have the right kind of soles so I take them off. I've brought strawberries, I can't afford to fall.

It might be the steepest path in Paris, it's certainly the steepest park. You've said you're somewhere near the top. I think you often make it hard to get to you. And it's so hot; with no shoes, the stone nearly burns.

The Buttes-Chaumont is a grass amphitheatre and eyes feed on passers-by once picnics are over. I look down to dodge pebbles and glass, then back up at the audience. Rows of gay men, mown hair and shiny chests, circles of girls, rosé, suncream, a pregnant woman, head on husband, smoking.

But I am only looking for you. I don't want to be squinting when you see me, I don't want to fall with these strawberries. I want to see you first, choose how I walk towards you, when to smile.

You catch me before I catch you, though; you half get up,

shoulders off the grass, lie back down, wave. You are not alone. I knew that, but I thought there would be lots of us, not just one other person.

We're not sure how close we have to be before we shout hello, or another opening line. I've prepared a few, but sound doesn't carry in the park, there are too many other voices and noises and wind. So we wait until I've nearly sat down. You go first. 'Hey Jude.' You tell me I've arrived for the first drops of rain.

No, I want to say, I just brought strawberries. It's you who brought the rain. I look at the boy next to you. I kiss him first because it might make you jealous. A third person can be so difficult.

I sit down, maybe too close, but the picnic blanket's small. And anyway, it's not a blanket, it's a Carrefour bag you've ripped along the side seams. You've budged over a bit, but I'm just sitting on a handle really. 'Sweet spot,' I say, but I can feel stones through the plastic. I feel hotter than I should. I want to make you laugh, you laugh so loudly. 'Just go straight to normal' never works, it's always a bit strange for the first minute or two. I think we're both trying too hard. I know that I am. We normally warm up so well that each time we meet, we expect to go straight to heat but it's not like that.

You ask me what I did last night, then I ask you. We have two days to fill in. We do it in sketches, taking it in turns to draw lines, all of it unchronological, because that's how people talk. The other person, your friend, whoever he is, doesn't say much. He texts, he can't decide whether to keep his cap on, he comments on the rain. You turn to me and it's us who talk.

We say nice things to each other and put each other down in equal measure. You think I think you're old, you think I think you're not serious. You think I hate all Americans in Paris. Not true. Actually, I've always thought Chicago's a good place to come from. That lake is like a sea. I say you have a tiny insect on your eyebrow, but it flies away before I get to brush it off.

We look at each other for just too long until one of us says 'What?' It's me this time, but it's happened before. We're trying to look into each other's minds, but the 'what?', whoever asks, neither of us answers. What? Nothing. No, really, what? Nothing. I want a cigarette because everyone else on the hill is drinking bottles of beer. I steal one from our chaperone, but it's a Gauloises bleu. 'The statement cigarette,' you say, 'straight to the lung. You won't like it.'

We haven't been alone since it happened. Not really, really alone. We've sat next to each other at canal-side gatherings, gone by ourselves to the bar when others were dancing, you held my hand to pull me down a corridor, pushed me against the wall and kissed me, briefly, but it was outside your front door and it was open. Never really alone. Ten minutes in McDonald's doesn't count. We spent it queuing and I couldn't stop laughing because of the haircuts, and because you are an adult and still you wanted chicken nuggets. You said it was an American thing. You got a Happy Meal, you told me you were still a kid inside and fed me a chip with your thumb and index. That wasn't the time to say the 'what?' we want to ask and get an answer.

Now we're in a park, on a steep hill. You came with a chaperone and I came with strawberries. As you say, I also came with the rain. It's funny; the drops are fat (on skin, they leave a splash the size of a €2 coin), but the sky is blue. We wonder where the blue will blow. We lick our fingers to find out. We hold them out to each other. They stay wet. No wind.

Everything is in limbo. Half the hill cup their palms to the sky, as if counting how many raindrops they catch will tell them whether they have to leave. Most groups are making signs of moving. Picnic blankets are held ready to be turned into makeshift umbrellas and mothers check if there's enough paté in the packet to make it worth taking home. Still, there is a good chance the rain might never really come. If the drops are fat, they are also few and far between. The other half of the hill is sticking tight. They will ride out the storm in Speedos and sundresses. I say something about the 'Club Tropicana' video, and speak-sing the only line I know.

There should be a rainbow somewhere but we can't see it yet. You doodle on the plastic bag with your finger and test the water: 'Maybe we should just go now,' you say, 'or it will rain, and everyone will run, and . . . ' You stop at 'and'. I don't want to go, I just got here. I want to risk it. I want to stay with you. I don't mind the rain, these dots of cool, it's refreshing.

'The strawberries,' I say. I hold them out like a reason. They're from a place where strawberries are in season and the fruit is heavy. 'We've still got the strawberries. We could go and wait under the willow.'

You ask the other person what a willow is in French. '*Comme ça?*' he says, taking out an earphone, and pointing. '*Un saule pleureur.*' A weeping willow, the same.

It's unspoken, but this sameness is taken as a sign and a yes and so we get up to go. We stand up easily, because our feet are already so much lower than our heads. You get to the willow first, and hold it open like a bead curtain. It's cooler under here. We've gone from grass to ground, the earth is dry as ash, worn-out brown with scuffed, twine-like roots. You say it's lovely here and I agree. You lay down the Carrefour bag, and this time the other person gets the handle.

We settle. I dust my hands off on your shorts (the chaperone is on the phone) and reach for a strawberry. A few feet away, there are two young men, a wooden chopping board between them. A Swiss army knife levitates halfway into a saucisson sec, and a quarter of camembert overflows its edges onto the wood. They are drinking a pale red wine and raise their glasses to us – a stained glass window to say welcome. They are both in soft shirts and one is wearing a country cap. I say I like his hat and he says *'Merci'*, and then, 'Thank you'. He's heard we're speaking English.

I tell them they are perfect. 'The breadboard, the hat, the wine. Just two of you.' (You put your finger on one of my back dimples, then.) 'It's like a Marcel Pagnol novel.'

He laughs, tips his hat and asks if we'd like some cheese. He says it's spring camembert, that the milk is different, and so the cheese is special, sweeter, pours. He pulls the sword from the stone and cuts us two slices. Really, he says, we should eat it with honey, and maybe hazelnuts.

The man is right, the cheese is special. I shuffle down so my head is on the plastic bag and look through the fronds at the people outside our willow. A black man and a white woman, the wrong age for each other, rubbing noses, play-kissing. Two old men sitting on a bench, sharing *Le Monde*. Then us, under the willow. My head is against your thigh, you put your hand down and stroke my hair, and for a second, I shut my eyes.

I would stay like that for hours, but I open my eyes because something in the park changes. The air thickens, quickens – there is suddenly a different feeling.

A group of children has poured over the concrete crown of the slope and start to run, no, charge down through the picnics. Their shoes land heavily on unopened boxes of biscuits, they knock over plastic cups of wine and lemonade. They do not see barriers in bodies or blankets. They do not see barriers. And nobody can stop them, because they are quick, because they are small, because, for some, unplaceable reason, it is as if they exist on a plane that's not quite ours. There must be fifteen of them.

One running boy stops beside a family of three. He is perhaps the smallest of the gang. His arms are bone, his belly convex. A child slightly older pulls him on; the mother of the family holds her own son tighter.

'Are they alone?' you ask me, American accent suddenly stronger. 'Where's the adult?'

People are shouting because their babies' fingers have been trodden on. Other people stand to see what's happening. The chaperone peers out of the willow, fag dripping from his lip. '*Mais putain, ils sont feraux,*' he says to us.

At first we watch the children like a play, from cheap seats at the back, but soon we realize that our willow is where gravity will take them.

There is one bigger boy who seems to be the leader. Still, he cannot be a teenager yet, he can't be older than twelve; his hips are hand-sized. But his skin looks scuffed – the type of dry and dusty that normally comes from working with bricks. Even in this heat, he is wearing two jumpers. The cuffs are dirty, and he's hooked a thumb through one of them.

The boy looks like he has recently grown, as if he still hasn't mastered the new length of his legs. And when he gets to the bottom of the hill, he comes into our willow, parting the wicker walls, and walks straight towards the men with the picnic.

They have their backs to him. The wild boy with the double jumper treads plainly, flatly, hard, on the spring camembert and grabs the cap off one of their heads.

The man jerks his head around to face the boy. He sees the hat in his hand, the stamped-on cheese, and the man grabs the knife next to it.

The hat is hostage. The audience is captive. The Buttes Chaumont goes silent. The slope takes an in-breath as one.

But the knife seems to mean nothing to the boy. He holds the stolen cap in his fist and kicks a dark cloud of dust onto their picnic. Even standing still, there is something odd about his legs. I wonder if he has been drinking. The skin on his face is different colours. You reach for my hand, and you hold it.

The man and the boy stand opposite each other, four feet apart. Sun and rain, they face each other.

'TU N'EST QU'UN ENFANT!' the man shouts. You can see his face burn from here. The knife in his hand has a short blade, and is shaking slightly. 'ELLE EST *OU*, TA MAMAN?'

They both hold for five more seconds. And all of this time, you hold my hand.

Then the child stamps his left leg forward as if he is about to charge.

He doesn't, though. He laughs, a laugh which doesn't come from his head or chest. Then he drops the hat, and runs.

The other children, all of whom had stopped to watch, follow their twelve-year-old leader. The tension is broken, the park bursts into applause. The children run on, run down, run to the gates, and disappear.

The words *sauvages* and *animaux* roll up and down the hill now. Tziganes. Roms. Did you see them? The children? They were children. They can't have been more than ten. No, ten years *old*. There were more than ten, they were everywhere. '*Il faudrait tous les enfermer*,' are words said too.

For a while, we look to see if they'll come back. We also look to the sky. We still don't know if it will really rain. People are leaving, perhaps because of the undecided sky, perhaps because of the children.

But the sun holds and soon the normal sounds of the park come back. You'd let go of my hand as soon as your friend sat back down.

Adrenalin is making my blood feel thicker or thinner, one of the two; it has the same effect as the cigarette. I ask the man with the picnic if he's OK.

He tries to use his knife to cut a slice of saucisson. His hand is shaking even harder now. The man he's with takes the knife from him, cuts him a piece, feeds it to him and touches his face as he chews it. The cap is reached for, and pulled back into their picnic. They have an unopened goat's cheese and the man rolls it back and forth, from one hand to the other.

What is this day? I say something about the Brothers Grimm, and the tale where wheels of cheese are rolled down a mountain. You ask why I see everything through books and films and music. I want to say that it only happens when I'm with you. When I'm with people that I like.

We try to write a poem but the only paper we have is a pastel-coloured perfume advert ripped from a magazine, and rhymes don't come, so we talk about when we were young, and the best and worst things we've ever done. I tell you a story about the time I drove a speedboat, you tell me about doing work experience at your dad's shoe-heel business. You ask strange questions, like what side of my mouth I chew on. You say that you're interested in the small things. You notice that the chaperone is not listening and you change your mind and say 'all things'.

At the end of the afternoon, we say goodbye to the men from another time, and leave the willow, strawberry leaves scattered where we were sitting.

You tell me not to pick them up. 'They look like crowns when they dry. I like our mess.' And so I look at you, and I look at you, and see all the times this has happened before, and you look back, and then it's your turn. 'What?'

Nothing. To leave, we walk slowly, even though it's downhill. Your shoes are on, mine are off, but raindrops have dried on the stone and cooled it down. Midges collect in the last staffs of sunlight, and the bins are built up with old picnics gathered up into plastic bags.

Out of the park and on the real road, the side by Botzaris, I hold your arm so I can put my shoes on. We kiss goodbye on

the cheeks, and lightly because of the other person and because
we think we'll see each other later. We make half-plans, you have
half a finger on my wrist and write on it in half-moons. We are
half-alone, and then –

'Girls,' the chaperone says through his cigarette. He taps his
watch. *'Il faut qu'on aille là,'* and you let go.

'Hey, Jude?' You say as you walk away. 'Don't make it sad.
You got stuff to do till we meet?'

'I've got a thousand missed calls,' I tell you.

'See you,' you say. I turn around to see if you look back, but
if you did, I missed that too.

In the end, we do not see each other again that night.
Instead, we drink too much in different bars with different
people. Perhaps I knew that as soon as I walked away from you.
The chaperone, the children. Nothing ever happens as you
think it will.

After we left each other, the air lay heavy as a blanket. I
decided to think that it wouldn't rain, so that it might. All it
needed was a chance.

Métro

They are going to take the métro. Pip suggested they meet at KFC.

'*Mais non*,' Clémence had said (she was glad this was on the phone and he couldn't see her). '*Kentucky, non. C'est pas correcte, ça.*'

Instead, she'd said, the fruit shop, the one where the pigeon flew out from the pineapples.

'The night we made the ratatouille?'

'*'Touille*,' she corrected, and soon after that he'd hung up.

But the fruit shop it was, and now Pip was waiting for her, summer freckles muddying the bridge of his nose, his hair freshly cut, looking at his watch, lightly bouncing on his back heels. He knows which door she'll come from – seriously though, there is somewhere they need to be and she is nine minutes late now – and finally, it opens.

It's the middle of the day, burning, and Château Rouge is busy. Dark men sell charred sweetcorn, darker men sell denim leggings. It's so crowded at the top of the stairs to the métro that RATP men in mint green uniforms have blocked it off and let the crush through in short bursts. There is a lot of pushing.

So yes, it's true that it's busy, but Pip can see her: she is not trying, she is not walking quickly. A taxi stutters to let her cross in front of it, but she waves it on, and waits. She's pretending she hasn't seen him, eyes anywhere but straight ahead. When she's close, she takes out her phone, looks like she's reading a text, smiles. She makes it obvious; she knows what she's doing.

Just as she looks up, Pip looks down. He has stopped bouncing, and is scuffing the back of his heel now, as if he's trodden in something.

'No pigeons this time,' he says when she gets close, pointing behind him.

'What?'

'I said, no pigeons this time. In the fruit shop. No pigeons.' Occasionally, he forgets she's French and speaks too quickly. 'No pigeons,' he repeats, *'pas de pigeon,'* and this time he vaguely flaps his arms.

'Oh.'

'We're late, we should go.' He wishes he hadn't done his bird impression. 'It's hot today. Are you OK? How are you?'

'I'm fine … tired. *Crevée.'* Clémence raises her shoulders with each word, but they are already so high. He can see the tension in her neck. She always used to get pain there, and he would smooth the knots as she sat on his lap on the métro. Pip moves to touch her but stops himself, and puts his hand back in his pocket.

'Yeah. Me too. Tired. You look great though.'

'Beaming?' she says. She says it 'bimming'. 'You get a tan?'

'I went to the sea for a day.'

'*Chez toi? Sercq?*'

'No. Le Havre. To see an old friend.'

'It looks OK. Good. Bronzé is good for you.'

Pip looks at Clémence and thinks how her face could only be French. The nose of someone who could give speeches, eyes that made him swallow, hair that she wrapped into a bun that fell out as she walked. The fineness of her frame, the fineness of it all. A month ago, maybe two, when everything had still been going well, Pip had emailed his father a picture of her. Eddy took three days to reply. When he did, it was with the word 'beautiful'. Pip was glad his father had chosen this word and not another. Attached to Eddy's reply was a scan of a photo of Esmé from before Pip was born. Pip had not replied, but looking at Clémence in front of him now, and remembering the photo of his mother, he had to admit there was a slight similarity. Almond eyes, he had always got stuck on almond eyes.

'We should walk to Line 2,' he says. 'Too many people here.'

And so they go down Boulevard Barbès. It's lined with shops, but the street itself is where the selling happens. Sim cards, mangoes, chants of malboro-malboro. When they were together, Pip's arm would be around her. She had been his, and they would leave her alone. There are few rules in Barbès, but that is one of them. Now that they are not touching, men try to sell her perfume and cigarettes and say she is *ravissante*, or worse, as soon as she has walked past.

'Doesn't it bother you?' Pip says when they are on the platform.

'*Quoi?*'

'The men. All of it. I could have hit them.' He could have, but he didn't. 'I wish you didn't live round here.'

He checks the métro map, even though they know where they're going. Nine stops, no change, his finger an inch from the plastic so he doesn't have to touch it. This is how he has adjusted to city living, by seeing it as a sort of maths. He leans over the track to look for the train. He's done that since they met and it's always annoyed her – it won't make the train come quicker, and what if he falls?

'It's coming,' he says, turning back to her. He always seems a bit proud, as though he was the one who made it happen, his face like a child's again. When it stops, they push on. It doesn't look as if there's enough space for either of them – he's so tall – but once they're inside, four more people squeeze in after. The human body is soft and yielding, she thinks. We believe we are bigger than we are, but we are just like gas.

Pip leans close, and puts his hands on either side of her. 'Sorry,' he says. 'There's no room.' It's a wall he's built around her with his arms. Now she will not fall, and if she did, he could save her.

One more woman pushes on, pushes Pip and Clémence's heads together. 'Fuck,' Pip breathes, 'it's hot.' Their eyes snag for a second, then break free. All these other faces around them – painted eyebrows, purple weave, ponytails and saggy cheeks.

'Sweat,' he says after that. He's not whispering. 'I can feel other people's sweat. It's like going back into the womb—' He stops short. 'Sorry. I didn't mean ... I didn't mean about that. It's just the smell. It isn't normal.'

'We speak English in France, you know,' she says. He's always loved the way she says 'France': it rolls, it falls. 'All of us, we do,' she goes on, 'we understand you.'

'I don't like this many people close to me.'

'Lonely child,' she says. '*C'est typique.*'

'*Only* child,' he corrects.

Two stops later, at Stalingrad, people pour out. The need to stand tight leaves with the crowd, so Pip lets his arm-wall fall.

It is just one man, alone, who steps onto the train.

How do we tell, almost instantly, the eyes which are best avoided? Neither Pip nor Clémence looks at this man, but they catch him in the corners of their sight. His legs do not bend at the knees, instead they move like wood. Each crash-landing sends a sweet-sour wind their way.

The second splits, and it becomes a story. Two things happen entirely at once. Just as this man comes on board, just at the very moment he sets foot on the train, a baby in a pram starts to cry at the other end of the carriage. From someone so small, it is a strong, high, wrenching sound. And you can almost see it land on the man.

At first, he cannot tell where the noise is coming from. His forehead jerks as if his eyes are chasing an imaginary wasp. If they allowed themselves to look at him, they'd see that one side of his face is gristled with scabs. He has a tall can of red Amsterdam in his hand and squeezes it until his matte fingers meet. The baby howls again, and then the man makes his own noise, as if his throat and his teeth have taken the corners of a cry and ripped it in half. He turns to face the infant. His head twists after the wasp one more time, and he starts to stagger towards the pram.

'*Non – non – putain,*' Clémence says, letting go of the metal pole and grabbing Pip's thin T-shirt instead. She turns her face as far away as she can. 'I can't look,' she says. She needs Pip to know she cannot look, that she is a girl, that this makes a difference.

The man is making his terrible noise closer and closer to the baby, but he is not there yet.

'What's happening?' Clémence stares at Pip's T-shirt, his chest, the faint push of his nipple. '*Il fait quoi, là?*' He must look for her.

'It's OK,' he says. 'He won't do anything . . .' He can't, Pip thinks, it's a *baby*, there are rules.

But the man is getting closer. The mother is moving to put herself between them.

Clémence turns and quickly flashes her eyes in their direction. The man is so close now. The mother wants to turn to her baby, but she cannot turn her back to the man.

Men, Clémence thinks, *men.* There are all these other men, in suits and shiny glasses – proper men, safe men – and they are staring at their newspapers.

'I . . .' She looks pleadingly at Pip, her forehead is chewed, she can't speak. The terrible man is shouting now, standing three feet from the mother. Cries are filling the train.

Pip's body is tightly tensed as if he might leap – he *might*, he *could* – but he stays exactly where he is. 'It's ... going to be fine.' (There are rules: you don't stand up, you don't look, you don't hurt a baby, there are rules.)

There are no rules. When the train comes into the station, it stops with an almighty lurch. The shouting man remembers his can and tries to stop it from spilling, but he loses his footing, he tips away from the pram. As the doors open, though, both feet slam flat to the floor, sturdy. His rough face chases the wasp, and he turns back to the baby. No one gets on, and no one gets off. No one moves. The doors, about to close, begin to beep.

But the mother is a mother and she takes her chance. She takes a sharp step towards the shouting man and uses both hands to push. Her eyes are shut tight; there are times when no one can look. It happens very fast. But the man falls out through the doors as they close, his can hitting the floor of the carriage in front of the pram and spinning, spilling, on the spot.

The man roars one last time, but the door is shut. The base of his fist lands hard on the window; for the beer, for the baby. But the train moves on, the man is gone.

Clémence is still holding onto Pip's top. She is still holding her breath. It takes her a second to realize she can let either go. They have three more stops until theirs. Do they have a conversation? Perhaps. A film they'd seen, a mutual friend, a new café on his street. Maybe. But the whole time, the whole time, her hands and heart vibrate.

She stares and stares at the métro map. Normally she sees Paris clearly in its coloured lines. But now it's a tangle. She does not know where she is.

They talk to make noise. It's only when they are about to get off the train that they notice the baby has stopped crying.

Two middle-aged sisters – they must be sisters, they have matching eyes – have moved to sit next to the mother and child. They're perched on the fold-down seats, leaning over the pram, singing a lullaby. It is Portuguese, or Brazilian Portuguese: open, bouncing, squashy, and the baby is silent.

Off the train and on the platform now, Clémence stays still, watching the sisters sing until the doors slam shut. Humans are mostly, mostly soft and yielding. When the train pulls away, still, she stands. Instinctively, her forearm moves to protect her belly.

'Clem,' Pip says, a gentle tug. Finally, he puts his arm around her shoulder, and guides her to the exit. He was going to say something about a happy ending, but he cannot. They walk up the stairs of the métro and as soon as they are back at sea level, he lets go of her.

'It's this way,' he says. 'I checked before I came. It's not far. It's easy.'

As they walk, she says that it's good of him to come. He says that he had a free day, and besides, he shrugs – he doesn't mean to shrug – it's for both of them. His eyes fall to her neck. So tight. Maybe he could still make it better. *Come away with me,* he almost says. *We don't have to do this. I could take you – all three of us – far away.* But he looks down at his watch again. They're just in time. Fine, it will be fine.

The doors to the clinic are white, as they thought they would be. Each waits for the other to push them open. Here, the journey ends.

Beni and the Kids, Part II

There was a barman at Le Paris who had been fired over thirty times. He was called Jamel and he was second-generation Algerian: face gutted with acne scars, Kangol cap, fifty euro patent brogues. Sofi didn't like him.

'*Ça va, meuf?*' he said to her as she wiped down the bar one late summer, late afternoon. '*T'es délicieuse, toi. J'oublie.*' I forget. '*Un milkshake. Fraise. Et mets du vodka.*'

Beni couldn't get rid of Jamel because he owed him so much money. He would come in with a friend who had gold teeth and a shaved side-parting and they'd eat lamb tagine out of takeaway foil and drink straight spirits from behind the bar.

'Beni and Alessio owe me thousands,' Jamel told Sofi this particular day, looking at her hair as if he might touch it. He had a cigarette behind his ear, and a toothpick in his mouth, which he dislodged from one tooth and passed with his tongue to another. '*Allez.* Just give me twenty from the till.'

Sofi said she couldn't, that it would get docked from her pay. Honestly, man, I already have nothing.'

When Sofi had first met Jamel, she'd taken the piss out of his cap, but since then, there'd been rumours of a shooting or stabbing – something bad he'd been involved with, or done. It was hard not to tread more lightly after that.

'Honestly,' she said again. 'Look at my shoes. I'm like Julia Roberts. I have to colour them in with a marker.'

Jamel ordered a steak and asked for it bloody. When Sofi was washing up, leaving her watch and bracelets on the bar, Jamel grabbed them and ran out, the greased bones from his tagine kicked all over the floor.

'That little shit!' Beni said when she told him. 'I'll kill him.' But Sofi wasn't allowed to tell the police because of all the money Jamel was owed. 'You're getting new ones – a new watch. We'll sort it out between us.'

'It was only from Argos,' she said.

'I'll get you a better one. I'll get you the best there is.'

He spoke certainly, comfortingly, like thick bread.

Beni promised to take a few of the kids to a Paul Simon concert too – a day trip to Bercy; Sofi would finally see Paris – but that didn't happen either.

There were good days, bad days, days with fierce blazes of both. The only other time Sofi cried was after Pip had been in to see her. She had disappeared during evening service, and Arthur the Cornish king found her smoking a spliff in the doorway of the African hairdresser's opposite.

'Your eyes are raining,' he said, then coughed, embarrassed.

'Your English is worse than mine,' she told him. 'Sorry. This is yours.' She offered him back the joint. 'I jacked it from your pocket.' She had a bottle of whisky at her feet.

'Who was that guy?' he said. He'd wanted to ask this.

This question seemed to make Sofi sadder.

'Old boyfriend?'

'No,' she said. 'No, not really. Just someone I used to know.'

Arthur helped her up, and she told him she didn't know why she couldn't stop crying. She put a finger on his tattoo as if she thought that might help. *Triangles*, she thought. *The world's not round at all. Everything always ends up in triangles.*

His shaven head shone brown-gold in the streetlight. He had a short white scar on his hairline and he wrapped strong, chalky arms around her. She felt then, that even if her legs fell loose, she would still be standing. That was the first time they kissed.

After the second winter in the snow dome, Sofi had to leave. She was getting calls every day from Crédit Mutuel, and from Bouygues, the phone company she could never pronounce. Before the calls stopped, she phoned home. Her dad said her mum would be happy to have her back, that it worried her what Sofi's life was like there. He did what dads do and passed the phone to his wife. Sofi told her mum that she was sad, and that she'd probably never get to Paris now. Her mum said she thanked God every day that her daughter had never made it to the Moulin Rouge.

By then, Beni had lost his spot in his corner. He came in less now, once a week maybe, and didn't stay for booze or breakfast.

The grapevine said he was fighting with Alessio, or suicidal, perhaps both, no one really knew. He never answered his phone any more. Sofi sent him a message saying she was leaving, and that she needed her money. She said she missed him, and the Beatles. She said she hoped he was all right.

Four days later, Beni called on the tinny work phone.

'Throw yourself a goodbye party in the restaurant. Invite all the kids. I'll come, and I'll get you your money. On my honour, girl, I'll get you your money.' The reception was so bad she could hardly hear him.

The party got out of hand. They smoked inside and made Long Island iced teas with far more than four spirits. They ate whole-fish-long panels of smoked salmon out of the fridge, and people kissed in the kitchen. When the day-sleepers from the port tried to come in – a beat woman in a miniskirt and a man she'd found – they gave them a crate of Beni's beer and then locked them out, so it was only the kids. Someone wrote Sofi a goodbye card, liquid eyeliner on napkin. Arthur held her, arms round from behind, and showed her that on the fifteenth step, on tiptoes – careful – you could look through buildings and see a tiny, bright slice of the Le Havre sea. Months and months, all those windows, she had run up and down the stairs and thought she had seen everything. But some things you don't get until right at the very end.

Beni never came, so she never saw him again. They kept drinking; drinking to him, ironically and not ironically, they drank from bottles. Glasses were broken.

Around midnight, Beni called her.

'Kid,' Beni said. 'The ketchup.'

'What?' she said. 'Are you here?' Phone to her ear, she did a full circle. She looked for him.

'Far away,' he said. 'Ketchup, look behind the ketchup.'

No one knew how Beni did it, because only one week later, Le Paris shut down. Bailiffs arrived and took everything from the inside, including the sinks.

But that night, behind the ketchup, he'd left her an envelope. Brown, addressed to no one. He left all that he could in her hands.

Death in Montmartre, Part II

A phone rings.

It's on top of a pile of magazines. Vibration on shiny paper, the phone shakes towards the bed. Rookie reaches for the phone, picks up.

Straight away: 'I know it's early.' It's Jude. 'It's too early, isn't it?'

'It's fine.' He's whispering. He hasn't used his voice yet.

'How are you?'

'Fine . . . fine.' Even quieter the second time. There are certain angles, lying in bed, that make it hard to speak.

'Are you busy?'

'Kind of, Jude, I was sleeping.'

'Would you meet me?'

He doesn't say anything.

'I can come over, if you want,' she adds.

'No, no, don't—'

Jude hears the creak of the bed as Rookie gets up. 'Hold

on a second, I'm just going to – *non, t'inquiete. Personne . . . personne. Une amie, seulement.* Sorry . . . wait.' She hears a door shut at his end. 'Yeah, OK. I can talk now. Are you OK?'

'You have a different voice when you talk to her,' she says.

'It's French.'

'No, not that. It's . . . sugary.'

'No, it isn't.'

'Comic Sans.'

'Is this what you wanted to talk about?'

'Not saying it's bad, just funny.'

'Is this what you woke me up to say?' he asks, his voice changing again.

'No. It isn't. I'm sorry—'

'It's fine.'

'—for being a cock.'

'You're not a cock.'

'Can we meet?' she says. 'Later?'

'Are you OK?'

'I think so.'

'That's not yes.'

'I don't know.'

'Caulaincourt,' he says. 'Caulaincourt. The café on the corner of Junot. Shouty barmaid.'

'In an hour?'

He thinks for a second about the girl in his bed. 'Two?'

' . . . OK,' she says.

'An hour and a half.' He stops. 'I can be there in an hour and fifteen.'

'OK,' she says again. Then 'thank you' but Rookie has already hung up.

That is when Jude starts to cry again.

She had called him from the bath, and it's got cold. The water is faintly green, faintly cloudy, but that's more from soap than anything else. She's scrubbed her legs until they are red raw and now there are tiny quenelles of her skin floating on the surface of the water. Before she called him, she watched her body through the bath. All of it distorted, vague waves making the straight lines of her legs shake. When she was on the phone, part of her thought: I don't care if the phone falls. Drop it into the water and let yourself turn to silt.

But she held the phone tight and, now Rookie is no longer on the line, she drops it onto the battered bathmat. Another thought cuts through her: this is fake depression, school depression, you can't even do depression properly.

Rookie doesn't shower. He spends the short time before he has to leave back in bed with his girl. Fifteen minutes of peace pressed against her sleep-skin. At the métro station, he jumps over the barrier and gets to avenue Junot in an hour and ten.

Jude is already waiting, hair still wet. (Even though it's short, her hair has always held onto water. If she gets caught in the rain, it takes hours to dry; one of the reasons it shines so much.) Her skin is bleached-looking, though, bleached-out. She's wearing sunglasses. Both elbows are perched on a Formica table, and her cheeks rest on her palms.

She offers him the chair opposite, thanks him for coming and asks if he wants a beer.

'No,' he laughs, quite genuinely. He's let his beard grow, rusty red, and you can hear it rustle when he opens his mouth.

'Old times' sake,' she says. 'It's Sunday.'

'I just woke up. Look at my hair.' He bends towards her and points to his partings. He has three. 'I've still got sleep in my eyes. Coffee first.'

'Let's go somewhere else then. I've been crying. Don't look, but my eyes are red.' She flashes her sunglasses to her forehead for a second. 'All puffy. Can we walk?'

'You look fine,' he says.

'Liar,' she says. She tries to smile but on the way to her face it turns into two tears – perfect spheres which hold over her pupil and then drop heavily onto her cheek.

'Come here,' he says and stands her up with his hands. He wraps his arms around her. His arms meet each other sooner than he expects.

'There's nothing to you.' He undoes his hug and puts his hands over her ribs. 'Where are you?'

'I'm here. I'm still here.' She shifts her hands into her pockets, which breaks his grip. 'I'm still here. Let's walk.'

For the first hundred yards of avenue Junot – a perfect curve, the beginning of a spiral – they say nothing. They walk uphill.

'It's not summer any more,' Jude says, pointing up to the trees. The leaves are starting to become stiff. In the flushes of summer, their fullness stops the sun from reaching this pavement, but daylight has returned to Junot. Jude has been inside for too long. Even with sunglasses on, she has to shield her eyes to look up to the sky.

'Again,' she says. 'It keeps on leaving and nothing's ever changed.'

'It doesn't *keep* leaving . . .'

'It does.'

'That's too much.'

'It's what it feels like. I think about what happened last month and I ask myself if it feels like a whole month ago. It never does. I do the same with years. It goes so fast. Two and a half years I've been here, and you, three. And what have we done?'

'Stuff. We've done stuff.'

'None of it matters.'

'It does.'

'Don't you think we've wasted it? You don't think about time like I do,' she says.

They've just arrived at their Spanish square. Jude sits down.

'That used to be my line,' he says.

'Don't *smile* like that.'

He nudges her over, and they sit on their bench in silence.

Jude has tissues – loo roll – tucked into her sleeve the way a mother does to an infant. 'Did I ever tell you why I came to Paris?' she says.

'You were madly in love.'

She looks at him blankly.

'Madly in love with me.'

She has to laugh at that.

'No? No, I know. To do that dossy French course at the Sorbonne.'

'No. Well, yes, that too. But part of it was to honour some – it feels so stupid when you say it – some promise I'd made to someone. Someone I – felt I, I don't know, *loved* or something.' She looks at her tissue. 'It's so stupid.' Her words are breaking down.

'It's not stupid.'

'Didn't I ever tell you that?'

He shakes his head.

'I don't think she ever came. Even if she did, I never saw her again.' Jude's eyes look as though she has been rubbing them. 'And now there's the American girl and all the rubbish in between.' Tears cross her cheeks, cross each other. 'You think it's funny, but it's confusing, Rook.' Her voice is breaking now. 'And it's sad. It *is* sad. It's embarrassing.'

'Not embarrassing. You're lovely. I always thought you were lovely,' he says, hand on her denim knees. He can say this now because he'd said it before, not just once, and all that was over. So far away it felt impossible. It amazed him how strongly, how consumingly the body could feel something, but that, if it is not returned, perhaps even if it is, one day that feeling just . . . melts. At times it frustrated him, at times he saw it saved him: why is it we can only really say what we feel when we don't feel it any more? 'That's the problem. That's your problem. You never see the people that wanted you. Want. You know what I mean.'

Her knee is so small under his hand.

'Then why do I only like the ones I can't have?'

He takes his hand away.

'I used to think that,' he says. 'Think that it was only people

I couldn't have. The girls who already had boyfriends. My mum's friends. I was in love with one of my mum's friends. Black girls who passed me in the street. Impossible girls. You.' He stops what he's saying and looks up at her then with fondness. Such fondness. In front of him is a face he has loved. His eyes seem to tip down rather than up when he looks at her like that. 'But it's not true.'

'It's not a choice to be like this,' she says. 'It's the way it happens.'

'It *is* a choice.'

'Not.'

'It's the torture of it, Jude. You like the minor keys.'

'I don't.'

'The nearlies and could-bes.'

'You don't know what you're talking about.'

'The maybes.'

'I get it.'

'It's what a teenager does.'

They look at each other.

'You're not a teenager any more.'

She says he doesn't have to tell her that.

Rookie looks away. Jude looks at his hair. She thinks how different red is from orange. His hair is the red of foxes, the red of bloodwood. It has a different texture to all others, red hair. There's something about his moustache that reminds her of a sea creature.

'We always fall in love in patterns,' he says. 'Not even *in* patterns. *With* patterns. The people are – sometimes I think the people are completely irrelevant. This American girl you like.

If she turned up right now and said you were the love of her life, do you think you'd still feel like you feel now?' He looks at her. He's trying to read her face like music. 'Wet eyes, wet hair, all . . . wet with love?'

'Yes.' Jude blows her nose very loudly. 'Yes, I think I would. I do.'

'You wouldn't.'

'That's not fair . . . You can't tell me off for not changing and then tell me I'll never change.'

'It's not just you. It's *society*. All of us. It's fucked up.'

She manages to laugh again, a light laugh at him. 'You were lovesick a minute ago. What happened to you?'

'I don't like seeing you like this,' he says. He scratches at a sparse part of his beard.

Jude says sorry.

'It's not your fault. I just . . . This girl. Does she even know? Have you *said* something this time?'

A pause. 'We slept together. We've been sleeping together.'

Those were not the words he expected. He doesn't know why it still feels hard to hear them.

'So?' he says, quickly. 'That doesn't mean anything. Have you actually told her how you feel?'

She shakes her head.

'Human brains,' he says. 'They're so simple, Jude. No one ever knows unless you say it.'

That's when the noise breaks into their conversation. It's an 8-bit version of Chet Baker. It's Jude's phone, from inside her bag. She takes it out.

'Fuck.' She stares at it. 'It's her.'

'Which her?'

'The American.' The way she is sitting has changed completely. 'She never calls me. What do I do? It's her.'

'Answer it, you weirdo.'

'I don't – I don't know.' She's looking at her phone like she's never seen it before. 'Oh fuck. Fuck.' She turns the phone to face him. 'She's hung up. What do I do now?'

'She'll call again.'

'She has a boyfriend. I don't know.'

'Just call her back.'

Before she can, Chet Baker sings again.

'It's her.'

'Of course.'

Jude reaches out and touches her friend's temple. A raised vein, heat, soft. He shuts his eyes.

'OK,' she says. 'I will. I'm going to take it.'

Jude leaves Rookie on the bench, and walks away to speak; the only word he manages to hear is a shy, but solid, 'hello'.

Less, Loss, Other Words that End in S

I f you were to see them, you would not guess that they are breaking up. They are in bed, alone together; so it's not very likely you would see them at all.

They have shifted down the sheets, the pillows above their heads, like clouds. They lie like the letter S, twice. Sofi is the first, Arthur is the second. He can feel the tops of her knees push, bone hot, into the backs of his.

The differences between them, how small she is, the length of her hair, strike him again and again. Extraordinary thing, he thinks, that I can lift, whole, off this world.

It's Sofi who called it their double-S. She said she didn't like the term 'spooning', thought it sounded metal, cold. She made a joke about once being in a three-piece cutlery set. That wasn't cold, she said, so far from cold, so she could understand it even less. 'Double-S,' she says now, again, 'like at the end of kiss.'

'Shush. With as many S's as you like. You talk and talk.'

Arthur zips her lips with a finger; they break open and she takes his finger between her teeth.

It is not clear – and never really has been – which of them likes the other more. There are things that other people look for, then things that count.

Sofi still cannot believe how handsome he is, and tends to say so, stopping him in front of shop windows and talking to his reflection. 'Classically perfect' is the sound bite she'd come up with, and stuck to.

She likes to kiss the side of his body under his arms. Skin never got used there. 'This is where we'll never get old,' she would say. She re-drew his tattoo. She wished she could scratch him, lightly, along the padded outlines of his ribs, but she bit her fingernails. It was the only way that she could keep them clean. She left the faintest grazes only when her teeth hadn't made a clear cut.

She liked the places he was hard where she could never be hard: his chest, solid in soft squares around the bumpy haloes of his nipples; his bum, 'wrong word for it,' she said, so firm she could knock on it like a door and did. The other place he got hard.

She tested him, in her head. *If he touches me on his way back from the toilet, it's true he loves me.* A few days before: *If it's him, not me, who breaks this hand-hold, it's him, not me, who will end this.*

She would ask him if she had kissed him everywhere yet.

'You already asked me that.' Creamy voice. Thick, spread. 'Loads of times.'

'Did you answer?'

'Probably.'

'What did you say?'

'Probably. That's what I said.'

And no one had ever made him laugh like she did. She would push his face away with her hands, deciding he was laughing *at* her.

'So what I thought it was *Maori* Poppins, so what? Easy mistake, it's not funny.'

'It *is*—'

'Not funny to laugh at me.'

He wasn't, he was. It didn't matter. Sofi made him laugh and no one had ever made him laugh like that.

'It's not my fault,' she said. 'I'm Polish.'

'When it suits you.' He took her head, a planet in his hands, and clamped it into his chest. 'Hear that heart?'

'No.' Her voice dampened by his jumper. 'You don't have one.'

'It's for you. It beats for you. All of it's for you.'

'You're not allowed to laugh when you say that.'

When they'd met at Beni's, both of them had just meant to be passing through. They called it a 'way to' place. But both of them had stayed. Smoked, worked, walked. Spent so much time together, but like brother and sister, for over a year. At first, Sofi thought he was too *soft* to be sexy: his hair, his skin, his voice, all of it soft as felt. And Arthur thought she was too ... too ... ? He didn't know what, now. They spent so long not fucking that they fucked for so long when they started, as if to make up for lost time. They were new again, it was new – new, confusing, tears by the sea, and fights by text – when they were allowed to see each other naked.

He had watched her like a film at first. Well-edited, smooth. It was like she moved in scenes – standing in a door frame, on tiptoes, hands reaching up to the top corners, gauze bra, naked everywhere else; pushing him into the loos on a quiet day at the bar, sucking him through his jeans. Scenes he could play and replay. The first time they had slept together, he could hardly get home. It wasn't butterflies in his stomach. It felt like a bird in there, beating its wings. He thought he'd walk in front of a car. He sat still in a café not far from where she lived and let his head explode with her.

Now he'd seen her breasts so many times they no longer shocked him. She'd plucked her eyebrows as they watched TV, marvelling at each thick hair's bulb – 'Look, Ar! Like a plant bulb, an *onion* bulb' – and showing them to him. He had looked all around her face and seen everything that was wrong with it: pinker splashes where foundation faded, how the tops of her ears pushed forward slightly as if reaching for what he said. Her legs had got a little fatter; he'd met her mother. And all of this, all these things, had built up like seconds into a minute. That minute felt so full, so full he thought it would burst. It was love. Still is. So hard to know which one loved the other more.

Arthur would talk about 'starting the day' to get them out of bed.

'As if the day won't start without us. As if it's our responsibility,' she'd say. 'We used to get up so late.'

'Go out into the day. We need light.'

'Open the curtains, I don't mind.'

'I don't want other men to see you.'

'I don't mind.'

'We'll get scurvy here.'

'I've got fruit.'

'Bananas aren't fruit.'

'They are.'

'Potatoes. They're like potatoes.'

'*Fruit.*'

'You shouldn't eat so many.'

'*Iron*, Arthur. It's good for you.' She pronounced the 'th' in his name with an 'f'.

'Not iron. Potassium. It causes blindness. Come *on*,' he'd say. 'The *day*,' like it was leaving. It was the only time when he pushed his voice.

Then she'd say 'Fine', firmly, and find pants, back-crabbing on the bed to pull them up. She'd put makeup on (still not much, but more than she used to, more every year) and finish her hair before she reached for the rest of her clothes. Sometimes she'd have her shoes on, and a bag in her hand, ready to go, before she chose a dress to wear, or one of his shirts.

'The *day*,' she'd say. But now it was him. He wouldn't have moved. He'd be watching her.

'Your breasts.'

He'd put a finger in her belly button and pull her to him like that.

'The *day*, you dick.'

'My dick, then the day?'

'You don't like the word "dick".' She took his hand and pushed his strongest finger into a damp dip in her pants. 'You think it's too English ... childish.'

'I was playing with the words you gave me.'

'Playing?'

'Playing. Fuck.'

'What?'

'No one has ever – oh *fuck* – no, don't ... carry on ... No one has ever ...'

'What?'

'I just feel like – I mean – fuck – you're the – I don't know ...'

'Finish your sentences.'

'So good.'

'I don't know what you're saying.'

'The best.'

She would talk during – her hands everywhere, she'd touch him everywhere – which he found strange at first. It wasn't talking like they do in things you see on the internet, or like other girls had tried.

'You concentrate so much,' she'd say when he was deep inside her. 'I can see it in your eyebrows that you're thinking.' He'd kiss her to stop her looking at him. 'Is it true that all boys think about Margaret Thatcher?'

Sometimes he wanted to say 'shut up', but even in his head that sounded wrong and he'd see her nipples – pink beads, soft and hard at the same time – and say, 'Your *brother*. I think about your brother.'

'I don't have one. Why do you have to be gross? Turn me over. Come. I want you to fuck me here.'

After a year or two, they stopped counting. They didn't know what to count from anyway.

'First kiss,' Sofi says.

'You kissed Meryn after that.'

'We all did. It was a party.'

'Then you went home. I didn't see you for a month.'

'You told me you loved me.'

'I did not.'

'You did. When you came to stay.'

'You were telling me about Sark. About that girl.'

A muscle in Sofi's belly, thin and tight as a wire, contracts.

'How strong it was.'

'You said that was hot,' she says.

'It *was* hot. But it got me. I wanted to make sure you weren't ...'

'Weren't what?'

'I wanted you to know how much I wanted you.'

'Do you still feel that?'

'Didn't you hear my heart?'

Now, in bed, alone together, his thumb follows the shape of a bikini. It's February, the month furthest from the sun, but she has a tan-line all year round. Belly dark, breasts white, like she'd bent and dipped her front in bleach.

'Not bleach,' he says, kissing them. 'Don't say that. Milk.'

They roll, return to their double-S. His back is so big in front of her. She puts herself in the middle of it, his shoulders at her hairline, her lips where his broadness begins to narrow, still thickly, into waist.

'Your arms are like two of mine, maybe three.' She sounds almost sad. 'Hey, Arthur?'

'Yeah.'

'Is this what life is?'

'What do you mean?'

'Are we grown up yet?'

'What do you mean?'

'Is this what we meant when we said "When I grow up"?'

'I don't know.' Had he said that? Had he thought it? He feels as if the bed has disappeared from underneath him. As if he is floating, static in the air.

'Where do you think you'll be in twenty years?' she asks, blunt fingers resting on his ribs.

'I don't know.'

'Where do you think *I'll* be?'

'I don't . . .' Harder. 'I don't know.'

'Which country?'

'I . . .' He stops. She blows on his back as he thinks. 'Where do you want to be?'

'Do I have children?'

'Do you want them?'

'I . . .' She's stopped blowing.

'It doesn't matter. Yes,' he decides. 'You have children.'

'Lots of them?'

'Lots.' Whatever it looks like, this is not a fast conversation. Between each sentence, the silence is such that they can almost touch it. He speaks even slower than he used to. All the boys she's ever known talk more slowly now they're men. 'They're healthy.'

'I'm glad.' She blows again. And then kisses his side. A line in slight curve. Orion's Belt. The skin of his torso that will stay young. 'Peter Pan. You'll look good old though. You look good. Salt and pepper suits you. So handsome.'

She pushes him back, until both shoulder blades are flat on the bed, and pushes her forehead into his chest. Both keep their eyes shut tight.

'Do I have them?' he says into her hair. He is not sure, but he feels a pain somewhere.

'Yes. They're just like you. Exactly the same, all Cornwall and lovely. I think they'll be lovely.'

Neither of them moves for a while. It is not that they are breaking up today, right now, as you read this. It is not the last time they will lie in a double-S in this bed, not at all. It might be years.

They don't need to say it, but they both know, that when they made each other older, they gave each other away.

Borges in Bed

It started with a line from Borges. Pip wasn't sure if he had remembered it right. His son couldn't sleep, and he was trying to help him.

'Could you say it again?' the boy asked. He was lying flat on his back, but his head was three inches off the pillow.

The boy did not look comfortable. Pip could see tendons, cello strings too close to the skin, tugging at his son's collar-bones. *Six years old. His bones are a third of the size of mine, they are as thin as sticks.* For one thick second, Pip could not wait for the boy to grow. He would have folded up the next ten years of his life in order for the boy to be less breakable.

'I don't remember it exactly, J.'

'But you just said it, Da.'

Pip licked his thumb and used it to wipe off the snot which had dried in a small cobweb under the boy's nose. 'It's something like . . .' and he repeated what he'd said.

J shut his eyes tight until they disappeared into folds of skin like stars. *That's where he'll have wrinkles one day*, Pip thought. *He shuts his eyes so hard.* J had clenched like that the first time he tried to swallow half a paracetamol, when the Calpol had run out. It hadn't worked. 'I've gone all closed at the back,' he'd said, pointing to his throat. So Pip hid the pill in a buttered bread sandwich, and got his son to take it that way.

J let his head lower back, slowly, into the pillow, as if he thought someone might have taken it from under him.

This tiny child doesn't trust anything, but he's so small not to trust things. J had one leg outside of the duvet, and one underneath it. Three nights earlier, he had said, quietly, that one half of his body was always hot, the other always cold. Always the same sides. He asked his dad if that was OK, and then he asked if he was going to die.

Now, this evening, he was silent. Pip felt his son's breathing start to slow down, he saw the tide of the duvet change. The first few times he had seen this, it scared him. The words 'peter out' came into his head. He had never thought those words before, but that didn't matter, they came to him now. What if his son's lungs petered out? *Peter out, peter out, I can't bear it if he peters out.* And he had shaken J awake.

Then apologized when he realized nothing was wrong. Pip thought about his own breathing and his own heart, his own everything, when he fell asleep in the bigger bed next door. His body slowed down too.

He let his son do the same now. He stroked J's forehead to help him on his way, to show that he gave him permission to go. He would not be that kind of father, Pip told himself, not the kind who got in the way.

Pip sat on the edge of his son's bed. He could feel the long corner edge of the mattress through his jeans. He felt, for a moment, as if he were sitting on a tightrope. The light coming from the corridor led to the noise of the television. J said the sound helped him sleep, unless it was guns or bombs, when he preferred it if the volume was kept low.

Pip kissed his son between the eyebrows, the weight of it pushing J's head further into the pillow. When J was even smaller, Pip had held him in his arms the way he'd seen it done in films. Cradling. He would kiss J's head again and again in tiny, staccato beats. He used to wonder whether he kissed him so much he would stop his hair from growing. Until he was two-and-a-half, J's hair was nothing but a suggestion, see-through in sunlight. After that though, it turned blond, then brown, and it grew fast, now, on the weekends. Pip got up slowly and walked to the door. He pulled it to behind him, leaving the light on.

In the small bed, J was not asleep. His left hand was flexed open as wide as it could go, as if each fingertip were trying to escape from the others. His right was clenched so tight his fingernails – they grew fast too – dug into his palm. When he realized how different his hands were, he let the force in each of them go. *My left side and my right side, they never feel the same.* It occurred to J that he might be broken.

When he thought that, new thoughts followed. Broken, he must be broken, and reasons sprang out, flaring, wild, hard, like his left hand's fingers. It was because he'd swallowed chewing gum. It was because he'd bitten a girl at nursery once, and blood dotted out through her Aertex. It was because people near him broke. It was because everyone was breaking. It was because he had tried peanuts. J had heard of allergies, he knew about illness. He had seen programmes about these things on the television, had heard words when he was supposed to be sleeping. He imagined black lumps growing all over the inside of his body.

That was how his brain worked. If you could see the way his thoughts moved and grew, you'd talk of estuaries or trees, things that fork, and double, and double again. It did not help what his father had said. He couldn't stop thinking about it.

That night, J was sure he did not sleep for a single second. What he could see in his head felt as big as a cinema screen. He looked all around this space, from floor to ceiling, from curtain to curtain. If Pip had been there still, he would have seen his son's pupils dance beneath the surface of his eyelids.

There were lots of things happening, all at once. Here are some of the things J saw:

He saw his home burning. He saw it from outside, as if the bird feeder had become a camera. He saw licks of orange, and butane blue; charcoal clouds of smoke so thick they smudged out the windows. He saw the fire start from the kitchen, then he saw the fire start from his father's bed. Then he saw it start from his own head (that week at school, a classmate had, without such words, described spontaneous combustion).

He saw groups of teenagers – or, twelve-year-olds at least, older than him and twice as high – running along the road towards his house. They had white faces, then black faces and then their faces were a mixture of the two. He saw baseball bats in their hands, then huge curved swords, big guns and finally axes, blades flashing silver in the light of the street lamp.

He saw a snake at the bottom of his bed which turned into the type of spider that was poisonous. After that, it was a scorpion, and finally, it was a snake again, cold, wet, moving towards his knee in a stretched S.

He saw a man in a hood break into their house. The man climbed up the drainpipe and climbed in through the tiny window in their toilet. Then he put his hands round J's father's neck and killed him. When J looked again, the man in the hood *was* his father.

He did not sleep. He saw everything that he could.

In the morning, Pip went to wake his son.

It was often the other way round. Before his boy was born – after they'd decided, at the very last minute, on that very hot day in Paris, to give him the *chance* to be born – Pip imagined a young child leaping, bounding onto the parental bed. But this boy, their boy, would walk round to where Pip slept, alone now, and tap at the highest point of his outline, hoping to find a shoulder.

This morning, though, Pip went to wake his son. J had kicked off his duvet in the night, and his limbs, which had recently thinned, looked longer than the day before, and were French-plaited in the sheets. His mouth was slightly open, his bottom lip glazed.

Pip drew the curtains slowly, so as not to shock sleeping eyes with full sun. He felt that if Clémence had been here, that would have been the kind of thing she would have done. He liked it when he felt that. Pip picked up the fallen duvet and held it out with high arms so it fell straight. He laid it lightly over J's feet, which were sole-to-sole, as if in prayer. Pip's hand was drawn by muscle memory, by magnet, to the boy's face and he stroked the highest part of his cheek. 'He-llo,' he said in a conscious whisper. 'It's been morning for ages.'

It was grown up, somehow, to be the one doing the waking. Pip was glad for moments like this.

At breakfast, Pip asked his son if he had slept well. J tried to pour himself cereal, but the box slipped and feather-light puffed rice skittered out across the table.

'You were scared last night, weren't you? Before I tucked you in.'

J picked up the Rice Crispies he could reach and put them in a little pile next to his orange juice. *Look at his cheeks flush, look how he concentrates; such a sober child.* How odd it was, Pip thought, to talk of a child as sober.

'It was good advice I gave you,' he said. 'Last night. Wasn't it?'

Because he had never liked high-chairs, J had three extra cushions stacked on his seat. He was careful not to move too much because sometimes all the cushions slipped.

'You were out like a light after that,' Pip said. 'Weren't you? It's a good thing to remember.'

And he said that sentence from Borges, or something like it, again.

J did not want to hear. He tensed his ears to fill them up with the sound of the blood moving in his veins. It sounded like the sea, when you stood at the end of a pier. Pip poured milk into his son's bowl.

He felt good after that. There were moments when he thought he might not be doing so badly. He was young to be a father –

both he and Clémence had been so young; it was how young they were that people always talked about, and then, now ... but he was making it work. Would make it work. Twenty-four was a fine age, surely? In his throat, coffee turned to hope.

'I'm like your dad and your brother, both at the same time, aren't I?' he said.

J did not know what it was like to have a brother, and so he didn't know what to say.

'We can be like brothers too, if you like?' Pip noticed every time he asked J a question. It felt stupid at times to ask questions of someone so small.

'If you like,' the boy repeated. With the back of his spoon, he squashed soft Rice Crispies into the side of his bowl.

Someone else's mother rang the doorbell then, to pick up J and drive him along the Uxbridge Road to school. Pip said, like he said every day, that it was very kind of her.

At school that day there was only one point, when they watched a cartoon in class, that J forgot about what his father had said. When he remembered though, it landed at the base of his stomach, and in his head, between his ears, high up, fizzing, on top of everything. In the afternoon, J locked himself in a low-walled toilet cubicle for nearly twenty minutes, until the teaching assistant came to check that he was OK.

After school, the same someone-else's mum took J to her house, which smelt of radiators, sweets and stock cubes. He didn't like her son much, but he liked the lady and thought she smiled a lot for how old she was. He asked her how old she was exactly, and she said thirty-two.

J said his mum was those numbers too, if you took the three and the two and swapped them round. He said that was the age she'd stopped at, and he added that she was French, as if that might explain it. The lady didn't know what to say after that, so she brought J a toy to play with. It was meant for someone younger than him. J sat on the sofa until his father came to pick him up.

It had been nearly four years since the accident.

They – Pip, Clémence, J (a baby then, face the size of a palm and body wrapped in triple blankets) – had been driving to the south of France to visit Eddy and Esmé's new house.

The motorway made the baby cry, so they'd switched to smaller roads. The hedges all looked the same, they hardly passed villages. They were late, they were lost. Clémence was angry with Pip for not having satnav, and the back of Pip's neck burned at the thought of disappointing everyone.

Eventually, he pulled into a layby, and Clémence crossed the road to ask an old man for directions. The man walked with a stick and his back curved forward in an echo of its handle. His white jumper was stained. He seemed friendly. Pip watched them through the window: the man pointed with his stick at first, then with wide, arthritic hands. Clémence nodded with each new point, then Pip saw her say 'merci' with a slower bow of her head. She'd turned back to the car, and ducked to see him through the window. She'd smiled, and mouthed 'See?' Pip had played this scene in his head a thousand times.

A second later, Clémence turned to wave goodbye to the

man, and stepped into the road. The car – a car that nobody saw coming – dragged her body nearly twelve metres.

To see it silent, it almost looked like the car had brushed her away. Brushed, swatted, it looked that easy. But that said nothing of the sound. Of bones and metals; of soft meeting hard and becoming unrecognizable. The brake was more violent than the impact.

The nearest hospital was in Paray-le-Monial, and Pip and the baby had waited there, red seats in a plastic corridor, nurses stopping now and then to stroke J's head and offer milk and tea. The families had arrived the next day. Clémence's father came up from Marseille, Eddy and Esmé arrived, grey-faced, in a taxi. The doctors told Pip many times that what he remembered from those moments might not strictly be true – that the mind contorts things after trauma – but he knows he shouted at his parents when he saw them. Shouted and shouted until he could feel spit falling from his mouth. He only stopped when the baby started crying too.

They spent three days in a bleak hotel near the hospital, then nearly a week in Paris to make what Eddy called 'arrangements'.

'Don't you dare call it that,' Pip had said. 'It's a fucking funeral.' When he had to tell Eddy a second time, he grabbed his father by the neck of his jacket in a café on rue Montorgueil. He'd held a finger, hard, up to Eddy's face. In his grief, Pip was fearless, and seeing grief, Eddy conceded.

It seemed everyone agreed that Pip should go back to his parents' house with the baby, and so he let himself be led.

'*Juste pour l'instant,*' Esmé had said. 'Till you find your feet,' Eddy added, by email.

His parents' new house was big and old, and had a lot of land. When Pip had been there for a week, he called his father.

'Where the fuck have you sent us?'

'Provence.'

'How will she ever get better if you won't let her live anywhere normal?'

'She likes it there. It's where she grew up. Where *we* grew up.'

'It's in the middle of nowhere.'

'It's not too far from the airport.'

'She doesn't fucking drive.'

'It's a big house. A lovely big house.'

'She's alone in it.'

'Not with you there.'

'But I'm not staying. I can't stay.'

'It'd be good for her.'

'You're so full of shit. There's no way I'm going to let him grow up ten miles from the nearest village.'

'Look, Pip—'

'I'm not going to do that to him.'

'I have a meeting now.'

'Bullshit.'

'And you've got a fucking tongue on you. Your mother never brought you up like that.'

'No. *You* did,' and by the time Pip added 'you prick' Eddy had hung up.

Two months later, on one of the weekends when Eddy was home, he commented on the length of Pip's hair.

'You're not looking after yourself,' he said, and he suggested that perhaps Pip should see the same doctor as Esmé had.

Esmé ended dinner abruptly. She took Eddy into the next room. The next day Eddy made calls. A few calls. Three or four. He got a job for Pip at an accounting firm. 'Entry level, but not bad. Big place. Lots of room for progression. Easy. London. They're going to have the intern find you a flat.'

Pip had cut his hair, and packed their bags, and so it was, and here they were.

That night, J could not eat much of his dinner. It was fish fingers. They had been done on the grill, and for slightly too long. When he cut them open, the rectangles of fish had shrunk inside their cases, It looked like there was glue around them, like they'd been stuck in. He thought of papier mâché. The peas were plump at first, but now they were cold they had wrinkled into raisins.

Pip never thought that he would be hungry at this time – it was seven, though meant to be six-thirty – but often ended up accidentally eating with his son.

'Dip it in the ketchup,' he said, mid-mouthful.

'I think I'm full now.'

'It's nice with the ketchup.' Pip picked up a second fish finger, dunked it in the red and put it in his own mouth. There was something about eating food which had cooled that made him even hungrier. 'Peas are good in the ketchup too. You can mix them in,' he said, and he did. *Kids' food*, Pip thought. *Baked beans, smiley faces. It tastes of things not being complicated.*

J said he'd finished.

'After tea, do you want to do some drawing together?' Pip asked. Until recently, he'd forgotten how much he'd liked drawing when he was a boy.

'I thought you said we called it "dinner" at our house.'

'After dinner then.' *He remembers all of the things I say. How is this possible? I made this boy, I made him.* 'Have you finished?' He took a spoonful of his son's peas. 'Do you want to draw then?' *Stop asking him questions.* 'You like drawing, you're good.' Draw with the kid, Pip told himself, if you think that's a good idea.

'No,' J said. 'Can we watch a film? Or just me. Can I watch a film? You don't have to watch it if you don't want to.'

Films stopped you from thinking. Pip said yes and after he had finished J's peas, and rolled the last fish finger up in a slice of bread, he turned on his laptop, and angled it so that they could both see the screen. They didn't have a television.

'What about . . . ?' Pip said the name of a film.

'Is it long?'

'What do you mean, is it long? Do you mean is it good?'

'Maybe.'

'Yeah, it's good. Do you want an apple?'

'No.'

'Chocolate mousse?'

'No.'

'Really? No chocolate mousse?'

'OK.'

Pip went to the fridge and got a green and silver can of beer, and two mousses. He handed one to his son, with a large spoon meant for serving. 'We should have had apples.' Pip opened his beer. 'Apples are healthier.'

Because of the slight deafness, Pip turned his head a little when he looked at the screen. This made J feel like his father was looking at him, and making sure he was OK, which felt good. The film was funny. Laughing made J's stomach feel empty at first, and then it felt fine. Pip had another beer and then laughed even more, and that made J feel better still. Soon though, the film was over.

'But you said it was long.'

'No I didn't. I said it was good.'

'Can we watch another one?'

'No, it's nine o'clock. Bedtime.'

'Just *one* though.'

'More film? No. I have a friend coming over.'

'Who?'

'You don't know them.'

J didn't say anything.

'There's nothing wrong with a friend. You have friends,' said Pip.

'Are they nice?'

'Yes.'

'No, but ...'

'What?'

'Is it a boy or a girl?'

'What is this? Are you some kind of policeman, now?'

'No.'

'You have to go to bed.'

'But you're not going to bed.'

'I'm your dad. I'm allowed.'

The boy tried his hardest not to, but he yawned.

'See?' Pip said. 'You're tired.'

J let his body go limp, and his father carry him into bed. Pip brushed the boy's teeth there, head on pillow, with a tiny bit of toothpaste and hardly any water. J's eyes were shut the whole time. They were shut until his father left, and with him, the light.

J was not asleep. His ears were open. He waited. He heard the door open. He heard a woman's voice. He heard his father laugh again. He heard the woman laugh.

The cinema screen in his head started playing films and films and films. Fires again, and hearts stopping working. Falling down stairs; his father falling down stairs. The boy heard more laughter. He imagined kissing. He tried to close his eyes but they were already closed. He tried to open them but it was so dark what he saw didn't change. They lay on top of each other. Worse, they fell in love. Fires, axes. He put his hands over his head.

He must have stayed like that for an hour, longer. When he let his arms go, and stopped clenching his eyes, and tensing his ears so he could only hear blood, he thought for one half of a second that he had finally found blankness. Then he heard a noise from the next room. A different noise to the one before, and he did not know what it meant. 'I can't stay here any more,' he said, out loud, to no one.

When he came out of his room, he saw that his father was lying still, with his eyes shut, eyelashes wet, in the lap of a woman. The woman looked as if she didn't know what to do.

(To J, she was a woman. In fact, she was nineteen – though it was not strange that Pip thought her older. There was something like a shadow underneath her eyes. Her clothes were sandy-coloured. Her hair shone like polished wood. It was the way her wrists were thin and her eyes like almonds that Pip liked. They reminded him of other women he had loved – his mother; Clémence; Jude, still. All of the women he had loved. This girl, this new girl, had brought them back.)

'Is this him?' she said. To Pip maybe, or to the air.

J nodded. 'This is my house,' he said.

'Are you OK?' she asked the boy. He was looking at his sleeping father and down at a dark red stain by the sofa.

'Is he hurt?'

'Oh, no. God no. It's not blood.' J looked up at the word blood. 'No, I mean, it's nothing bad like that. He spilt his drink, is all.' The girl felt hot suddenly. Her bra strap, yellow, had fallen over her arm; she pushed it back up over her shoulder. 'Your dad's sleeping. He's fine, he's sleeping. Are you OK?'

'I can't sleep.' J took a step towards them, then stopped. His toes curled into the carpet. Despite the dark beneath her eyes – light smudges, like thumbprints – she was pretty, the woman, the girl, and reminded him of someone.

'Is he OK?' J asked her.

'You can sit next to us if you like.' It was a sofa for three people.

'Is he crying?'

'I don't know. He's been . . . I don't know.'

'That's my dad.'

'I know.'

J climbed onto the sofa using his knee. He sat next to the girl. His feet did not touch the ground.

'Why was he crying?' J asked. He hadn't quite yet learnt to whisper. Some words were soft, others pushed out at full volume. Pip did not wake up though, just stayed, somewhere else, with his head on the girl's lap.

'I'm not sure,' she said.

'Has he been thinking too?'

'Probably. Don't we all think?'

'Are you doing it as well?'

'I think we all do.'

'I know. But did he tell you about the thing?'

'I don't know. Maybe. Which thing? About . . . ' The girl pointed, loosely, kindly, at a photograph of Clémence in a small frame on the table. 'About your mum?'

'No. Not about her.' J shook his head. 'About the thing that he said. That nothing ever happens like you think it will.'

The girl did not look troubled, like J had been. She looked down at the man's head, passed out in her lap, and thought that it was probably true.

'He said: "Nothing ever happens like you think it will. *Exactly.*" For it to work, you have to think it exactly.' J sat on his left foot, because it was cold. 'If you think it in your head then it will only happen there, and not here. You can stop it from happening here.' With the word 'here', he touched the sofa, like the sofa was the real world, and the whole world. 'He said he read it in a book.'

The girl just looked at the boy. She didn't have any brothers or sisters either; she didn't know how to be with children. Half of the girl, more than half, wanted to go home.

'It's hard though,' J said, and his forehead moved, trembled, like water in the wind. 'I've been trying to think of everything. *Everything* bad, that I don't want to happen.' He looked up at her. 'I *have* been trying. If he wakes up, will you tell him I have? Will you tell him I tried?' J was starting to cry now. Pink had poured into his cheeks – he changed colour just like his father did; in so many ways he was just like his father – and hot tears, she could tell they were hot just from looking at them, swelled in his eyes. 'But I'm tired now,' he said. 'I'm tired but,' tears at the tip of his nose, on his chin, all over his face, 'I still . . . still can't sleep.'

'Oh. *Oh*,' the girl said. 'Come here. I don't think he meant that.' J found space for his head in the side of her waist and nestled into it. 'I don't think you have to do that. It's not up to you to do that.'

J could feel the heat of his father's head against his own. The girl could feel the heat, and weight, of both of them. She realized that there are certain things which make you an adult. The simple presence of someone younger than you. The girl had never done this before, but she said, 'There, there. There, there. There, there, there.'

For a while, J cried. Then crying turned into breathing, turned into slower, turned into something like sleep. There was silence, the screen in his head was finally blank.

That night, the house did not burn. There were no scorpions, hooded men, knives. Just a father, a son, and a girl to rest their heads upon.

Other People's Shopping Baskets

Days turn into weeks turn into years. It is Sunday, Sunday again, and the supermarket shuts in ten minutes.

People who shop at this time have not chosen to shop at this time. They are rushing, and thrust just enough for Sunday night and Monday morning into their trolleys. Crisps, chicken, wine for a kind of communion; cornflakes and milk for breakfast.

Pip has just walked in through the automatic doors. He says 'shit' in his head as his eyes scan the queue. Thirteen people, more, stretched out into clots and clumps all along the biscuit aisle.

Marvellous, he thinks. *There's only one person on the till, and it's a fully fledged child.*

The gluey-skinned teenage boy at the check-out holds a £5 note to the light to check for the hologram.

Don't fanny around with fivers when the whole world and his wife is here.

Pip looks down. The whole world and his son. His son.

When they walk next to each other, he only sees the top of the boy's head and the tip of his nose. *Half of me. Half made of me.* He reaches down and dusts J's blond hair with his knuckles.

'Get *off*,' J says and winces away. 'Eugh.'

He has recently discovered rudeness. Pip still finds it novel.

'Seriously? Are you serious? You make me laugh. You're not fifteen. Go and get the bread.'

'*Fine*,' J replies and walks off. The way he says 'fine' makes Pip hate American TV shows.

'*Brown* bread,' he calls after his son. 'With bits in. Healthy, OK?'

Pip wonders suddenly what it will be like when they walk next to each other and are head-to-head. He's going to be so tall, people keep on telling Pip, tall and heartbreaking. Just like his daddy. It always occurred to him, after people said it: wasn't the term 'heartbreaker'?

Pip has sundried tomatoes, orange juice, beers, and lasagne for two in his basket. He needs garlic bread and apples. He finds them. Then he finds his son, who has brown sandwich buns in one hand, and a jumbo bag of brioche in the other.

They get in the queue to pay. It's curved round to the frozen section now. The kid on the till is still checking each note and doesn't know the code for any of the fruit. Pip props his beers on top of frozen cauliflower florets in an open freezer so they'll stay cold.

'I don't like lasagne,' J says, bending over and tapping the packet in the basket.

'Stop. Now you're just trying to be annoying.'

'I'm not, *ack*shully.'

'It's what you order when we go to restaurants.'

'Not any more.' J pauses. He wants to get the next bit right. 'Meat is animal.' He looks up at his dad. He feels brave. 'Dead,' he adds.

'Oh no. No, not at all. I'm not going to have a vegetarian for a son. I refuse.'

Pip realizes that the woman in front of them in the queue is laughing at their conversation. He sees movement in her shoulder blades, and in her hair, which is long, blonde, shines, has a slight wave at the ends. It's the kind of hair men want to touch.

'I'll have to leave you here,' he says to his son. 'Right here in the supermarket. You'll have to live here.' It's not strictly intentional, but he's speaking louder so the woman in front can hear. He likes to make a woman laugh; he hasn't always been able to.

'I don't care,' J says. 'I'll just eat chocolate.' He points at the wall of biscuits.

'You'll have to pay for them, and you don't have any money and then ...' The queue moves forward a bit. 'You'll go to prison.'

Pip wonders if he's gone too far. The woman in front turns around.

For that first half of a second, he doesn't look at her face. Her chest is distracting. She doesn't have a trolley or a basket. Her arms are up high as if to hold a baby – and he looks at her chest from left to right to see what she is carrying. So many things. Nectarines, pesto, super plus Tampax, a four-pack of yoghurt, herbs, rosé. A tin of foie gras balanced in the crook of her elbow.

As she turns, she keeps her eyes on her arms so she can concentrate. The tin of foie gras steadies and she looks up at Pip.

'He's ...' She was intending to say 'he's so sweet' but she catches Pip's eye on her way down to the child, and goes no further.

His face. She looks at him and knows his face.

He knows hers too.

'Oh my God,' he says. He doesn't mean to breathe in quite that hard.

'Shit.' Her tampons fall. 'Hi. *Hi,*' he says. 'It's you.' He can't believe it. 'I can't believe it's you.'

He looks at her armfuls again. 'Why don't you have a trolley?'

'I don't – I never do. Things get—'

'You look amazing.'

'—squashed.'

Sofi and Pip are looking at each other and trying to see how many years it's been in clues like clothes and eyes. His jumper is soft, powder-grey, and stubble on his cheekbone catches the strip-lighting. Egon Schiele angles still, but sanded down now. He is noticeably handsome. She is wearing bright red. She's just been on holiday in Croatia and her skin is still tanned.

Sofi looks down at the young boy. 'Fuck me! He's not *yours,* is he?' J's feet are slightly apart so he can stand strong and his eyes are bright blue and huge, almost too big for his head. 'Fuck! I'm sorry for swearing. But is he yours?'

'I'm my *own,*' J says. Skin like eggshell. His lips are so pink.

'You have a son.' The bridge of Sofi's nose suddenly stings and she thinks she might cry.

Pip nods.

'I'm so happy for you.' Now, a nectarine falls. 'How old is he? You're married?'

'No – no. Clémence, she – that's his mum ...'

J has picked up Sofi's box of tampons and holds it up to her with two hands.

'Sorry. He's eight. Nearly nine.' Pip reaches for the box. 'I'll take those. I mean, not forever, just until you get to the till.'

'Who are you?' J asks Sofi, this time holding out the nectarine.

'Uh ...' For some reason, she stares at the things in her arms. Children have a way of getting to the heart of things. 'That's a hard question.'

Pip steps in and takes the nectarine from his son. 'We knew each other when we were young.'

'I'm Sofi,' she says to the boy. 'I knew your father when he was a boy.'

'Not a *boy*,' Pip says.

'A bit a boy.' Sofi's never understood why people shake their head in disbelief. But that is what she is doing now. 'Fuck, I'm so happy to see you. See him. Really I am. I didn't ... How *are* you? What are you doing? You look ...'

'I'm good. We're good. We have a new place. It's really nice. Isn't it nice?' Pip angles towards his son.

'My room is bigger now. Do *you* have a big room?' J says to Sofi.

'What about you?' This is Pip, again. 'You look – you're like ... black.'

'Holiday.'

'You look great.'

They're smiling at each other.

'That bar,' he says.

'Terrible bar. I mean, great bar. It was a fun time. It was bad for me.'

They're smiling at each other, but somehow smiling *on* each other too. It's the type of smile that changes the spacing of the air and it's strange. Because yes, they are looking to see how many years have passed, and how. But they are also looking at each other and seeing themselves as if no time has passed, seeing themselves as they had been, as everyone has been, so much younger.

In one of Sofi's smiles, she says sorry – both of them feel it – for the last time they saw each other.

Then, 'It was just the Isle of Wight,' she says.

'What?'

'It was the Isle of Wight I could see. From Le Havre. When it was really clear – on a really clear day, I looked out and I thought it was Sark. I liked that. But it was just the Isle of Wight.'

The queue is moving fast now. They can see how much time they have left together, and with each step it gets shorter.

Pip's son asks Sofi what Tampax are. Before she can answer, she is at the front of the queue. She bends forward slightly and lets all the things in her arms drop onto the conveyor belt. The check-out boy stares at her with a slightly open mouth. As she finds the cash, she takes out a business card. She keeps it between two fingers as she gets her change, then she hands it to Pip.

'You have to call me,' she says. And this time, she means it.

He doesn't have time to look at it properly before he slips it in his pocket. He wants to know what she does. He notices that the card is matte white, has beautiful lettering. She's wearing a jacket that looks expensive. Her smile is wrapped up in lipstick but it's real again. She is a proper woman. She looks like you could say hello to her. He imagines that were she to sit in the window of a café, men would come in to it just to pay for her coffee.

She's just been given her receipt. She has her bags in her hands. 'Call me,' she says again. It feels right that she would kiss him on the cheek, but the child is in the way.

'Bye bye, little one,' she says, and they both say 'bye' back.

She has nearly left the shop when Pip calls after her.

'Sofi,' he says.

She turns. She is standing right in the way of the electric doors. They start to close, then reopen, start to close then reopen. Limbo. The sun is setting and the only part of the sky they can see is cool moon yellow.

'Do you want to come for dinner? We live just there.' He points in a curve, which means 'down the road'.

'What are you going to have?' she asks. She pretends to take a look at what he's buying even though she's too far away to see.

'Lasagne. Peas? Kids' food. I don't know. We bought bread.'

She nods.

'It's just the two of us. Me and him. There's enough. Enough lasagne. Now this one's decided he is only going to eat –' he turns to his son, 'broccoli.'

'Chocolate,' J says. He's looking at the rings on Sofi's fingers. Loads of them: red, turquoise. There's something about her he likes, something easy about her. She's happy and she's not even trying. *She's cool*, J thinks.

'Yes,' she says. 'Yes, OK. I would like that.'

'Great,' he says. The sticky boy at the till is waiting for Pip to enter his PIN. 'That's great.'

Pip realizes his chest has been tight, like there was a hand inside, gripping it. As a woman decides not to leave them, the hand lets go.

Sofi points to the pavement just outside. 'I'll wait,' she says.

3

For a while I could not enter for the way was barred to me. I turned again to the house . . . as if we ourselves had left but yesterday.

Daphne du Maurier, *Rebecca*

Going Back

I went back for you too.

That was the first thing I wrote, and afterwards, I wrote over the words again and again until they became like nests on the page and lost their meaning. For a short while, I did not know what to write after that. Just this – I went back for you, for both of us, for all of us, everyone, it depends how you see it. I didn't feel that I was alone.

I went for one day, and all the way to the coast, I went by train. No plane, no pilot, no Badoit. I wanted to go back slowly. If you look at the trees along the tracks, trains go fast, but if you look out far, sometimes it feels like you could be walking. And I went back from the other side too: France.

I've been spending a fortnight in Normandy with my other half. We met in France and so we try to go back every year for our anniversary. It's not beautiful from the bigger roads, but they half-timber houses and it's famous for Bayeux mint chews and the brightest paintings of sea skies and yacht steeples. Cider comes in wine-size bottles with champagne corks. I think you'd like it.

A friend of ours has a place here, in a town with weekend homes and crazy golf. The roofs are pinched and gothic, but there are snatches of the sea from the kitchen window and enamel tiles of turquoise swallows on the gateposts. Next to our bed, above a bare bookshelf, there's a map of Europe. It's the type of map that pretends to be old – countries' edges drawn in calligraphy, zigzags in dark blue for the sea, the same, the zag just sharper, in green for mountains. The paper's dip-dyed in tea, and I was looking at it, following borders and beaches, and suddenly I saw how close I was. I found our island and put my finger on it, covered it completely.

I knew I had to go, and said that. Just with my lips at first, and then the words became sounds and felt so loud in the room. I heard them as if someone else said them. We were leaving Cabourg in a week, and I felt, as people say they feel, that if I didn't go now, I never would. That evening, we went for dinner at the Grand Hotel – Proust's hotel, they call it. He featured a lot on the menu. Madeleines for each course, a savoury tilleul sorbet as a palate cleanser. Just before dessert, I said I had to go away. Just for the day. When I said where, I think it was understood. Lives are long, and when you love someone you let them keep the parts that came before you. Our knees knotted together under the table. We ended the meal with Calvados, I paid. I looked up timetables, woke up first, and set off for Sark before breakfast.

The train to St Malo – just one carriage, shaky on the tracks – was dark red with dusty seats, and when I arrived I had an hour before the ferry. Another time, I would like to stay longer, or go with less in my head. I wonder if you ever went to St Malo? The sand is the colour of brushed teeth, and the boats look expensive. The ferry from there to Guernsey was fast, new, neutral. Called a 'Condor', which I thought was a strange choice.

St Peter's Port seemed higher than it had been before. Real estate is booming and it was crowned with sky-high cranes and between them tall spires – I hadn't noticed all the churches last time we were there. The houses on the hill were all white but faced the sea at different angles, which changed the way each one threw back light.

I had a cappuccino at a port front café and they made it with a heart in the foam. It was one of those days when the sky is enormous. Warm to look at, biting to be in. There wasn't a cloud and the sun burnt white. It looked more like the moon, and it was cold enough to feel the air wherever it touched your skin. It made you want to breathe deeply. For a while, after I'd finished my coffee, I watched a young couple on a bench – maybe one of the benches we'd sat on – on the stretch of pavement outside the café. They were dressed for different weathers; the girl in a sundress and shoes that might go see-through in the rain, the boy in a children's-book blue beanie and a jumper thick enough to turn a boy's body into a man's. I could not work out whether they were in love, or friends, or brother and sister. The boy smoked, the girl stole drags, how their hands met was like a dance.

(I am sorry for the detail. It's just that I want to tell you everything. I want you to have been there with me.)

For the off-season, the *Sark Belle* was full. That's what the ticket woman said, anyway. 'Sark for you too?' she said, cheek fat with chewing gum. 'Whole world's heading there today.' She blew a bubble as she counted my change.

I hoped she would be right, but the world that got on the ferry was the wrong one. An American family boarded just behind me, and sat close. They had never been to Sark before, and called it Sark Island. You'd have hated it. Every time, Sark Island. Is it big, Sark Island? Will there be other children (this was the child speaking) on Sark Island? I felt, then, this bizarre, buried sense of ownership. I wanted them to know that I had been there before. The dad had creases from an iron on his jeans. They talked about planes flying over the island, how high in the air they have to stay for it to be legal. Either it's changed or they got it wrong. I turned to them, and the son, they only had one, had his mouth open in an 'O'. He was at the age when you stare. The father noticed, smiled an apology without looking at my face, and lifted the child up away from me and onto his denim lap.

The crossing was gentle. Sailors from the Sark Shipping Company walked around in pale blue shirts and smiled at people. Seagulls bobbed in the open water, or congregated on certain rocks, a hundred white heads keeping each other warm. The wind, and there wasn't much – it was the air itself that was cold – was behind us. We could see the boat's motion in a circle around us, but after that, the sea looked smooth and shiny as a mirror, face to the sky.

I realized that what I was scared of most was blankness, that it would mean nothing. That I had let my eyes rest on memories too many times for them to still touch me. (The man on the other side of me kept on sniffing. He was reading the Bible, and he had a gnarly cauliflower of tissue pressed into the page as a bookmark.) I tried to work out if I was afraid that the island would have changed, or more afraid that it might have stayed exactly the same and that I had changed. Constants are comforting, terrifying, both. The Bible man sneezed and said sorry into his tissue.

That was when the little boy with no brothers or sisters ran to the window and said he could see it. Sark Island.

I wrote and wrote and wrote. Here, to you, and on a 'to do' list too. It was a 'to do' list that didn't make sense. Things from the future, things I'd done already. I just didn't want to see the island from the distance, flat and far, like a postcard, because it had already become that.

People talk about edges. Being on them, taking them off. I felt at that moment that I knew exactly where the edge was, and that it was beside me. Close to my skin. I don't know. Nostalgia is one of the hardest things to write down. Even the word – it tangles. Perhaps the only way it can exist outside the body is in music. *New Scientist* says that music is the closest thing to time travel. I read it in someone's loo once. Everything that happens in between the first and last time you hear a song concertinas into nothing. In your head it's the first time again, but everywhere else it isn't. That's the sad thing: everywhere else it isn't. And it feels like a tugging at the base of your stomach.

As the ferry neared the island, it crossed the stretch of water where the three of us once threw flowers. I think I remembered the spot right. It was at the last moment where the land still looked like we could reach out and touch it. I imagined our flowers lying on the floor of the seabed. I imagined them whole, and that they had kept their colours, because what they'd promised was true. The boat pulled closer to the harbour.

Honestly, I think I half expected to see Pip leaning on the seawall. I wondered if he'd be even taller, if he'd still be blond. I wondered if the island was somewhere time was trapped and if everything would start all over again. I saw him in a thick pea-coat for winter, I saw him reading, I saw him in my head, but only in my head, lots of ways. The man next to me must have stopped holding his tissue because suddenly the wind caught it and blew it up into the air. It passed in front of us like a tiny cloud, paused, then disappeared. The *Sark Belle* docked. Heavy ropes were tied and the sides of the boat leant on Uniroyal tyres and old barnacles.

I walked with the American family, the Christian with a cold, and all the rest of the world headed to Sark that day, through the harbour tunnel. Algae on the walls, diesel in the air. There ahead of us was the Toast Rack. I think it was the same one, just a bit rustier, as if the toast had burnt. It took us up the hill slowly, a soft jerk with every gear change. The American woman shut her eyes, breathing out through her mouth, fingers pushing on her husband's stocky knuckles as if they were her own pressure points. We got off at the top of the Avenue. Monkey tails still dipped green and muscular into the gardens of NatWest. The other trees were getting their leaves back. There must have been a flash heatwave a couple of weeks before because some of the buds had blinked through early.

Do you remember how the gravel on the Avenue was so fine that it looked like someone had brushed it? Because the roofs are low and flat, I realized it's the only place on the whole island where the shadows are straight. The bakery that had been new, and once shone like glazed pastry, had no customers. I couldn't even see any bread. The lacquer has chipped. I looked through the window and the girl at the till was eating crisps. Instead, I went into the Island Stores to buy water. They'd swapped the greetings cards and chocolate bars around. I had a sudden fear that someone would recognize me and busied myself by the freezers.

There is – and I don't know why – a shame in wanting to go back.

When I paid, I recognized the woman completely; her hair was shorter, her lines more etched, her necklace the same. She smiled at me as she would have done to anyone, but then they must have seen a thousand faces at their till, and we only saw theirs as we handed over Guernsey bills. We had a place and practice to attach to them. To them, we were just girls who bought a lot of butter.

Still, the Sark faces stay with me more than most. I see them on buses, in cafés. I still see backs of heads and imagine that when the person turns around the face will be familiar. Sometimes I think that was the summer when my eyes formed. Maybe not 'formed', but saw things, and thought what they would be in words. I looked so hard at everything.

At the other end of the Avenue, past the post office with its blue postbox, carriages were still for hire – those carthorses with bellbottom fringes over their hooves. There were bikes for hire too, with once-white tyres, and bells with Spice Girls stickers on. I wanted to walk, though. And it felt different, not to be cycling. I realized how fast we'd gone.

The first place I went back to was Bonita's. The gnomes were gone, and the grass was shaved short as a head. There were leaflets on the gatepost announcing it as 'Bonita and Son' now. I wanted to go in. It would be easy, I told myself. I imagined myself opening the gate, getting to the door, knocking. I fast-forwarded to tea, broken biscuits, own-brand cola, Bonita smiling, being able to talk about you. Four times I walked up the path in my mind, and four times I didn't take one step.

So I went to the Coupée instead. I'd forgotten the thickness of the concrete spikes. They seem to ask you to touch them, because so many people already have. The harder rocks in the gravel stand out now, but smoothly, and shine, polished by passing hands. I counted the spokes as I walked across and there are twenty-one on each side. It felt, in a strange way, as if each one was a year. As I walked across, it was like I was growing up again. Or going back, year by year, to when I was last here.

I want to ask how it was for you between then and now. I got it wrong and right. Wrong has to go first. Right last, because it's right, now. I want to tell you that I went to Paris. Not just for you, but a bit for you. At the start, anyway. I looked for you there and I thought I saw you on the métro and I imagined again and again what I'd say if we spoke. I lived there for three and a half years. The Eiffel Tower was a stupid place for me to say I'd meet you. No one who lives in Paris ever goes there.

When I'd crossed the Coupée, I climbed the low hill to the fields where the Czech boys used to stay, but there were no more tents there. All the grass was high and the same colour. I found Cider Press Cottage, and then my way back to the beach where we swam naked. In a few months, when it will be warmer, day-trippers will push the path clear, but right now it's thick and wild. I pulled my sleeves long over my wrists, found the bare bits of thorned sticks and picked a slow way through.

I was glad there was no one else on the beach. Just birds surfing on driftwood, and the sea with a champagne foam that was thick, milk-white. It was too cold to swim, but I remembered the heat of that last day – the sun burning through hair, drying shells, changing shoulders – and that made it warm enough, it really did, to dip my feet in.

And all around the edge of the island, Sofi, on the wall of the cliffs, there's a line of yellow, two metres up from the sea, that wasn't there before. It makes you think that the sea used to be a different height, that it's getting less now, or that Sark is getting taller. I thought it would feel smaller, like a family house you knew as a child, and go back to as an adult. But if anything, the island seemed bigger. It was easier to get lost.

At a certain point, maybe three o'clock, the sun changed sides and lit up a different half of the island. I went back to the Avenue, back to the café we always wanted to go to. The gate was white and heavy, you have to lift it to make the latch work.

The waitress was pretty, in this very precise way. Her eyes looked drawn with a compass, and there was eyeliner in her tear-ducts. She brought me cake with my coffee. It wasn't as good as yours. Not enough salt. No nail clippings, no long gold hair you would spot at the last moment and finger-pinch out of Pip's slice.

Pip with his blond freckles and blonder eyebrows and bobbing Adam's apple. I heard from him just once. He contacted the tuition agency and they gave him my parents' address. He sent a letter. His handwriting was even smaller, but he'd filled four sides. There was something formal about it – fountain pen, navy. I got the impression he had written it out a few different times.

He asked me where I was. He said he had been living in Paris, but was leaving in two weeks. He said he thought of me. He told me about where he'd lived, and a concert he'd seen the night before. German opera. He told me about the books he had read, and wrote down his favourite lines, with the edition and page numbers in different pen in the margin.

Halfway down the last page he told me, as if he were telling me about the weather, that he'd got a girl pregnant. That they hadn't been sure, but now they were, and that he had a feeling everything was going to be OK. Her name was Clémence and she was French. He said I'd like her – that we had things in common – and he made a joke, or perhaps it wasn't a joke, about calling the baby Jude. That way, he said, it didn't matter if it was a boy or a girl.

And in the line before last, he said he had seen you. He said you were in Le Havre. He told me the name of the bar, and said he was worried about you and it would be good if I could call.

The letter arrived too late though. Or rather, I arrived too late, at Christmas. My parents had left the envelope on the hall table for six months, like they expected me home any evening.

I recognized the handwriting straight away. I took the letter up to my room and opened it as I lay in a crooked star on my childhood bed. Pip had left no address post-Paris, and when I tried to call Le Paris, the number no longer existed. This was years ago. I had missed you both.

When I tried to eat the cake in front of me, I couldn't swallow. I missed you both. One cloud, one of the only clouds that day, blew between the café and the sun, and light lost its shine for a minute or so.

Pip's house, their house, the house that became our house – was the last place I went back to. I almost left it so late that even if I changed my mind, time at least would get in the way.

I could feel it even in the path. It is unusual to go to a place day after day after day, and then not to go at all for such a long time. The body reacts. The approach to a house is a strange thing. The weight of what waits. An empty house is harder still – it's both life and time which have come undone.

The house, the garden, they were changed, unchanged. It was as if I could see two things at once: the reality now, unmoving, and then things I had seen before, playing like a film on top. Pip with a book tent on his chest, the outline of Esmé's black sunhat, how quickly you could climb a tree. Maybe we've done this to our minds with cinema, maybe we've always done this. It was something like cross-cut or collage. For a moment, it was like you and I, and Pip and everyone – all of us from summer – existed again. Flowers in wicker crowns, we lay in a wide, tangled circle with each of our heads on someone else's lap.

It seemed to me that I had never looked at the house as a whole before. I'd seen the island from the other side of its windows. From back crabs in the garden or from the gazebo where we ate lunch, I had caught it upside down, or in the corner of my eye. Now, I stood alone at the bottom of the garden and looked at it straight on. With trees that had grown taller, and ivy at its corners and the cream-blue sky, it was framed like a painting.

They had not been there for a long time. The curtains in Esmé's upstairs room were drawn, the windows thickened with double-glazing. A child's swing in the garden made it clear someone else had lived there since. Leaves had gathered on the seat, the house was empty now. A 'for sale' sign next to the bird bath looked as if it had been there for years. I stood there, and the air felt thin, and like on the first last day, I took in everything.

The first time I came home from Sark, I felt time pass by looking for blackberries and tasting them. I'd go for walks and check there still were some left, and as they got sourer and the ones that were light red refused to get darker, I knew that that summer was over. Blackberries are still the way I see the furthest end of summer fall.

This time, if I cried on the ferry home, it was not strictly sadness. The sun was setting. Plane trails crossed one another and made tartan in the sky. There are times when the universe makes tears inevitable. Actually, I could not work out which it was: happiness or sadness. It was one foot on a tightrope between the two, and sometimes they feel the same.

Back at St Peter's Port, the boy and girl I'd watched in the morning were still sitting on the bench. Perhaps they'd never even moved. She was wearing his jumper now. She'd curled her feet up under her, was sitting on them. They weren't talking any more, just leaning on each other, slow, unworried. I remembered a teacher years ago, telling our class that every young person is beautiful. We'd looked around at one another then, and pushed one another and laughed. None of us understood what she meant.

But it's how unfolded the skin is. Possibility, time. How much time there is.

That night in Guernsey. I don't remember it ending – not *an* ending, anyway – but sometimes I think about something you said before we stopped. Your head was higher than either of ours. My cheek was on your chest, Pip's head, light, was down by one of our hipbones. I think it was mine. One of your arms was stretched up and your underarm looked like it was sprinkled with tiny iron filings. I ran my finger over them and kissed you there, then kissed your arm, then your neck. Soap. I remember how the hotel room smelt – everything we normally keep inside us was in the air. You shifted down the bed, ran a thumb over my forehead and whispered into my temple. You said something about 'first time', and maybe you meant with three, or with a girl, but I said 'me too' because it didn't matter which of those you meant, it was true.

I probably still do not understand it – love, whatever it is, whatever those feelings were. What makes us catch it, or why we throw it, so often, in the wrong direction. It's never wasted though. I say this with no motive, just gratitude that you were kind, but that summer, and for a while afterwards, I did love you, Sofi. I loved you completely, and it was my first time. I can say it now, there's no harm in it. No one ever minds someone having loved them.

I want to find a way to send you this. I want to tell you that I am happy. Look back over your shoulder at me. I hope, wherever you are, you too are happy.

I am nearly home now, and suddenly it's not cold, as though the air has caught on that it's just been day. The clocks went back a week ago, and the length of the evenings is still surprising us. By this time, though, it's almost dark and the person I love now is waiting for me.

But that's how it was. Just like that, I walked back into childhood, and it was an island. If it's an island, it has rules that don't make sense anywhere else. If it's an island, it's the smallest one, where the sun shines white, and we went there, and we knew we could not stay.

Acknowledgements

I would like to express my real and lasting gratitude to:
Tor Henman, coach supreme to an all-blonde girls' football team, who knew I watched *Masterchef* and wondered if I'd like to join her as a private cook on Sark.

Andrew Miller, who employed us, and his fun, charming sons, who were fortunately a very different family from the one is this book. You have a cameo on page 69. I truly do promise that Sofi's kitchen hygiene was not based on my real-life practices.

The Men of Balzac – thank you for letting me be your pseudo-secretary for nearly two years. Most of this was written at your desk, fuelled by your Nespresso capsules.

My very first readers – Jethro, Dave, Sophie, Raoul, Laura – beloved friends who were kind enough to send positive post-cards even though what they read then was skeletal, if not terrible.

Shakespeare & Company, and Charles and Clydette de

Groot. It is a wonderful thing you do. The Paris Literary Prize changed my life wholly.

Hedgebrook writers' retreat on Whidbey Island. You have created a place of generosity and hope. Women writers – look it up, do everything in your power to go.

My editor Victoria Pepe and my agent Karolina Sutton, for taking a chance on this book. I have felt in safe – and exceptional – hands.

Aline, Anna, Ania, Philippa, Freya, Alex, Marie-Cybèle, Amanda, Paul, Natalie, Ralph, Leila. Friends who, in particular, read, supported, shared. My family: my beautiful godson Alex, Hanna, Babsy, Musa and Nina, the Winterburns, Trina, Sarah, John, Marianne, Ellie, Jacob and their baby-to-be, and my clever, kind Uncle Charles, an English teacher and majestic pianist, who never got the chance to read this, but gave me more book tokens, films and music than I thought was humanly possible.

My parents. If this is a novel about only children, I am glad to be yours. I wouldn't have it any other way. Thank you for sending emails that make me laugh and make everything OK.

H – perhaps it's ill advised at this age to mention the person you love. I don't care. Thank you, forever. Right now, you're in the room next door listening to 'Yumeji's Theme'. I think about you, and think about you, and think you're a miracle.